Praise for *Cabot Wright*

"James Purdy has succeeded better than anyone else around at the moment in re-creating the U.S.A. and presenting it simultaneously as his own invention and as a faithful reflection of reality—not an easy feat. *Cabot Wright Begins* is a delight all the way through."
—Paul Bowles

"It might loosely be described as a bravura work of satire— a satire on pornographic fantasy, a satire on New York literary life, a satire on affluent eccentric mid-century America. Except that satire is perhaps too narrow a term to convey the kind of comedy that Purdy writes . . . but rather the vehicle for a universal comic vision."
—Susan Sontag, *New York Times Book Review*

"His funniest novel. . . . Few modern novelists have refused so steadfastly to reproduce their last novel all over again, and Mr. Purdy's courage in denying his admirers with another dose of the old familiar mixture seems to me justified by the regularity with which he produces unexpected yet unmistakably good Purdy products."
—Angus Wilson, *Observer*

"Purdy builds his fiction like the hall of mirrors in a fun house. Which is the real image? One is never sure. Purdy's vision of modern life has the bonecrushing savagery, the hallucinatory richness and total horror of a bad case of delirium tremens."
—Conrad Knickerbocker, *Life*

CABOT WRIGHT BEGINS

OTHER NOVELS BY JAMES PURDY

Gertrude of Stony Island Avenue

Reaching Rose

Garments the Living Wear

In the Hollow of His Hand

On Glory's Course

Mourners Below

Dream Palaces: Three Novels

Narrow Rooms

In a Shallow Grave

The House of the Solitary Maggot

I Am Elijah Thrush

Jeremy's Version

Eustace Chisholm and the Works

The Nephew

Malcolm

JAMES PURDY

CABOT WRIGHT BEGINS

LIVERIGHT PUBLISHING CORPORATION

A Division of W. W. Norton & Company

New York • London

Copyright © 1964 by James Purdy. Copyright renewed 1992 by James Purdy.

First published as a Liveright paperback 2013

For information about permission to reproduce selections from this book,
write to Permissions, Liveright Publishing Corporation,
a division of W. W. Norton & Company, Inc.,
500 Fifth Avenue, New York, NY 10110

For information about special discounts for bulk purchases, please contact
W. W. Norton Special Sales at specialsales@wwnorton.com or 800-233-4830

Manufacturing by Courier Westford
Book design by Chris Welch
Production manager: Anna Oler

Library of Congress Cataloging-in-Publication Data

Purdy, James, 1914–2009.
Cabot Wright begins / James Purdy.
pages ; cm
ISBN 978-0-87140-352-0 (pbk.)
1. Rapists—Fiction. 2. Wall Street (New York, N.Y.)—Fiction. I. Title.
PS3531.U426C25 2013
813'.54—dc23

2013013133

Liveright Publishing Corporation
500 Fifth Avenue, New York, N.Y. 10110
www.wwnorton.com

W. W. Norton & Company Ltd.
Castle House, 75/76 Wells Street, London W1T 3QT

1 2 3 4 5 6 7 8 9 0

for

JEANNETTE DRUCE *and* BETTINA SCHWARZSCHILD

CONTENTS

CABOT WRIGHT BEGINS

1

BERNIE ON THE PROMENADE

o one knows how the arteries and nerves of the man next to you make him see you and the world that surrounds you both.

Early Saturday night Bernie Gladhart paced the Promenade in Brooklyn and looked across the river at the skyline of Wall Street, now like a series of extinct craters, unlit and uninhabited, by reason of the weekend departure of charwomen and the thousands of other cleaners who keep the skyscrapers ablaze all the evenings of the working week. Bernie was the most downhearted of men, even though he was pacing with a purpose and had a wife and home waiting for him in Chicago.

It was Carrie Moore, Bernie's wife, who had sent him to Brooklyn in the first place, with a mission to get the story of Cabot Wright from the convicted rapist's own lips, and to write the truth like fiction. Bernie had been in New York a month looking for leads on Cabot Wright, and had had no luck. He had been everywhere, hunting . . . nothing. And now on Saturday night, a holy time in America when all men must find fun, Bernie's discomfort and homesickness were acute.

Carrie, a semi-retired miniature painter, believed confidently that her husband Bernie had, as she always put it, a "great book inside of him," if only for once he could start out with the right subject: his other books, unpublished, were all about himself and had been perhaps too personal to have wide appeal. Not only was Carrie certain that Bernie would write a great book, she was also convinced that it would reach the big public. Great books, if long enough and full of topical description and contemporary comment, were now coming into even wider public favor. The lengthier and fuller of comment, the better. But good subjects remained scarce, no matter how hard one hunted for them.

Carrie's third husband (Bernie was the fourth), Harold Winternitz, a LaSalle Street broker, had given his former wife a lifetime subscription to two great New York newspapers, and Carrie continued to read them absentmindedly through force of habit. It was the papers which put her and Bernie onto Cabot Wright, for such a purely New York criminal as Cabot otherwise might have escaped their attention in Chicago. Carrie had always been an *aficionada* of local crime, and was even a kind of authority on Illinois murder cases. The Cabot Wright affair, though far from murder, attracted her interest from the beginning and she cut out many of the writeups about the young Brooklyn rapist and pasted them in her clipping book. Despite Cabot's being guilty of something, there remained in her mind a queer feminine doubt that he had been

motivated to his deeds—more than 300 rapes in Brooklyn and
Manhattan—by the overpowering lust attributed to him by
the press. Yet nobody could deny that Cabot had been convicted in court by a jury; the world considered and wanted
him to be motivated by the passion attributed to him by the
most famous journalists of our time.

One winter evening, sitting in the basement of her South
Side Chicago home (inherited from Harold Winternitz), Carrie pored over the New York newspapers. Suddenly her eyes
fell on a small headline tucked away between the shipping
news and the report that the nebula of Andromeda was possibly inhabited by humans:

NOTED RAPIST RELEASED FROM PRISON;

CABOT WRIGHT RETURNS TO BROOKLYN

A photo showed Cabot, without his handcuffs this time,
staring away from the camera into the confluence of the Hudson and East Rivers. You could not see in the photo that his
hair was red, nor could you sense the warmth of his lips; only
direct sunlight brought that out. He looked vague, if not ordinary, of medium height, with athletic shoulders, but with a
somewhat pinched look of inattentiveness, perhaps caused by
prison food, confinement and bad company.

"Here's our subject for you," Carrie handed the newspaper
to Bernie.

She studied her husband's face.

"You will have to dig some, of course," she warmed to her

plan, "but if you would, you've got it at last. All you need do, Bernie," she gulped her toast soaked in coffee, "is present the truth as fiction."

Bernie scanned the news story and the photograph, but his face told her nothing.

"Think of what this could mean to us in the future, if it all works out the way I think it can, and you write the story as I feel sure you will," she talked on in the face of Bernie's rigid immobility. Her tones were more than pleading, they had a hushed quality he could never remember hearing from her before, like what you hear in the voice after conversion. "And you can do it, Bernie, love. You can write this book because you've got a subject at last."

Bernie smiled then briefly. There were two things he could never resist—encouragement and praise. He got both by the wagonload from Carrie, and it was the secret of their marriage's success. Older than her husband by at least twelve years, counting only her "alimony" house among her possessions in the world, Carrie tried to make up for any lack that she feared her young husband might find in her, by an incessant campaign to build up his self-esteem, courage, hope, faith. She was a church open only for him, with services in full operation twenty-four hours a day.

From the beginning of their relationship, before their sudden marriage, when Bernie only "roomed" at Carrie's house, she had given him not only praise and encouragement but the becalmed feeling of being supported at every level, even though, from the first, it had been Bernie's cash that brought in the groceries, and kept the light, water and gas on. But the house—as she had a way of reminding one—was Carrie's and it was from her that emanated the atmosphere of a home; the people who came to the house and who made "society" for them, were Carrie's friends first and foremost before they were his. It was perhaps Carrie's owning her house (none of his people had ever owned anything) that first communicated to Bernie the sense of being not only wanted but "at home" all the time. And finally he came to feel he was at home permanently, and this was important for a man like Bernie, who had been both an orphan and an inmate of a reformatory. Thus when he began his life with Carrie, he found more than he had ever dared hope for. Now suddenly, to Bernie's uneasiness, Carrie had more in view for him than happiness—she promised him he could be a famous writer.

In one of the many unpublished books he had written on the subject of his own life, Bernie had traced his origins in tedious detail. Coburn Maxwell Gladhart, the "scion of a broken home" (a phrase, from the day he had stumbled on it, he had taken for his own), had had his first big trouble as a boy, the result of his inexplicable impulse to steal bicycles from a factory parking-lot. He spent a brief stretch in jail at the age of 16. Once out, he was immediately in trouble again. As a second offender, he was sent to a reformatory, and there through the good offices of a young evangelistic chaplain, he was set straight, became interested in religiously-oriented psychology and, when paroled, found his way. He sold cars part-time, working the rest of the day as a bus-boy in a large university cafeteria. Here, one cool fall day, Carrie Moore, attending a Women's Art League tea in an adjoining building, had stepped to get some cigarettes, and spied him behind the coffee urn. Whether it was his prison pallor, his shy tough manner, or his look of need, she had fallen in love with him at sight, and hardly a month afterwards (they had begun seeing each other every night) she began divorce proceedings against Mr. Winternitz. Her marriage to Bernie took place two weeks after this divorce.

Only Bernie could have explained to anyone how holy it was to live in a *house,* after all his years of not being anywhere except on the outside. He was able to explain his feeling convincingly more by looks, gestures, and sounds than by words, for despite his passion to be a writer, he was limited in verbal facility. He loved the "at home" feeling above all also, and it was, as he saw later, perhaps the only thing he had ever loved. It was certainly the main thing that Carrie brought him.

That was why being sent suddenly to Brooklyn by Carrie was, as Bernie came to see every Saturday night (that holy handful of hours in America), a frightening mistake, and he was sure it would end in some permanent hurt, barring a miracle. If only, after all his wandering away from what he wanted, he could get back at last to the wedding-bower (Carrie's pet name for their bedroom)! Then everything would be all right, even if no book or writer came out of the experiment.

CARRIE MOORE HAD always been an extremely plain woman, though she had a good figure before she got plump. Like many plain women, she demanded a great deal of her husband around the house. Friends agreed that Bernie was a martyr to Carrie's sexual appetite, which had the reputation of being enormous. Curt Bickle, an obscure Chicago novelist and close acquaintance of Bernie, claimed that Bernie kept in training by consuming many boxes of raisins per week, plus canned frozen oysters, young onions, steak, protein pills, a thick molasses resembling car oil, and as many stalks of celery as he could masticate.

Every night in Chicago at 9:15 p.m., Bernie mounted the winding staircase, in his dressing-robe, to Carrie's huge bedroom at the top of the landing, and for fifteen interminable minutes, man and wife thrashed vigorously together among the bedclothes. Roomers who had returned home early heard Carrie, at the end of the quarter of the hour, cry out, "I'm going! Dying! I'm going, you hear?" Bernie, battling to keep his virile member belligerent, fought out the quarter hour, until his wife's cries signalled success; then he retired from the fray without having spilled a drop of himself, keeping what he had bottled up, as it were, for the exigencies of the next night. Sometimes, though, through feeling or lack of control, he lost command of himself, and then Carrie's cries of "Dying! Going!" were even more anguished. She never insisted outright that he reach consummation with her, for vigor, not self-satisfaction, were the requisites she asked of a husband. While she rested after the encounter in the wedding-bower, Bernie would go down into the basement and resume reading the Chicago papers over some warmed-up instant Sanka. If Carrie felt sufficiently revived and wakeful, she sometimes joined him, and together they would work crossword puzzles or watch something furtively on their midget TV screen.

After Carrie's brainstorm about his writing a book, they

spent more and more of their evenings discussing how to do the story of Cabot Wright. Sometimes, as in the nature of a reprieve, 9:15 p.m. would nearly slip by without her stepping upstairs for the encounter. She never tired of telling him what a great book he had "in him," and though he shuddered a bit, she emphasized that it must not be a short book, for length was a necessary ingredient of great fiction.

The more Carrie in her enthusiasm talked on, the more Bernie stared at her, immobile and drawn. Was Brooklyn, he wondered in such moments, her Siberia for him? He was, after all, her fourth husband; perhaps this was her method of ridding herself of him—by a mental plan.

On and on she went, in her flat mid-Western prairie drone, while he brooded and tried not to listen.

"Just a few days after publication," he heard a sentence here and there, "we'll see who's buying our book in the stores, eh, Bernie? With that subject," she laughed her satisfied late-evening laugh, "the young good-looking rapist from the right side of the tracks . . . who could fail with it?"

Not only was Bernie averse to leaving Carrie's house because of his "at home" feeling, a more practical consideration made him regard his departure as ill-advised. It was on Carrie's basement telephone that he conducted all of his car deals, his "little business," and whatever she may have thought of car-selling, it brought him a living. He was, besides, nearly as attached to his boss, Wurtheim Badger, as to "home"; selling cars was about the only job a paroled convict could get at that time in Chicago, but Wurtheim had been more than the man who gave Bernie his chance—he liked Bernie personally to the point of ribbing him unmercifully, teasing and making jokes at his expense, for he felt his little prison gradu- ate was a natural salesman, and could sell anything. The first winter as car-salesman Bernie had worked so hard that, as he pointed out to his boss and Carrie, "his ass had got as bony as an Arkansas mule's."

Now in Brooklyn, sitting day and night at his typewriter, Bernie nostalgically recalled Wurtheim's ferocious kidding of him, his belittling of Bernie's occupational "disease," his mock concern over any responsibility for an employee's physical dis- ability. In connection with Bernie's dwindling posterior, Bad- ger liked to tell an interminable anecdote about a Brooklyn cabbie who "went on this rigid diet because his stomach was so big he couldn't enjoy his wife in the usual textbook posi- tion, but instead of losing his fat where he should have, he lost it on his ass where he couldn't spare it!" Bernie recalled the story in full, hearing again the cadence of his boss's voice, his crawling narrative, unfunny the first time he heard it but now, in this strange place, not only unamusing but chilling like a postcard, falling out of a file, from a dead man.

Having been translated from Chicago to Brooklyn, almost without knowing why or how, changing professions from car- selling to full-time novelist, Bernie took up his new place of business in an antique sprawling tenement palace off Jorale- mon Street. It was called the *See-River Manor,* and it was a monster hive buzzing with Puerto Ricans, ruined Cubans, native whites and mulattoes ending their days on relief checks and handouts from friends and relatives. He didn't go to a nice residential hotel, as Carrie had advised him, for the simple reason that his source of money now was Carrie, not car-selling, and while generous with her body, Carrie had never been so with money. She had half-starved her own daughter in infancy, according to the friend of the family, Mrs. Curt Bickle.

If Carrie was stingy with spending-money—Bernie found himself living on the peanut butter sandwiches and fresh oranges that a fellow-convict years before had told him was a perfect diet—she was generous about paying long-distance phone calls at her end of the wire. Had Bernie been able to live on long-distance calls, he would have been well fed, because he called Chicago twice a day, early afternoon, when it was yet expensive, and late evening, when the rates were in effect, reversing the charges every time he called.

Maybe Carrie was approaching menopause, he mused, and had gone crazy and thought up this book for him. That was what was wrong with her, she had gone nuts and sent him to Brooklyn. All they talked about on the phone now was the novel, she never mentioned the wedding bower. Cabot Wright seemed to be some kind of change-of-life baby, so far as she was concerned. Even if he ever wrote the book, it would be hers, rather than his, it went without saying.

Then a funny thing happened. Though Carrie's maniacal interest in Cabot had left him rather cold in Chicago, it began to communicate itself to him in Brooklyn over the long-distance wires. Bernie began to feel not only that he was close to Cabot in some inexplicable but really connected way, he also felt at the same time that his meeting with his "main character," similar to the sudden appearance of a historical personage come to life temporarily, would be not merely unwelcome but maybe impossible to endure.

Bernie's new business day therefore settled around the telephone, much as it had in his car-salesman days, reporting progress to Carrie instead of Wurtheim Badger. In his in-between hours, to satisfy her later questions, he went hunting Cabot. He was already writing his novel—it was almost one-third finished—but Carrie insisted he must meet his subject before completing the script so that the story would be "authentic." Bernie simply went out and talked to people, to anybody who would listen. No one was ever able to direct him to Cabot, but it helped him to report to Carrie that he was doing something all day long besides writing.

As the weeks went by, Bernie became more and more certain of one unwelcome consequence: Cabot *would* appear. He was unsure of all the rest—that he would finish the novel, that it would be published, that he would ever see Chicago again, that he would resume his role as leading-man in the wedding-bower—all these things were improbable and dubious. But he was now sure that Cabot Wright would appear.

To convince Carrie that he was really hunting, he continued to ask around concerning the rapist. Newspaper vendors and men with shined shoes who stood around looking informed, cops, messenger boys, soap salesmen, the drivers of the Post Office trucks, sanitation men—all expressed mild interest when he questioned them and they noted his Chicago accent. Was he a detective? A writer. They nodded respectfully and seemed relieved he was not a detective. A few tried to be helpful.

"If I was you," a newspaper vendor who had heard of Cabot Wright told him, "I would just begin walking around the streets and by-ways here in Brooklyn. Go up and down. After a few blocks, ask anybody . . . Look on mailboxes inside the doors of apartment buildings that don't have doormen in front. Or where they do, ask the doormen. They're a snotty lot, but they know everything. Remember the character you hunt has a notorious name, but also remember the public memory ain't five inches long. They can't even remember their last famous general. The last human of importance the American people have been able to keep in the working end of their brain is your own Chicago triggerman, Dillinger. After him they kind of lost hold on keeping who's who straight. So don't be surprised if they don't remember who Cabot Wright is, or if they do. By all odds he's forgotten, but you could run into one of these cute newspaper-headline memory men, nuts for keeping old information on their tongue's tip. Such a wiseacre would remember, and then he might do one of two things, direct you right, or horn in your business. Don't tell him. Best thing to do is keep walking. Brooklyn is large—76 square miles—but the part where he done his dirty work can be covered in a few afternoons of easy strolls, and you'll come up with something. Glad you're not a dick, though. People like to help a guy with an idea. So good luck and don't sit down on the job."

OUT OF A city of over 8,000,000 people, how was he to find one man seriously in hiding? Cabot Wright had probably changed his name and appearance and would never be easy to verify from the only two available photographs. He may have undergone spectacular changes (grief and guilt damage the face and heart), and might vary chameleon-like daily as he strove to merge into the anonymous crowd.

Looking out over the waters that compose the confluence

of the Hudson and East Rivers, with Wall Street on the north and the Statue of Liberty on the south, Bernie was fevered again by his mania for belonging. That was why he had begun to steal as a boy, in the first place. He had wanted to be "inside" with the people whose houses he had to burglarize. Now in Brooklyn he felt left out of everything all over again. He didn't like to seem unemployed even to the kind of people who lived in the Joralemon Street tenement. (He told a man on his floor that he worked on a night-shift so that he wouldn't wonder when he saw Bernie around in the daytime.) Gradually Bernie realized that people in Brooklyn were even less interested in how he made out than they were in Chicago.

At night, half-asleep, he would see himself back in the reformatory and relive those days in agonized boredom. He remembered the faces of all the men and boys who had been "in" at the same time as he; he could still hear their talk and laughter, and could see the guards watching him and them. He had been over this thousands of times in his own mind and with the prison psychiatrist, but now it all appeared to him as a movie he had seen four or five times and had not enjoyed at the first showing.

He had begun burglarizing wealthy people's houses—he repeated to himself—because he wanted to be at home inside the house he robbed. Now again, in Brooklyn, he found himself in front of something like a closed house. He was hunting a man his wife had commissioned him to find, an unknown whom he was writing a novel about, whose whereabouts and person filled him with anonymous feeble irritability coupled with a forced conscious lack of interest.

"Do you really think I'll ever run into this man?" Bernie

asked Carrie during one of their interminable telephone con- versations. "Take a look at the Brooklyn telephone directory, for example," he told her, "and see the number of Wrights listed, blurry column after column of the same name. Anyway a convicted rapist who has served his sentence wouldn't want his name in a directory in the first place. Or take a look at the number of red-heads in Brooklyn, since Cabot has red hair. Even among all the people who have Jewish, Italian, Negro, and Puerto Rican fathers, redheads are common, let alone the Wasp diehards."

"Wasps?" Carrie wanted to know what he meant.

"It's a word they use here. White-Anglo-Saxon-Protestant."

Carrie admitted that the thorns and the difficulties were real but, she insisted, "They are not going to stump us!" and made kissing sounds of love, encouragement and goodbye over the long-distance connection.

Hanging up the receiver in the airless telephone-booth of the tenement, Bernie wondered again whether she had played a huge joke on him. Was this Carrie's method of ridding her- self of him, by sending him away? He remembered Zoe Bickle, Curt's wife, who once while drunk had told him that Car- rie actually hated all men, and would like to exterminate the breed. Failing that, Zoe had said, Carrie always got rid of her husbands one by one, after draining them.

2

MRS. GLADHART HEARS
MRS. BICKLE

C arrie Moore had arrived at her "plan" for her husband only after enlisting the support and encouragement of another person, who had come wholeheartedly to her aid. She realized that without the help of a confederate she would never in a month of Sundays have got the strength to send Bernie to Brooklyn. She could not bring herself to tell him before he left that there was somebody else behind it all, though by his steady examination of her face in their long talks in the basement, she wondered whether he suspected. He might have hesitated more than he did, had he known somebody else stood behind her, for he could obey and follow only Carrie. To believe that the directive was not entirely hers would have filled him with a cankering doubt about her belief in him. For that reason Carrie was careful to say nothing of her accomplice.

The friend who nudged Carrie into action was Curt's wife, Zoe Bickle, a handsome woman of forty-five, whom Bernie hated, and with whom Carrie herself had kept up a running battle for years. As the wife of the novelist and on her own, Zoe Bickle knew some of the right people in New York publishing and enjoyed being involved in "the real literary current," even though she seemed cynical about publishing, perhaps because of her first-hand experience of it. During the early years of her marriage to Curt, when they lived in New York, Zoe had worked as an editor in a venerable second-rate publishing firm. Her subsequent isolation in Chicago was due in a large part, one supposed, to the failure of her husband as a writer, but even now she held an editorial job with a Chicago encyclopedia, by which she supported Curt, and even did "free-lance" editorial jobs for her old employers occasionally.

Living only a short block apart, the Bickles and the Gladharts saw one another every Saturday night, a custom they had kept up for over ten years, when either Zoe Bickle gave a party to which the Gladharts came, or the Gladharts gave a party to which the Bickles came. More or less the same guests usually attended each party. At the Gladharts there were jazz records or a well-known jazz pianist, and everybody brought his own liquor, owing to Bernie's impecuniousness. At the Bickles, instead of music there was "discussion," and liquor was available if not exactly plentiful. At the Gladharts, with the musical background, the emphasis was on relaxed behavior, and the evening usually ended in a perfunctory type of sexual encounter in which married couples switched partners and unattached persons found a room not in use. People drank heavily, there were often quarrels between the married couples themselves, and on occasion physical violence. Invariably furniture was broken, again in a perfunctory way. The to-dos were sordid rather than exciting, perhaps because nearly everybody was approaching middle age. Even when there was a sprinkling of young persons and even children, advanced for their age, who painted or wrote or underwent trances, they seemed to add no exuberant or gay note.

One night at the Bickles the party was so solemn, with discussions of Buddhism, Unamuno and peyote, that Carrie, very drunk, took Zoe Bickle aside and confided her penchant and passion for the Cabot Wright case. For the first time in their acquaintanceship, Mrs. Bickle responded warmly to a topic that Carrie brought up. Zoe, it turned out, was a great follower of Cabot Wright, and said she would give anything to know how Cabot was faring now that he was out of prison.

Bringing her chair close, Carrie spoke into Zoe's ear:

"Do you think anybody could write his story?"

And Mrs. Bickle without batting an eye replied:

"Somebody has to."

"I mean as fiction, say," Carrie explained.

"As fiction," Mrs. Bickle boomed agreement, absolute belief, surety.

"You think Curt will want to write it?" Carrie felt her way, even though she had decided the writer must be her husband.

"I think Bernie could write it sooner," Zoe Bickle immediately replied.

Zoe's irony was wasted on Carrie. Whether she had uttered her remark as a witticism or a cry of bored impatience with Carrie or her own husband, the remark itself was seized on and carried off by her incredulous but triumphant auditor.

"I'll tell him you said so!" Carrie had risen at that moment, not wanting to lose what she had heard from Mrs. Bickle by any sudden modification or amendment. "I'll tell Bernie," she added for positive clarity, even though she had no intention of mentioning Zoe. All she had needed was this final psychological push, and Zoe had pushed her over the unknown brink.

"Sweetheart," Mrs. Bickle began, in slow realization she had made Carrie a present of something the latter dearly wanted. "Carrie!" she called, but her friend had already made her way into the throng, and that moment was the beginning of everything, for all of them.

ONCE BERNIE HAD departed for Brooklyn and Carrie was alone, she panicked. The one person she could have spoken to, Zoe Bickle, she hesitated to call, for the very reason that it was Zoe who had given her the courage to send him away. Though Carrie realized that Zoe could not have meant everything that her sentence had conveyed at the moment she uttered it, it had now become the truth. Carrie even knew she had acted on it because she wanted it to be the truth.

At last Carrie saw there was nobody else she could call except Zoe. They were old friends but not really close ones, yet out of everybody else in Chicago they were two women in a similar, almost identical, situation. In some ways Zoe's situation was worse than hers, for Curt Bickle was one of those contemporary men more common than book and drama reviewers realize—a man not only willing to be supported by a woman, but incapable of turning a hand to support himself. Also Carrie and Zoe were married to husbands who wanted to be writers rather than men who were in fact the authors of anything.

There were, of course, dissimilarities too: Zoe was positive for example, that her husband would never be a writer, at least in the public sense. In a way she now counted on his not being one, for she wanted to face as squarely as possible the truth of her situation: she had put everything on a losing horse. On the other hand, Carrie believed without proof or evidence that her fourth husband, Bernie, was a writer, that he would be known as one, just as she was equally sure that Zoe was right about Curt's not ever going to succeed. Too, Carrie counted on Bernie's being not just a writer but a successful one, and she clung to her almost irrational belief he could write the story of Cabot Wright.

In the past, Zoe had expressed mild interest in Bernie's literary ambitions but she had never before told Carrie to go ahead and let him try his wings in Brooklyn. Though they never discussed it, Carrie and Zoe had only one tacit agreement between them: Curt Bickle would now never make it. He might as well go on with what he was doing, studying and annotating the book of *Isaiah,* despite his Gentile origin and lack of Hebrew. True he had all the training needed for a writer, with his university background, controlled sensitivity, and flair for phrases (his thin-blooded prose appeared once every seven years in *The New Yorker,* cut a bit, with more commas than he had put in, but it was unmistakably his voice), while Bernie, untrained and without experience, as Carrie never tired of insisting, had the heart, the life experience, and the feeling.

If you get lonesome enough, Carrie knew, you'll even call the police. Zoe Bickle, in many ways, was for her a good deal more upsetting than a police lieutenant. She would ask Carrie more questions than a policeman, see through all her evasions and lies, and give her a hard time. Carrie finally realized she could delay her call no longer when she learned that Zoe was going on a trip.

When Mrs. Bickle answered the phone, Carrie said: "Zoe, precious, you know who this is. I hear you're going to New York in a day or so, but do you think you could do the impossible and come over? I know you're afraid of the streets after dark." Then Carrie briefly explained her situation and Bernie's mission in Brooklyn.

Hanging up, Mrs. Bickle was not quick enough to hide her astonishment, even shock, from her husband. He asked her what was wrong.

"She's sent Bernie to Brooklyn on the basis of something I said."

Curt Bickle's grim look turned his mouth to a paper-thin line. (It was his thin mouth that had originally captivated her, she remembered, as she looked at him now without desire.) He forced a yawn, then looked quickly at his wristwatch, while Zoe explained why she thought she'd better run over to Carrie's despite the hour.

"She's in a real fit, Curt."

"How could she send Bernie to Brooklyn on the strength of something you said?" He seemed hurt, and suspicious that what she had done might prove dangerous for both of them.

"Maybe I'll be able to answer your question when I come back."

She went out and walked quickly, looking about carefully. The danger of the streets (four or five women had been mugged in the neighborhood during the last month) worried her until she reached Carrie's and rang the bell.

She had hardly freed herself from Carrie's embrace and dry quick kiss when she began with the hardest question itself:

"You mean then that you sent Bernie on my say-so."

A bit startled by such suddenness, Carrie was nonetheless relieved it had come so soon and so sure.

"I'm afraid so." Carrie felt she might as well allow Zoe full responsibility.

"Do you have a cushion anywhere for this chair?" Mrs. Bickle half stood up to show how uncomfortable a seat she had found.

Carrie produced a fat nondescript sofa cushion.

"You'll have something to drink," Carrie mumbled. Thinking over her own invitation she said, "All I have tonight is some beer and a bottle of wine that's been opened some time, I'm afraid."

"Not a thing just now." Mrs. Bickle had adjusted herself to the cushion and lay her head back. "Perhaps I'll have the beer later. I'll see."

"Got a headache?" Carrie peered at her friend.

Zoe shook her head. "Today was Tuesday," she was barely audible. "That's my long day at the office. Tonight I cooked Curt's dinner for him."

"I thought he was the cook." Carrie's voice was gray as slate.

"It was his evening not to feel up to it," Zoe said.

"Curt's still wrapped up in the Old Testament?"

"*Isaiah*," Zoe nodded.

"What do you think he'll ever do with it? When he gets done with it, I mean," Carrie wondered.

Zoe had to laugh at the solemn manner Carrie always assumed when she touched on the subject of Curt Bickle, or indeed writing.

"I think maybe you worry more about Curt than I do," Zoe commented, and it was not the first time she had made this observation.

"Oh well now, Zoe."

"What do you hear from Bernie since his trek east?"

"He called just a few hours ago," Carrie brightened a bit. "We're keeping in touch by phone. Twice a day, as a matter of fact.

"Look," Carrie went over to Zoe's chair and stood like a pupil who has brought a paper to be corrected. "I mean, Zoe, have I been a maniac, do you think, in sending him to Brooklyn?"

"You do manage to make me feel totally responsible, if not exactly guilty, darling."

"You wouldn't of course remember a sentence you spoke. Oh, it was at your house, and I guess neither of us was bright and shining sober."

"I'm sure of course I must have given you a sentence or two then," Zoe's voice was hard, if not precisely unpleasant. "I hope you're not going to collect sentences I say when I'm in my Saturday cups."

Carrie waited a moment before she said: "I wouldn't have done it, if you hadn't said what you did. Mind you, I'm not blaming you."

Whipping out her compact, Zoe looked in it at her mouth which she had opened wide. As she closed it and the compact, she demanded:

"What was my goddam sentence?"

Carrie walked over to the mantel where one of her own miniature oil paintings had been placed. She did not reply.

"All right! I'm beginning to see what you want to lay at my door," Zoe said. She studied Carrie in the silence that followed, and wanted to shake her for not keeping up her personal appearance better than she did. Carrie obviously never went to a hair-dresser, she was at least twenty pounds overweight, and her complexion seemed never to know soap, let alone creams or bases. Yet sex was the only thing that had ever held Carrie's interest over the years, and one would have thought, well———.

"You thought then," Zoe fairly assailed her, "you thought *of course* that I thought Bernie could write the novel about Cabot Wright!"

Zoe had then exploded in laughter, but the sight of Carrie's pale intent face stifled her merriment. "Of course I said it, Carrie," she watched her from the corner of her eye. "I won't back away from any part in it."

Carrie nodded now. "But you didn't mean what you said," Carrie struggled to subdue her own threatening arms, held forward suddenly toward Zoe.

"I must have meant all of it," Mrs. Bickle weighed everything, and struggled with the attempt to understand her own confusion.

"But you're not sure!" Carrie shot at her.

"Well, sweetheart, sincerity is not quite so simple or convertible as everybody always makes out. As a matter of fact I think Bernie could write a book. Don't ask me to explain. Curt and I have argued over it. It's a feeling *I* have."

"But you feel I've been a horse's ass in sending him to Brooklyn."

"That's a risk we all run when we decide to do almost anything." Zoe had regained some of her more ordinary composure. "I mean you did right!" she now went on in a loud voice to Carrie. "But you can't expect me, poor lamb, to be quite so devout about your husband's prospects as you are. I'm not devout about Curt's, as you must sometime have observed!"

"I'm not going to blame you, and I didn't call you here to do so!" Carrie paced up and down.

"Well, it was a fateful utterance—mine, that evening," Zoe laughed.

"I had followed the case so long—the Cabot Wright one," Carrie began again.

Mrs. Bickle nodded for her to go on.

"And you see, I knew I was losing Bernie after all!"

Zoe Bickle could not suppress her look of surprise.

"Something fairly desperate had to be done," Carrie told her.

"I believe I'll have that beer now," Zoe loosened her feet from her high-heels and lay back in the chair now.

Carrie gazed at her for a moment as if inquiring about her health, then went out into the kitchen.

She came back with a stein of beer and a paper napkin, almost pushing them into Zoe's face.

Zoe drank eagerly from the stein, made a grimace of displeasure, then drank some more.

"You send a husband away to Brooklyn on a wild goose chase of writing a novel about a certain criminal I'm frankly taken with," Zoe began now in earnest. "Then it would be nice, you decide, if it was me who had thought the whole thing up in the first place because, I suppose, I happen to have kept a writer all my married life who won't write a line . . .

"I'll tell you everything I think then, Carrie." Zoe went on. "Curt, my husband, is a writer, and he'll never write again. That's our funeral, as they say down south. Now in your case, my pet, you're married to a phenomenon of our own special epoch, a man who couldn't in a thousand years be a writer in the only meaning of the term, but who can and probably will write a book. Put that down to a feeling I also have. And then tell yourself this before bedtime: I, Zoe Bickle, did give you that sentence the night you were at my place and the fact I'd had a lot to drink is not to the point. Furthermore, I think you were right to act on it, whether you're losing Bernie or not—that's beside the point too. You took a gamble, but you know that. Why should you expect everything to work out successful? You're old enough to know better. Furthermore, it may be nearly time for a new husband. If we look back on your old marriage charts, you're ready, sweety, you are."

"Since you say you sent Bernie to Brooklyn," Carrie took her turn now to laugh, "let me ask you another: will he write the book?"

"It might have been easier if somebody had hit me over the

head tonight in the street." Zoe put down her stein of beer. "As a matter of fact," she went on to Carrie, "I'm going to New York on some publishing business of my own, next week."

Carrie let Zoe have all the time she needed.

"I do know people who count in publishing," Mrs. Bickle let Carrie in on something Carrie already knew. Looking at her friend gravely, she added: "You've heard of Princeton Keith."

"Afraid not, Zoe, dear."

"It's a big name for nobody, which is all big names in our period are," Zoe smiled.

A deep depression had settled over Carrie. Mrs. Bickle held out her glass. "You know, darling Carrie, I can't drink this beer. When a drink's flatter than cistern water—"

Carrie made a motion to take it and get another, but Zoe vetoed her offer by continuing to drink.

"Who is Princeton Keith?" Carrie wanted to know.

"Mr. Big in New York publishing. He's given me a job of sorts in his New York office for a month or so. While I'm there, of course, I can introduce Bernie."

Zoe put down her beer for the last time, after trying to drink a bit more of it, and showed she was going home by walking over to the door.

"We don't know what will happen in New York, sweety," Zoe said, "but almost anything could. And I did say that sentence to you. Whether truth comes out in drink or not is up to somebody else to say, but I said what I said, and I'll stick to it."

When she heard this, Carrie became almost voluble: "Now

you've come over here at this hour of the night, through a street that scares you, you can stay a bit longer. We've broken a good deal of ice tonight. I don't expect to throw my arms around you or go down on my knees and pour myself out, but I'd like to tell you a good deal more than I've been able to before."

Zoe sat down.

"You think, for example," Carrie walked about like somebody reciting from distant memory, "you think Curt, your husband, is a real writer, and that Bernie isn't."

"All right, Carrie! You said that. I didn't," Zoe countered.

"Well, I wish you had said what you thought. I can even read the blank spaces on your face. But then that's you. You work at never saying or showing what you feel or think or are."

"No wonder I'm so tired then," Zoe thanked her.

After a lengthy silence in which Carrie paced and Zoe smoothed her hat, Zoe spoke again: "I don't know the answer to your questions, dear girl. Who do you think I am?"

"You don't know that you don't think Bernie can write?"

"I don't know what writing is."

"Oh now, Zoe, stop it."

Zoe showed by a gesture the little interest she had in it all.

"You're too frail a girl to have held up a grown man like Curt so long all by your lonesome," Carrie muttered. "That's all that's wrong."

Yawning, Zoe waited for her to continue.

"You've decided to intervene on behalf of Bernie. You're in publishing. Good. But you don't believe Bernie is or could be a writer, though you think he can write a book. On the other hand you believe Curt is a—probably a great writer, and will never write a line."

Zoe's eyes closed, then opened without expression, her jaw set, then slowly gave. "Well, I'm surprised," she could only say. "You make the truth so simple . . . And I don't believe Curt's a writer, either, for your information."

"But you think Curt might have been a writer, whereas Bernie never."

"Look, angel, why should you want me to say something you fear you might believe. You want to believe Bernie is a writer. All right, dear. What's *your* proof? For yourself, that is."

Her back to Zoe, Carrie fidgeted with the hour hand of a broken ugly ormolu clock whose ancient gold flaked at the touch.

"I did bring you some stories Bernie wrote, a couple of years ago. You and Curt returned the manuscript without so much as a word. What did that mean?"

"It meant they meant nothing to us."

"You meant he wasn't a writer then."

"We didn't think that far, Curt and I."

"Oh, Zoe!"

"You're new to writing, Carrie. You'd be much harder on a jazz musician or a painter . . ."

"But Bernie needn't be a great writer."

"No, he needn't," Zoe agreed.

"He's got to write this book," Carrie told her.

"New York publishers," Zoe began with studied reluctance,

"can make anybody write a book." She examined her teeth in a handmirror because one of her fillings had come loose and her jaw ached. "Queens with crowns, scrub-ladies, Coney Island pickpockets, dope addicts, corset salesmen—publishers have done all of them. Got almost interesting books from some of them. What's that got to do with what you call writing?"

"All right," Carrie merely continued. "Do you think then a New York publisher could get a book out of Bernie?"

"If he's got a paragraph of information in him they like, they can. If the book's bad enough, they'll publish it, and if it's *bad* bad enough, the daily reviewers will love it, and it'll sell. Now, dearest," Zoe stood up. "I've told you all I know."

Zoe was thinking hard about New York when she inquired: "Does Bernie really know anything about prison?"

"He was in long enough to know everything, wouldn't you think?"

"Then what in hell do you want him to write a book about a rapist for?"

"The books he wrote about himself never came out right, Zoe. The Cabot Wright story is just perfect for him. He'll understand the main character but he won't be made nervous by him."

Zoe laughed, and took Carrie's hand in hers. "Listen," she began. "I want you to know who I'll be turning your husband over to, now you've gone and bought him a ticket to New York on the strength of a sentence I spoke when drunk . . . Princeton Keith is Mr. Jesus Christ Jehovah in New York publishing at the moment. How long he'll last is of course not in my field of knowledge, but he should last, considering the times. He's an ugly-pretty skinny man of 45, he's crooked and he hates writing. He loathes and fears writers and would write the Pope a phony contract. As I say, he's crooked as a dog's hind leg, and can open all doors. If, you see, he decides Bernie can be used, and if he thinks Bernie has a book inside of him—not a real book, you understand now, you've got to settle on something they can *print*—then he'll help. Princeton can smell a real book and a real writer from the first strike of a match in conference, and then he goes into action to prevent that book or writer ever being heard from. He's America in action—opposed to quality."

"Oh, Zoe, cut it out."

"Do you want me to make that kind of bargain for you or don't you?"

"If he can help Bernie, I'm willing to overlook all those dirty digs you've just given both of us," Carrie said.

Zoe kissed her.

"Bernie's got a book in him," Carrie said in an attitude of prayerful menace, "and I don't care what you or anybody else thinks of him, and I don't care how he comes to write it."

"Fine and dandy," Zoe sealed the agreement. "Then Princeton's our man. For your private information, I went to school with him. We're from the same little Illinois town. Of course he wouldn't admit now that he was ever further west than Philadelphia, or that his dad was a dirt-farmer. But he's a bit scared of me, respectful at least, and I do hard little writing and editing jobs for him occasionally, like the one I'm doing next week. And he'll see Bernie . . . Better give me his Brooklyn address while we're about it."

"I feel you saved a lot here tonight," Carrie mumbled, as she wrote out Bernie's address for Zoe.

Pulling her jacket down and tight around her, Zoe said, "Why don't you fill up this barn of a house with some roomers again, like you used to? You'd feel less spooky," she touched Carrie again with her lips. "By the way how do you treat beer like that to make it taste like poison?"

Suddenly Zoe added: "You wouldn't have let Bernie go if you weren't crazy with hope."

"You ought to know it was more than hope. I thought his going off would be the only way to keep our marriage, frankly."

"That's kind of a dangerous risk, now I hear this part of it."

Carrie exchanged a look of defiance and menace.

"You admitted yourself, Zoe, so many untrained, uneducated men have written books that sold."

"Well, thank God then I thought up Princeton Keith for us," Zoe exhaled a great breath of relief.

She still didn't seem quite able to leave, though she faced the door again. She turned back to Carrie: "I see myself or a little of me all over again right here. You're not as young as I was when I made my big step down, but you're not old yet. But don't think you're ever going to get fat on soap bubbles now. I spoiled my life and I certainly spoiled Curt's." Mrs. Bickle seemed to be reviewing everything that had happened to her. "Babied him all the time, and he's never written a book that can stand on its own two feet, though he's completed a dozen novels. I gave my life to somebody who wrote and wrote and never finished even one train of thought to the very end. And yet Curt's a real writer too. His machinery is stuck, that's all.

"Why would I paint you a rosy picture about writing?" she went on. "There's not the slightest mathematical or human probability that Bernie can write a book that will make a cat take notice, even with a master quack like Princeton around, and even if his book's published—probable in an age of poop like ours—it will bring neither of you a thing. Most books don't even come into the world with the noise of the still-born."

"You could be mistaken, too, Zoe, smart as you are." Carrie had turned deathly pale.

Mrs. Bickle smiled her hard broken smile, showing upper teeth too perfect to be real.

"Whether Bernie succeeds or fails, at least we'll find out what he could do, and he can come home to me. That's what I'll have to hold on to now," Carrie said. "He'll try there, and come back to me here."

You're a goddam big optimist as well as a half-assed reckless gambler," Zoe looked at her sharply.

Carrie stared at her friend with a questioning grin, just this side of terror.

"You can't stop short of what's the truth now," Zoe said. "It'll hurt too hard later unless you tell yourself what can happen, right now. You must acknowledge there's a strong chance Bernie won't come back at all. Why should you fail to realize what you've gambled? If he writes the moneymaking book you both seem to think he will, he might not need to come back to you. He's never, after all, seen money. But there's the other chance that he won't come back if he *doesn't* write it, if he doesn't write anything."

Everything in Carrie Moore's expression went so blank that Zoe had the impression she was looking at a frame that had lost the picture.

"You're telling me in plain English I've lost my husband."

"Well you must have known there was some *suspicion* of risk or you wouldn't have sent him on his errand because of one poor drunk sentence from me!"

Carrie went as far to the other side of the room as she could, and there began to cry in earnest.

"I know in my case, in my marriage," Zoe ignored her friend's distress, for she saw no reason to spare her now even in the name of kindness, "so far as Curt was concerned, I knew he would leave me if he succeeded, and if he failed, I knew, Curt being what he was, would stay. I suppose I wanted him to fail, deep down. Some potty little analyst said as much to me once, though I never could afford the treatments. But failure has kept Curt at home like a nice warm dachshund. If he'd made money in the beginning, he'd have left me on my behind. I could be wrong. But our marriage has bloomed in failure. We're happy, we've been happy since we accepted the bed we made for one another . . . But you're ambitious and you're nervous, and you're neither young nor old. You're special gamblers, you and Bernie . . . That's where I can come in, with Princeton Keith." She seemed to be studying Carrie without actually looking at her. "Next week in New York, I'll know more. Meanwhile, Carrie you should fill your house up with roomers. Keep yourself occupied. And paint some more pictures. You're getting lazy."

She paid no attention at all to Carrie's convulsive weeping. Going up to her as if she were completely calm, she said, "We're both wives who support our husbands in a way some women would never comprehend, let alone undertake. We're not so unusual in an age like the present."

She patted Carrie's behind goodnight.

"You'll see how much I will do, Carrie dear girl," she told her, opening the door to leave.

3

IN THE COCKROACH PALACE

he doors to the rooms at the *See-River Manor* did not close properly. Anyone looking at the flimsy lock on Bernie's door, for example, could be certain of entering his room merely by pushing a nail file through the aperture between jamb and lock. But what burglar, to use a word that always made Bernie smile, would want to break and enter his room, or anybody else's in the *Manor?* There was one thing Bernie had, of course, that was beyond price and that the sirens of fire-engines and police cars made him clutch in the night—the notes and manuscript of his novel. If a burglar took that, he took everything. But who in the *See-River Manor* or in all the world would want what he had written? Even the many scavengers who roamed the streets of Brooklyn at all hours—odd men and queer ladies propelled not by their need for treasures but by some obscure and consuming impulse to bear away unknown person's discarded things—even scavengers were known not to break or enter.

What now made Bernie nervous in the night was not the knowledge that his lock was easy to pick or that anybody could enter his room, but the secret he now kept to himself and had not shared with Carrie on the long-distance telephone.

One evening, as he walked up the stairs to his room, his skin broke out in goosepimples when he saw that his door, which he had locked before leaving, was ajar. Inside a gentleman wearing a straw hat was seated at his desk reading the last pages of his novel.

"Bernie?" the unknown visitor extended his hand without rising, thereby indicating his importance. He smiled, amused to see that Bernie did not recognize him. "Princeton Keith," he introduced himself. "From the Goliath Publishing House. You're familiar with our books, I'm sure."

Bernie stammered a phrase.

"As to this story about Cabot Wright you're doing . . . But of course you'll have to change his name to a fictional one! Can't use real names, you know." The intruder pounded on the stack of typescript with his fist. "But whatever you'll call him, so far so good!"

Bernie gulped, wanting to say *Who told you? How did you find me?* and Keith, an amateur hypnotist and ventriloquist since early youth (he had performed magic acts on a mid-west vaudeville circuit at the age of 24), read those questions on Bernie's lips.

Bernie, who was still standing in the doorway, was afraid to close the door behind him.

"Come in, please," Keith motioned him to sit down on his

own bed, for he had taken the only chair. "Be seated by all
means."

He examined Bernie Gladhart's face with interest. "You're
puzzled. You see a mystery where no mystery is. As is usually
the case, there is no puzzle and no mystery. Mrs. Bickle told
me," he went on to explain. "Wife of a writer named Curt
Bickle. But of course you know both of them. Curt never did
very well himself at the writing game. On the other hand,
Mrs. Bickle feels you have a chance . . . —She's here," Keith
added, flinging a hand in the direction of New York City, but
was then puzzled at a strange disconnected look which had
come swiftly over Bernie Gladhart's features.

"Mrs. Bickle's here to help you," Keith brought out,
consolingly.

"*Her!* Help me?" Bernie exploded. "So this is why I'm here,"
he understood the whole thing now. "Talk about put-up jobs,
for Christ's sake. So this has been a crummy hoax from the day
Carrie read those newspaper stories till I landed in this cockroach palace. Oh, Carrie," he apostrophized his wife, "when I
see you again . . ."

Ever delighted at discomfort in others, Keith regained his
own composure and good humor. "Now save your steam for
your book, my boy. Never waste energy. Prime rule of mine.
Fool to let yourself go, young as you are. How young are you,
by the bye?"

Frowning, Bernie merely retorted: "So that middle-aged
bitch is behind all of this." He ignored Keith and jumped
around the room upsetting ashtrays and empty cheese jars.

"And my cheap double-crossing wife . . . So it was *her* idea, huh," he menaced Mr. Keith. "As if she could have an idea that wasn't bed . . ."

"I don't know what suddenly bit you, or where," Keith continued, perfectly calm. "But I will tell you this. We'd like to publish the book. We want, that is, your idea . . . Only thing I'd kind of like would be for you to meet with the goddam culprit himself. The rapist. It'd be a great help to all of us." Mr. Keith looked wistful.

Bernie studied his face for traces of irony, sarcasm, tricks.

"I'm not going to require the impossible of you," Mr. Keith looked away from him. "I'm after all not hunting documentation but ideas."

The thoughts of both men at that moment were elsewhere. Bernie was thinking of the "secret" he had not even shared with Carrie. It was something he had only recently learned in Brooklyn, and he thought Princeton Keith might have got wind of it by reason of his peculiar statement about the "goddam culprit." Princeton Keith's thoughts were more portentous. Though he was considered the most brilliant editor in New York publishing, he faced a crisis in his career, one might even say Armageddon. He was not here reading a coffee-stained manuscript in a bed-bug palace by choice. He had not found a new book or new writer that had made money for his firm in several seasons. Other editors, obscure compared to him, had recently made several "finds" and fortunes, and though Princeton Keith had been the fair-haired boy of the Al Guggelhaupt publishing empire, there was a marked coolness now between editor and publisher, a strained, inhibited but crackling hostility.

"Find me a new book, or a new writer soon, or face the eventuality of our early pension-plan," Al Guggelhaupt as good as told Keith, always in veiled and indirect messages, as had Corinna, Al Guggelhaupt's wife, in saccharine expressions of "concern" dropped from her lips at terrible cocktail parties.

Reading the story of Cabot Wright that late afternoon in the *Manor,* while the sounds of Spanish caterwauled up the rotten stairwells, Keith's face relaxed for the first time in years without the help of whiskey or tranquillizers.

"I've got it for you, you old ball-less dynamo, Guggelhaupt," Keith had actually cried out half-through the manuscript, and now as he faced Bernie similar words fell from his lips: "I've got you something this time you can't put down, you cruddy old fourflusher!"

Alarmed by this verbal attack from his intruder, Bernie seized Keith's arm and intemperately shook him.

"Of course you've got a book in you!" Keith exclaimed, coming to himself. "I've told you we want it. What more can I say?"

Baffled at Keith's odd incoherence, Bernie changed tack and said, "What would you say if I told you that in addition to writing all this about the culprit, I've met him besides?"

Keith looked at Bernie deprecatingly, and astonished him by his reply:

"I'd simply tell you that it isn't at all necessary. When I suggested awhile back that it would be good to know the rapist, I was merely speaking from an ideal viewpoint. What matters is here," he struck the pages of typescript again, "and you wrote this without meeting him!"

Exasperated, Bernie was about to shout, when Keith, who had good lungs, beat him to the punch:

"And what would you say, Bernie, if I told you that not only have *I* met Cabot Wright, but that I used to know him and his family."

Obviously taken aback at this intelligence, Bernie sat down again on his bed.

Keith smiled at the writer's token of receptiveness, and went on immediately:

"Not only, Bernie, did I know Cabot, I know all about him."

"Except where he is now!" Bernie shot, in great anger.

Unruffled, Keith persevered: "Big fellow with flaming red hair, toothpaste smile, innocent gray eyes, stuffy background, Yale—but," and here the editor chuckled, "his Achilles heel, Bernie—he was a *supposititious* child. Rotten heredity, one can only suppose."

Rising from the novelist's typing chair now, Princeton Keith took the younger man's hand in his, clasped it firmly, and said:

"Change the poor bastard's name, a few facts, names of victims, etcetera, we've got a book. Nice meeting you, Bernie."

The editor snapped his fingers in a northerly direction as in the face of an invisible eye: "We'll make you eat shit and call it filet mignon, Guggelhaupt old boy. And Corinna will smack her white lead lips for more."

"Mr. Keith," Bernie caught the editor by his jacket, "would it interest you at all to know, if I can get the word in somehow while you have your mouth shut, that I've also met the Achilles heel you refer to?"

"The expression Achill—."

"Shut up," Bernie said. "And sit down."

He shoved Mr. Keith back into the chair.

"Who do you have reference to?" the editor asked with alarm.

Despite being forced into a sitting posture, however, Keith drew himself up, was again the serious distinguished New York editor, guest columnist in New York newspapers, nation-wide lecturer, member of TV panels, a face invariably present at great cocktail hours.

"Who do I have reference to? Who but *him*," Bernie informed his visitor.

"You can't mean it, Bernie, by God!" the editor leaned forward eagerly. "It can't be true."

"Why would I tell you if it wasn't," Bernie gave it back to him. "After all it's me who's got to produce . . ." Then looking both mysterious and powerful, he added: "He's right here too," and pointed at the floor.

"You mean Cabot, of course," Keith wanted this point made clear positively, and Bernie nodded.

"As I said," the writer told Keith, "he lives here."

"And you've talked!" Keith could not help shouting. "You've said lots to him!"

"Almost nothing," Bernie replied, somewhat depressed by the smallness of his "secret."

Keith stood up again, now holding Bernie's typescript tightly against his three-button suit.

"Give that back here," Bernie snatched at the manuscript.

Making Keith sit down was much easier than taking a manuscript away from him, when he wanted it.

"I'll have five copies of it made!" he calmed Bernie. "I've never lost a manuscript, not in twenty years. We'll have a contract made up for you. We want the book," he said.

Then pausing as he thought over something, Keith added:

"Don't tell our culprit we know each other, Bernie, or he'll be on to the fact maybe you're writing something."

Keith studied absentmindedly a heavy silver ring on his hand.

"To think he's stopping in a place like this," he suddenly exclaimed. Catching himself, he looked up and away from Bernie, like a man come out of sleep. Out of the corner of his eyes, nonetheless, Bernie could see the editor examining critically his cheap Chicago clothes and the stained wall-paper with its morning-glory design.

"Of course a lot has happened to Cabot since I knew him," Keith sighed, still as if to himself. "Coincidence of this sort," he went on, "you two chaps in this same establishment, well, I mean, coincidence which is so common, so abundant in real life, dear fellow, isn't tolerated by many publishing people. Be glad I'm an exception. You'd have hurt your cause had you told most publishing people he was here. They like the workable story. I'm different," he sniggered.

Bernie considered Keith's ill-concealed judgment that if the *See-River Manor* was too seedy a place for Cabot Wright, it was, all in all, just about adequate for a writer such as himself.

"But you're sure it's really him now?" Keith inquired with

concern just short of hysteria, going up close to Bernie, his eyes still worried by something in the cut or the cloth of the suit the writer wore. It was this final scrutiny of his clothes by Keith that made Bernie decide he would loathe him from that moment on.

"It's him all right," Bernie nodded.

"Well, fiddle," the editor reassured him now. "Here or not here, we won't need old Cabot in any case. And after all if we do want to check a detail or two, or there's some color lacking in our palette, we can always use the old imagination. Expenses aside, too many cooks spoil the broth."

Keith patted the typescript again. "Bernie, don't forget, we're in business, old man. And this is a book. Don't ever let anybody say it's not. Thank God, Zoe Bickle's in town. We'll use her, Bernie." He flashed his smile. "We'll use you most," he whispered. "And we'll use *him* if necessary," he employed Bernie's gesture pointing downstairs. "We've found what I've been looking for, and I hope you feel the same. Just great to see you, Gladhart."

He had gone then, taking the precious thing that the fire engines and police cars had kept Bernie awake over, night after night. But Princeton Keith left behind a greater sense of security and hope, coupled with some inexplicable hurt and shame, than Bernie had ever known.

He went out into the hallway to make a phone call to Chicago. When he got to the booth, however, his hand refused to take the receiver off the hook.

4

FIRST ENCOUNTER

I 've seen somebody I don't know who down there, and it can't be nobody; it's got to be him—Cabot.

Bernie had indited these words in the typescript Keith carried away with him. It was Bernie's only record of his first Brooklyn discovery, and this was the secret he could not as yet share with Carrie on the telephone.

When he told Princeton Keith he had "met" Cabot Wright, he had not told quite all, for he had not really encountered Cabot in the social sense the editor assumed he meant. Rather he and Cabot had looked at each other in common surprise, as we catch a glimpse unexpectedly of our own worried face in a store window and do not immediately recognize who is staring back at us.

It had occurred in the following way.

Like all New York tenements, the *See-River Manor* allowed you to hear all sounds individually and collectively under its roof, resembling in this regard a huge listening-booth in a music, or record, center. Soon after his arrival, Bernie had discovered that when he stepped into his tiny clothes closet to hang his coat (it contained nothing else), he could hear a stream of sound—music and talk—percolating from below. Another week or two passed before he noticed the loose board on the closet floor. He picked it up cautiously, found it covered an empty space originally occupied by a hot-air register, and looked down. There, one floor below, was a kind of student's room, with huge dictionaries and reference books, a forlorn yellowed habitation in which somebody must spend his time morosely. As far as Bernie could tell, the room was empty.

Just a day or two before his meeting with Keith, hearing the sounds again, this time the monotonous speaking of a young man, Bernie quietly removed the board. He recognized the occupant as a man he had seen on the street, several times on the long promenade, always at night. In daylight now he could see that his hair was red. Was it Cabot? Later that evening, looking down into the room once more, he had been caught in his observance by the occupant himself who had shouted: "You up there! DON'T YOU BEGIN!"

Bernie had been taken too much unawares to put back the board at once. They confronted one another between ceiling and floor, interminably. The young man, when interrupted, had been examining his face in a small hand-mirror affixed to the wall by a nail. Strangely enough, after shouting at Bernie, he lost interest in his observer, and after feeling his way about the room by touching objects of furniture, like a blind man, sat down in a dilapidated easy chair minus a cushion, and seemed indifferent to the fact that Bernie still gazed at him from above.

After putting back the board, like a sleepwalker, fearful, trembling as when one hesitates to open a telegram bearing a message that may change one's life forever, Bernie had gone down to the vestibule in which all the mailboxes were lined up. In all the days of going in and out of the building and looking automatically at his own mailbox (the only mail he expected to see were his rent and light bills—what reason had Carrie to write him, when they spoke on the phone twice a day?), he had never before noticed the names of his fellow tenants. For the first time now he looked at each name, going from box to box and finally coming to the number of the room beneath his own. In black lettering on gold he read the seven letters: c. WRIGHT. Several days later Keith Princeton called on him.

AFTER BERNIE HAD recovered from the shock of Keith's visit enough for his hand to obey him, he managed to take the receiver off the hook joylessly and telephoned Carrie in Chicago. He wanted to scream at her that he knew all about Mrs. Bickle and the book being *her* idea, but he was in control of himself now and instead dutifully began telling Carrie his "secret." As he quietly explained that at last he had discovered Cabot Wright's whereabouts right in the *See-River Manor,* he realized that Carrie was not really interested or surprised and, to his incredulous certain horror, he was certain somebody was with her in their—in her—bedroom. After a very brief conversation, she made her goodbye kissing sound, but he could not bring his hand to hang up the phone. Then hearing voices and someone laughing, he realized that Carrie inadvertently had not put her own receiver back on the hook. They were still connected and he was about to shout and warn her, when what he heard silenced him . . .

What Bernie heard in the wedding-bower as he listened with frozen attention in Joralemon Street, was the product not only of Carrie's own nature, but of Mrs. Bickle's visit to her house.

Zoe's visit had struck terror into the painter's inmost being, and only after her neighbor's departure did she realize how shattered she was. Carrie had not been so "down" since Harold Winternitz had told her she represented every second-rate Bohemian claptrap of a dead era. Looking in the mirror, she saw that she was certainly old in the face, and if anything older in the body. Her peculiar logic might have told her that she was through; instead it told her she required someone young and disengaged of the opposite sex, and at once.

Carrie had grown up in an age which practiced promiscuous coitus as an injunction, if not a duty. Marriage, she and her contemporaries felt, was easier and more sensible than the single state, though not laudable or noticeably rewarding in itself—a gray *faute de mieux*. The best thing about marriage was the increased opportunities it afforded to meet a number of men sexually in relaxed homelike surroundings. Being single to her would be as awkward as appearing in the street bald of pate or deprived of makeup.

Even more than her craving for "success" and "recogni-

tion" in her husbands was her incurable need for "romance."
She wanted to be married to a writer, but she also needed a
permanent man in the wedding-bower. Carrie saw now, of
course, after Zoe's call, that she had not quite understood her
own motives in sending Bernie to Brooklyn. Zoe's remarks
made it clear to her that she had acted rashly and that her
lonesomeness, as a result of her rashness, would be an awe-
some problem for her.

For days after Bernie's departure she did nothing but sit in
her wicker rocker, with her hi-fi set playing for interminable
hours, opening up new boxes of cleansing tissue, blowing her
nose, wiping her eyes, and cursing Zoe and her first three
husbands intermittently with the popular bad words of her
girlhood.

Bernie's daily long-distance telephone calls, satisfying though
they were at first, since she realized she was "inspiring" him,
were finally too spiritual. They did not assuage or comfort her
need for romance in any palpable way.

She finally decided that perhaps the best thing to do was
follow Zoe's suggestion, and again let out her rooms to rent.
Roomers in the past, often between husbands, had somehow
kept up her spirits and her interest in life; when depressed, she
could invite one of the boarders downstairs for a drink and a
chat. Shaking off her lethargy and blues, Carrie walked over to
the five and dime store just before it closed one evening, and
purchased a neon-bright red sign that said BEAUTIFUL ROOMS
TO LET.

The sign had been up only a few minutes when she felt it
was "working." Early the next morning the bell rang and on

hastening to the door, Carrie had been pleased, if not thrilled, to see looking in through the frosted glass not the romantic stranger she hoped for, but something a good deal more promising, the familiar face of a friend who was a young handsome bachelor to boot.

Something snapped that evening in Carrie's brain, she later explained to herself. The moment she opened the frosted door, all she could think of was, "He is the answer to my prayers." Brooklyn and Bernie seemed as distant as Burma when she laid eyes on Joel Carmichael Ullay.

She had known Joel when, as a very young man, he had been part of a well-known Negro ballet group, and the husband of the woman who headed it. A Ph.D. and a beauty, this woman had danced out in methodical savagery her contempt for the white race, until she herself had become a woman of wealth and social prestige. Joel had broken with the great choreographer during her rise to eminence, and had got himself a good job in the Government. Rather light-skinned in strong light, he somehow looked beautifully dark and interestingly menacing in subdued illumination. A mole near his satin mouth increased his appeal which, after his divorce from the choreographer, he felt too unusual ever for another marriage.

Harold Winternitz, who deplored racial fraternizing unless on a strictly professional or cultural basis, often taunted Carrie during their short-lived marriage by saying he was surprised so "emancipated" a woman had never crossed the color line in bed. Stuck as she was in a Caucasian vacuum, he sneered, perhaps much of her misery had been owing to her monotonous racial diet.

If Winternitz had been a witness to her present meeting with Joel, he would have seen it was more than race which brought her this evening to full realization of her caller's startlingly exotic but obviously available charms.

When she finally showed Joel the large double-room that was for rent, she was already aware that Bernie's voice, which had been echoing every day from every room in the house, would now be as inaudible as one of her busted phonograph discs. She did not know how Joel felt, but his very coming and his persistent smile, the padded way he followed her up the stairs to view the room, made her assume that he felt enough. She was not wrong. Before he had made final arrangements about the rent, they were automatically in closest embrace, as if a kiss were the conventional requisite for finalizing an agreement, like strong liquor drunk by businessmen over a deal. Kissing her with warmth and generous wet lip and tongue, he had allowed his hands to rest first on her breasts, then on her buttocks, and the two clasped each other like stars before a cameraman who had shot this scene innumerable times before.

"Have supper with me later tonight?" she managed to ask, once disengaged. As he began his descent of the impressive staircase, the keys to his room in his hand, he nodded to her question without turning around or speaking.

After Joel had left, she could only sit down again in the wicker rocker, and practice calm. Had one of the Illinois tornadoes blown away the whole house, leaving her and the rocker intact, she could not have sat there more oblivious to outside happenings. She knew this was a principal, albeit spectacularly unforeseen, event of her life. All other attachments, loves, husbands, events in her life seemed faint and unreal. There had never been a Harold Winternitz, and there was certainly now no Bernie Gladhart. She cried a little as she saw Bernie disappearing. He had needed her, and probably still did, but it was a hurricane after all that sometimes made you wake up. She knew now he could never be a writer. Those querulous phone calls told her, for on a telephone one finally hears the real voice isolated from the flesh that contains it. What she heard coming to her from Brooklyn was only a mewling infant, missing its milk. It had been for her a kind of drug to believe the impossible, to believe in Bernie, but suddenly her belief was dead.

Carrie knew of course what was coming this evening, and she prepared to make herself ready. She rested, she drank bowl after bowl of nourishing clam soup, and every so often just a nip of brandy. She telephoned a fashionable Hungarian restaurant which, on being pressed, would send out a complete dinner for two.

There would be no more empty hours in the wedding-bower, she told herself, aloud. After all, she had tried the impossible with Bernie, and she was glad her punishment was over. Waiting for evening, dressed only in her foundation, but with her wired bra lifted to dizzy heights, she snuggled under a coverlet covered with lily-pads for design.

In bed with Joel late that night, Carrie scarcely was aware of the telephone's ringing, as freeing herself briefly from her lover's smoky arms, she achieved consciousness long enough to say a few words into the mouthpiece. She could hardly remember what she said, for her body satisfaction, akin to a coma, owing to Joel's expert lovemaking, prevented her from either recognizing what Bernie said in his puzzled voice, or saying anything much to him in reply.

In her special physical state, and her longing to be back in Joel's arms, she had let the phone fall to the floor, remaining connected with Brooklyn and permitting Bernie to enter the wedding-bower, and by the miracle of electronics hear everything as clearly as if he were listening at the door.

AT FIRST IT was difficult for Bernie even to take it in, let alone believe his own ears. He felt like a man who had tuned in the radio to hear the announcement of his own death. Yet he was unable to leave off listening, and the earpiece seemed to have become attached to his face.

Carrie's bed was always immediately adjacent to the phone, and her words to Joel Ullay came clear and merciless, leaving nothing in doubt. Bernie heard all, listening for what seemed hours at Carrie's expense both financially (collect call) and spiritually (her soul laid bare). He heard, that is, not merely their lovemaking which in its eclipse of his own left him feeling annihilated, but toward dawn Carrie, speaking in quiet sober tones, declared that Joel was to succeed to all bower rights from now on. This was followed by her analysis of Bernie's own spectacular failure as man and provider, then in turn by a vigorous new set of coitus, with cries of animal pleasure and yelps from an unidentified throat, at which Bernie himself seemed to lose consciousness, being awakened again by renewed cries and moans emanating from Chicago.

The last thing Bernie heard before he hung up once and for all was Carrie's telling Joel that not only was Bernie pedestrian in bed, but he would never, even by wildest chance, finish the story of Cabot Wright.

Bernie planned immediately to jump off the Brooklyn Bridge, but a headache of such exquisite pain and tender pulsation started that he could not even walk out of the *Manor*. He finally got to his bed, fell on it without taking off his clothes, and for the next few days did not know whether he was waking or sleeping. Early one morning when he came to, there was a woman sitting beside him. It was Mrs. Bickle, who had awakened him by the cool pressure of her hand on his temple.

5

ZOE SIGNS WITH PRINCETON

M rs. Bickle had arrived in New York during the big drought, the revival of the wig and white-lead lip makeup, fellatio as the favorite subject in best-selling fiction, the campaign by the Commissioner of Markets to put palm-readers, fortune-tellers, and purveyors of the occult out of business, and world sugar irregular.

Dropping in unannounced from the Gramercy Park apartment that Keith had obtained for her, Mrs. Bickle had no idea she would find Bernie Gladhart as sick as he was or living in such squalor. She called a doctor, a young Sephardic Jew, who prescribed sedatives and told her the sick man was undergoing a minor emotional crisis. He cautioned her to sit at his bedside until he rallied.

Obeying, Mrs. Bickle listened to Bernie; incoherent mumblings through the night, their chief topics being incarceration and the noose. Early in the morning, he seemed to take a turn for the worse when he recognized her beside him. It required

time and effort on her part, together with the doctor's predilect remedy of cup after cup of warm water with lemon juice,
to convince Bernie that they were not back in Chicago, and
their New York career lay still ahead.

"When you're stronger and I've had my beauty sleep, you
can tell me what happened," she assured him. "I suspect,
however," she added, "it's the place as much as anything,"
and she surveyed the filth and the mouldering walls and
ceiling.

"The place, hell! Carrie's gone and married a nigger," Bernie exploded.

A few days later when he was well enough to be sitting in a
chair, dressed in a monk's cloth bathrobe, he explained it all to
Mrs. Bickle.

"I suppose it's my fault, too," she said, "since I'm supposed
to have sent you to Brooklyn in the first place."

"You don't seem too surprised at my news either, come to
think of it," Bernie studied her face.

"How did you find out he was colored?" Mrs. Bickle asked
in reply. She did seem unsurprised. "I mean," she said, "after
all you were only on the telephone."

"Oh," he sneered. "Well, that's easy. She shouted his name."
He laughed three times. "When she was in culmination, she
called out, 'Joel! Joel Ullay!' and I remembered that was the
name of the dinge dancer she knew."

"I'm already in on the whole thing, Bernie. I may as well
tell you."

"You mean you heard it on the phone too?" he was nearly
credulous.

"Curt phoned me about it," she said. "News travels fast in that neighborhood."

"Well, then you can tell me," he snorted and leaned back in his chair. "Go ahead." He lit a cheroot, and began examining the ends of his fingers.

"I'm sorry, Bernie, about it."

"Skip the shit and let me have the facts," he told her.

"Somebody talks like he was going to live after all," Zoe couldn't refrain from a sigh of relief.

"Go ahead and tell me, Zoe, and then I can decide by myself if I'm going to die or live."

"Well, of course you're right, Bernie. It is Joel Ullay. He's moving in."

"*Moving?* He was clear in the other night."

Consuming his cheroot in enormous drags, he went on with: "Say, Zoe, did you ever hear of a guy that lost everything as quick as I did: my home, wife, job, my town. I ain't got a thing left, if you think it over."

She did seem to be thinking it over, and he turned away from her face with irritation and impatience.

"Go ahead and give it to me," he told her.

"If you can wait a minute, I'll give you Curt's version of it," she fumbled in her purse for a cigarette.

"Oh don't give me nothing. I hate people who got versions from out of somewhere, and horse around with pauses and commas and expression on words, and that jazz. Give me the news."

"All right, the gory facts then." She stared at the long ash on his cheroot and lighted her own smoke.

"Seems Carrie and Joel had a mock wedding at her house," she began.

"Well," he was impatient again at her pauses.

"They claimed they didn't want to go to the trouble and expense of a divorce this time, and in any case Joel's present girl friend would not cooperate at any level, it seems, though later she may be agreeable to a settlement . . . Everybody who has ever half-known either Joel or Carrie was there. Mostly South Side folks, of course. And it was a costume affair." Mrs. Bickle turned down the corners of her mouth to show what she thought of that. Bernie's face was stony, but he managed to inquire:

"You don't know who the bride came as, by chance?"

"Curt didn't mention how any of them came," Zoe replied. "But they were all pretty seedy costumes, and a good many only made a stab at dressing like anybody. There was a pillow fight early in the evening, and a good many of Carrie's American antiques and objets d'art got busted, and Harold Winternitz's Oriental carpet burned badly. The usual great jazz pianists, that U.S. Senator Carrie always keeps in tow, an old opera star or two, the university people, the young fry and children and finally the ceremony, with ring, 'preacher,' wedding march, and the rest. After that it was just like it always is at your house on Saturday nights." Zoe stopped. "Don't look like that," she couldn't help saying to him.

"How?"

"All ashes and thorns," she told him. "It had to end, Bernie," she went on as consoler. "Be glad, really, that it ended here for you instead of there. It would have been terrible for you had it occurred while you were in Chicago, believe me. You really would have been hurt. It's terrible here, too, I realize, but distance dissolves some of the nastiness, not the main part, granted, but some."

"Jesus, you have philosophy," Bernie said.

"Bernie," Mrs. Bickle proposed, "supposing I invited you out to a nice big restaurant with carpets and chandeliers and tall drinks and food. Wouldn't that make you feel more like living? I've got a message for you from Princeton Keith."

"Don't have the clothes or the appetite," he replied.

"You will," she said in a soft if sarcastic voice.

Looking at her studiously, Bernie brightened and went on: "Would you mind stepping over here and doing a little something for me in the line of a favor?"

She nodded.

"Bend down now," he said when she had approached him, "bend down and cover my face with nice warm cool kisses. I know you won't feel it when you give them to me, but fasten a few on just the same."

"Well, poor little hard-up you," Mrs. Bickle bent down and pecked him a couple of times. He took her hand in his.

"Did big old Keith tell you about *him?*" he moved his head in the direction of Cabot Wright's room, below.

She thought a moment before she said, "Is it really him, then?"

"No question about that," Bernie mumbled. "The rapist is down there all right . . . Go take a peek, why don't you. It's in the clothes closet, and you just lift up the loose board on the floor."

"I take your word for it."

"If I get to feeling better, I've got to show him to you," Bernie spoke now almost too low to be heard. "You know you look good here, Zoe," he still held her hand. "You look almost gorgeous." He kissed her fingers.

"You *are* homesick as well as light-headed," she sighed, but she bent down again to kiss him, and he held his mouth to hers.

Freeing herself, she heard him comment: "Just to think when I accomplished my mission at last and found my rapist, the lady who thought it up in the first place had just given the whole thing up for love."

"Life is full of incidents," she spoke as he pulled her down to him again.

"Don't do this because you think you have to or because we're both away from home," she cautioned him. "And for God's sake no little games of spite on poor old Carrie, please."

"You look good to me. I told you that," and he put his mouth to hers again.

After a night in Bernie's arms, Mrs. Bickle found that if she had not yielded to him as ardently as Carrie always testified she did, she had warmed him up from total despair, and on returning to her Gramercy Park apartment, taking off her high heels as she sat with a drink on her divan, she realized that she had replaced Carrie more completely than Joel Ullay had Bernie. She would probably never be Bernie's lover in any full sense of the term, though nobody can be sure what is coming so far as love is concerned. In any event she had better take over Bernie's book about Cabot Wright, or Princeton Keith would make her life a hell.

―――――

ON HER FIRST day in New York, Keith and Zoe had met for their talk at a fashionable hotel, in a huge court of potted palms, in an alcove protected by an awning, exclusively reserved for the publisher by the management at certain hours each day of the week. (A gentleman from a rival publishing house had once inadvertently approached Keith's reserved space a bit ahead of the editor; Keith had commanded him to be off; when the other refused, they had come to blows; worsted, the interloper had left with a bruised cheek and eye, cursing his assailant roundly.)

Studying Keith closely now, Mrs. Bickle discovered he was happy over two things, one that Bernie had a book about the rapist and the actual rapist in tow, and two that Zoe was here, on the spot.

"It's a little bit too wonderful for me to believe," he told her. "And I need a book like this, believe you me, Zoe, dear. My publisher, Al Guggelhaupt, needs it too, God knows. We've got to find something *good*. We're dying from best-sellers. All money and no bite."

Mrs. Bickle looked away.

"And to think," Princeton went on to exaggerate a bit, "that it would be an old girlhood sweetheart who would bring this all about!"

Zoe Bickle smiled, and even flushed faintly, trying to remember what Princeton had been like as a boy in the small Illinois town where they had grown up. He could have been nobody's sweetheart, she was sure.

Her uneasiness about Princeton was not prompted by his

inadequate memory of their childhood, but by the offer she knew he was about to make, which he had already referred to as something concrete and substantial.

When he realized what was wrong—her obvious distrust of him—for he was nothing if not sharp, he began to work on her, hard.

"There you've been for years," she heard his voice as she sipped the incredibly frondescent mint julep he had insisted on selecting as her drink, "hiding your light under a bushel, nursemaid to a ne'er-do-well hypochondriac writer, a wet nurse, if the truth were told, when you could be one of the best editors in publishing. But now I've got you here, I'm not going to let you go. You know I have this offer to make to you, or you wouldn't be sitting before me. We'll forget the other little job you came here to do. A ghost can do that . . . Let me put it this way, Zoe dear, you can send Curt money, enough to let him study Hebrew the rest of his life, if you'll see the light of reason here in New York."

Without waiting for Mrs. Bickle to say no, he named the sum of money he would give her.

As it was an incredible amount of money, she expressed her surprise by total lack of expression. Princeton repeated his offer.

She could only sit there, perhaps stunned, but looking bored and dull.

"I'm offering Gladhart half as much," he was clearly puzzled by her poker face.

"Just enough to put him on easy street," she quipped, to his relief.

As he rattled on with his plans, he was careful to watch the look of temptation come and go on her face. She had been not only poor a long time, he knew, she had not been praised or complimented by anybody for even longer. He was positive Curt never paid her the slightest flattery. As a matter of fact Curt seldom kissed her, and sexual matters, Keith decided, must be nearly forgotten between man and wife back there. But in New York, he saw, Mrs. Bickle was blooming, and looked ten years younger than her age; she looked certainly fine in the court of palms, and her good appearance would help him when it came to promote their idea, possibly even more than Bernie's having the perfect book, and the actual rapist under surveillance. It was all too goddam wonderful.

"Of course," Keith went on, in reply to a comment from Zoe that was both cynical and indifferent, "I mean to make you work for your money and I mean to pick your brains. My own career is—I'll be open with you—always in the balance."

She looked up quickly on hearing his last remark, but finding it, as she thought then, merely rhetorical, went on with her apologies for turning down his offer: "I'm afraid you want things I don't have," she explained to him. As soon as she had said this, she realized it was obvious she wanted to back out only because she had felt the temptation of his offer, and because the sum he had named was so huge.

"If you want more money," he said coolly, "that can be arranged."

"Now you've frightened me even more," she was truthful.

"The fact is, Prince, I couldn't write a novel if I tried, and I know next to nothing about prison, rapists, or indeed Bernie."

"Perfect. You don't need to know a thing about any of them," he informed her. "I want somebody who can write . . ." He pulled from a battered briefcase Bernie's manuscript. "The book is nearly all here," he thumped on the soiled stack of paper. "We need more facts, details, and less of Bernie's kind of mentality, which he calls imagination. We'll need to know more from the rapist," he paused suddenly and looked far away, out into Central Park, "and by the way, speaking of that," he spoke in hushed legal tones, "I've checked and doublechecked. The man below Bernie *is* the rapist. It's Cabot Wright," he explained, "living in the room beneath our Chicago car-salesman."

Now she was really surprised.

"We need you, dear Zoe, for the English language and for brains. Nobody else can give us those but you. I don't want to call in any ghost."

"You'll have to let me go on taking in the facts," Mrs. Bickle had then replied to his peremptory command that she decided at once about his proposal.

"I'm afraid I don't have time for the luxury of procrastination," Princeton Keith said swiftly. He looked both menacing and bilious. She was taken aback by his look of gritty cold determination, so that she flushed again, which he noted.

"If you don't say yes to this offer, Zoe, you're a bigger idiot than anybody who ever lived. One would even doubt you really love your husband, for I don't see how you'll be able to provide for his old age, which I imagine will be a costly one, on the salary you're earning now."

"I'm still getting over my surprise," she said, an odd tone in her expression, as if she hadn't heard his last speech.

"Over what, may I ask?" he was immediately cautious.

"Over your enthusiasm."

Keith sat back in his chair and groaned. "Look," he began, in exasperated paternal explanation. "I'm in business. I'm in business for Al Guggelhaupt. Could I have enthusiasm and work for him, do you suppose, or work for myself? What's more, I don't think you have enthusiasm either. It's what endears me to you. Besides, it's a dangerous emotion, primitive American, I judge, and it's the first thing to watch if one wants to avoid decline. I don't think, as I say, you ever had it, and you won't catch it from me, thank hell, and you won't catch it from New York."

"BUT WHAT ON earth do you see in Bernie's writing?" she cried, and she stared at the manuscript beside them on the marble-topped table.

"Dear little girl," Princeton patted her arm. "Be in touch," he begged her. "Do be in touch."

"No, Prince," she was gloomy. "You'll have to explain better than you've been doing, or I can't say yes to your offer."

It was his turn to flush.

"I'm where I am because of offers such as I've made to you," he said, grim. "And I intend to stay where I am."

"At the top," she smiled.

"All right, wherever I may be," he spoke now almost savagely. "And you can go back where you came from if you're happy there."

When Princeton suddenly became silent, to indicate he was thinking about terminating their interview, she let the words slip out again in only slightly different phrasing:

"But, Prince, you couldn't want his book for the idea!"

"And why ever not?" he countered.

She saw then he was in earnest.

"But anybody could think it up!" she said.

"Anybody could think it up after some boob had done so," he informed her.

She began to see faintly then what it was all about.

"You're impressed by his idea yourself, but you won't admit it," he scolded again. "Your towering pride, Zoe. Ten miles high—you've always been so."

"A young man from Wall Street rapes 300 women, is convicted on the testimony of one of his victims, is sentenced, gets out, comes home to Brooklyn." She shook her head.

"It's splendid, it's sumptuous, it works," he tore a paper cocktail napkin in two. "And it's a book, my dear."

"Do you mind telling me," she wondered, "if you get all your ideas from boobs?"

"I'd say so," he answered without hesitation.

"And where do you find them? The boobs, that is."

"That's the fine thing about New York," Keith intoned, half-closing his eyes. "They're nearly all here, the boobs. It's a city based on them, and if one feels he needs someone in any field, a walk around the block, a hop on the subway, a random telephone call—he's supplied. You don't think I'd be where I am without them?" he inquired. His voice now sounded like that of a man much older than his years, say that of an Al Guggelhaupt.

"Well, Prince, I guess you're in earnest," she conceded, mild, even melancholy.

"I'm not earnest, silly. I'm acting successful."

"All right, you've found one boob in Bernie, and I don't suppose I should protest too much if you find another in me. But I'd like to know the details as to how you'll use me. That's all."

"You'll put things together for me, Zoe, dear, and you'll keep an eye on Bernie, of course. When I feel I'm running thin, you'll pour me thick again. It won't be too hard. But, Zoe, I can't do it so well without you, and that's why I'm offering you that sum of money that made your eyes so wide. You'll have to stay. As I've said, I'll make it more than advantageous."

She stared at him.

"I've heard of offers like this," she thought again of the money, "but I never quite believed them."

"Everything finally happens, Zoe," he told her. "And here it happens again and again."

Some tears came into her eyes, and though tears never pleased him enough even to notice them, he dried hers quickly for her.

"You've been good all your life, dear," he told her, "and if you think you're going to be bad—and I know that's what you are thinking—you've the right to be so. Once you've got your money you can be good again all over—to Curt, to everybody. Your role, sweety, which you picked for yourself early, is to hang on some kind of cross more or less continuously.

What I'm offering you will frequently be pure inferno, so you should feel at home most of the while. If you won't do it, some other smart person will come along and do it for you. For while I mentioned the boobs, I didn't mention the brains. I pick them both."

"I feel I have already signed the papers," she was smiling, though disconsolate.

"Come, come, Zoe," he said. "No posturing and let's have a cup of hot tea now to make us both feel better."

He called to a boy in Arabian costume, and gave him the order.

"And I can't even think the offer over," she said when the tea had arrived and its warmth and excellence began to cheer her.

"Only until you've heard the whole proposal, my dear. I've only told you half."

She looked up then as if she had suspected as much, and an expression of uneasiness passed over her face and clouded her eyes.

"You probably can guess what the second part of the proposal is in any case," he was firm, but she felt he too looked pale and worried despite his jauntiness and cold confidence.

"I don't want you," she heard Princeton Keith's voice, "I don't want you merely as a writer, good as you are. And as a matter of fact while we're talking about writing, let me say something. It was you who were the writer. That's why your marriage to Curt, I suspect, never worked out so well as it might. He should have supported you, and you should have written, not him. You'd be rich today. However," he took out his pocket watch with the heavy chain, "I don't have forever even with you. After all, we are planning to publish other books next season too in my house. I'll come to the point. You'll have to see Cabot Wright. That is, you'll have to see a lot of him. You won't run any risk or danger that you wouldn't be running right home in Chicago. I've seen to all of that in any case. If necessary we'll get you a bodyguard, but it isn't that way of course. I know all about him, Cabot. He's harmless and, if you ask me, he always was. Then there's Bernie for protection for you. We want you, though, to talk to Cabot, and find out the things that have to be found out. Cabot's the kind of chap who wouldn't talk to another man, mind you, and never in an eternity to someone like Bernie. But I think he'll talk to you. I have a sixth sense about such things. Sometimes I'm wrong, of course, but hardly ever in a case this refined. As I said, it's not an easy assignment, and there's some danger, but I think that's why you'll take it. Don't refuse me, Zoe, or it'll break your heart. Just say yes, dear, and then I can run on back to work."

Mrs. Bickle didn't disappoint him after all. She looked at him hard and said yes.

6

SECOND ENCOUNTER

I t is doubtful if Mrs. Bickle would have ever been able to meet Cabot Wright or get one word or fact from him had she not, during a three-alarm fire, fallen through the skylight directly above his quarters.

Before her descent and encounter with Cabot, Mrs. Bickle had suffered mental and moral anguish, as a result of her having signed the pact with Princeton Keith and (from her own viewpoint) Madison Avenue. Though she felt more or less guilty, if not dishonest, after agreeing to carry out her assignment, she came to a quick decision that if she was to "see" Cabot Wright, the only sensible, if most unpleasant, plan was to cart herself bag and baggage to the *See-River Manor*.

Zoe Bickle, as Keith had reminded her so many times, had known nothing but genteel poverty all her life, and she had just begun to enjoy the luxury and ease of the Gramercy Park apartment. But it was for that very reason she moved to Brooklyn, for she saw that otherwise she would do her assignment from a false and distant standpoint, whereas, once uncomfortably settled in the *Manor*, she might at least be able to face the truth, even if she did not entirely understand it.

She had telephoned Princeton Keith about her change of address. His attitude toward her, now that she had agreed to what he wanted, was that of watchful waiting and studied indifference. He did not care how she obtained her story and, borrowing the attitude of his former analyst, he expressed neither approval nor disapproval of her action, and seemed unimpressed that she had decided to live in dirt, vermin and danger.

Bernie Gladhart had likewise cooled somewhat toward Mrs. Bickle after his first cordial reception in his weakened condition. His early Chicago impressions of her as a double-dealer made him uneasy once more, and every time he thought of her he was reminded that because of her remark to Carrie he had come to Brooklyn in the first place, and through her he had actually lost everything he cared about. And her sudden election by Keith to write the book for him—this was a final confirmation of his vision of her as the force which spun his destiny. He began to drink heavily, and was now seldom seen by her, for he decided she had sinister designs against him, when she rented a room in the *Manor* on the same floor with him.

Zoe no longer stopped to ask herself why she had accepted Keith's assignment. She felt somehow that the large sum of money (so large that it would have to be paid to her over a period of years) was no more important than the nature of the assignment itself. By reason of its intractable difficulty and ambiguous fascination, it had held her from the first.

Once established in her tenement work-room or, as she called it, her detection center, she was assailed neither by fear of rats or physical violence so much as by an uneasiness of more practical consideration. How was she to get herself introduced to the rapist in the first place? Even were this accomplished, how was she, considering her own personality, ever to be able to obtain information from him which would be usable? Thinking this over, she went into so black a despair that she was tempted to call off her agreement and go back home to Curt in Chicago.

She was saved by a fire that started in the building next to hers and that she mistook for a conflagration in the *Manor* itself. Frightened by the piercing clangor and nearness of the Brooklyn fire engines, Mrs. Bickle had hurried out into the hallway looking for an exit and quick access to the fire-escapes. In her haste, she inadvertently opened a door marked *Keep Closed,* tripped on the uneven stairs leading from the door, and before she could regain her balance had fallen into a glassed-in aperture, which gave under her weight and propelled her into the room below.

Most women in such circumstances would claim to have missed death by a narrow margin, but Mrs. Bickle knew that she had not fallen far, a few feet at most. Fortunately she landed on a Queen Anne sofa, which broke her fall. She was shaken up a bit, and she had several nasty scratches, but she stood up at once. When she was sure she had broken no bones, she sat down just in time to see entering from the adjoining room the once famous still good-looking face that had dominated the pages of the newspapers for such a long time.

Cabot Wright, as if to show that nothing remains the same, was wearing a hearing-aid in his right ear, Zoe observed to her disappointment. Somehow it was the last thing she expected. Deafness in the young is at first not without charm, and Cabot lost nothing of that because of the "aid." However, as Zoe was to find out on longer acquaintance, deafness, no matter in whom, is sad and annoying.

Like many deaf people, Cabot did not pay constant heed to what was said, and spoke in a rather loud voice, inquiring whether she was hurt, then not listening to her answer.

"Some bandage and a bottle of antiseptic," he said, as if to the wallpaper, and went out of the room. He did not seem surprised at her arrival, but showed no interest either.

When he had returned with gauze, bandages, and the antiseptic, she told him she didn't think her injuries warranted this attention, and then again realized he had not heard her. Aware that she must be speaking, he touched something connected with his hearing-aid and seemed then to expect her to say something again.

He kneeled down and bandaged one of the injuries on her forearm.

"Friend of a publisher or a writer?" he inquired of her.

This query seemed somehow even more upsetting to her than her fall through the glass partition. It made her feel he had been expecting her. She had forgotten, she realized, that Princeton Keith had known Cabot Wright, but why had

Princeton told him about her and not simply introduced them in the first place? "Because the only people who come here are writers or people sent by somebody," Cabot explained.

"Well, you'll pull through, I judge," he said at last, when he had tended to her cuts. Getting up from his kneeling posture, he pulled up a small footstool and sat there, a careful distance away from her.

"People warned me after I got out of prison," he began, "that writers would come. So I thought they would swarm." He smiled. "Not too many have got here, matter of fact, but they keep coming, a constant flow. But they all leave empty-handed, even though I give them what they say they want."

At that moment Mrs. Bickle saw what she was up against, and the thought that many had come to him, had asked for his story, been talked to, and gone away empty-handed, was startling and discouraging. She felt there must be innumerable writers composing novels, plays, and even perhaps narrative poems about Cabot Wright.

She allowed a sigh to escape from her, which he noticed, even if he did not hear it, for he said:

"Need something?"

"A glass of water," she shouted. She had begun to feel a bit faint, and she realized that either her fall had disagreed with her more than she had first acknowledged or seeing Cabot Wright himself at last had been too much for her.

He went into the next room, and returned almost immediately with an old-fashioned tin cup such as she had seen on farms as a small child. With some hesitation, she drank from it.

"You're disappointed," he studied her.

Looking up at him, Mrs. Bickle saw that he looked like the mythical clean-cut American youth out of Coca-Cola ads, church socials, picnics along the lake. Could he be—was it possible he was the real rapist? She compared him in her mind with Bernie, so much less attractive, the only other life-size criminal she actually knew. Yet the man who had brought her the tin cup looked—yes, impeccable.

"I suppose you know what I'm doing here," Mrs. Bickle began. "That I'm a writer or sent by somebody," she quoted him, a little too low perhaps for him to hear, but at that moment her attention was attracted from the not overclean tin cup to an amazing spectacle in the next room which she had till then entirely missed. In this room from which Cabot Wright had first emerged she caught sight of a solid array of clocks on the wall, of all sizes and shapes, from large ones like those seen in public waiting-rooms, down to small alarm-clocks fastened by force to the wall. There were rather pretty old-fashioned ones, with large black hands, and finally the remains of an ormolu likewise nailed to the wall.

He nodded to where she was looking. "A lot of those were here when I moved in," he told her. "This was some sort of watch-repair place. But I've added a lot of them myself."

He sat down again on the stool and stared back into his clock room, almost wistfully.

"The clocks have given me a funny new habit. Listening to them so long I began to take my own pulse every few minutes. I can't break it." He giggled, and she was surprised she had not noticed this mannerism in him before, as it was rather pronounced.

"Before everything happened to me," he explained, "I don't think I thought about clocks or time. Now it's almost the only thing—I won't say I think of—but that holds me, the old heart's tick-tock as it fills and empties itself of blood 75 times a minute!

"My biggest trouble, though," he continued, like one who had been expecting her to come and interview him, "well, it's not deafness," he touched the aid, "my biggest trouble for other people is I can't remember."

There was a look on Mrs. Bickle's face like a heavy shadow blotting out eyes and mouth.

"Literally can't remember," he looked up into her face like one modestly telling of accomplishment and ability.

"Only thing I have to make me remember is some police tape-recordings. You're welcome to hear them sometime." He exchanged a look with the largest of the clocks in the adjoining room. "That's why the 'hunters' soon tire of me. The tapes don't give them enough of what they want. Well, that's the way it goes. Where's the keenest place you can hurt a man? Not in his eye or groin, but where he can't remember."

Mrs. Bickle sipped from the tin cup.

"You're a different type of visitor," he turned now to Mrs. Bickle's case, "although I saw you regard my poor wallpaper with the same expression the others get when they look at it. I have, you see, four or five wallpapers, one under the other. They wear down gradually all of them to the original willow pattern over the calcimine itself, then robin redbreast, scenes at the forge, water lilies, peasants in ancient France. I've always wanted a room different from my adopted parents'. No carpets," he looked down at the bare floors, "no chandeliers," he nodded above where the plaster was coming through, "no dining-room sets or covered toilet seats."

Mrs. Bickle cleared her throat. She was listening very intently to his accent and she was puzzled. Each sentence he spoke seemed to be from a different geographical section of the country. Though all his speech sounded native American, for Cabot Wright was an American criminal in anybody's book, it was nonetheless, like his wallpaper, composite.

From almost the moment of her entry, Zoe Bickle in her head had begun to write her own book about him—the book, that is, she would have written had she not been under assignment. But now another thought gave her pause, for whatever she might one day hand in to Princeton Keith for *his* book, she saw with great clarity that her "subject" had neither the biography nor the personality that could possibly be fitted into the publishing list of the Guggelhaupt empire.

Her cogitations were interrupted by the door's opening. A young man in clerical garb stood on the threshold, removed his hat when he saw Mrs. Bickle, and for a moment looked puzzled and upset, then nodded slowly and put his hat over his breast.

"Reverend Cross," Cabot Wright identified him, "come in, sir. And what did you say your name was?" he turned to Mrs. Bickle, and, when she told him: "Let me introduce you to my preacher," which brought no change of expression in the young man who had just entered.

"Mrs. Bickle would like to be interested, Reverend Cross," Cabot Wright said in a stentor's voice. "She fell in, you might say," he went on, in a sweeping summary and explanation of her presence here. He pointed to the plates of glass lying near the sofa.

Mrs. Bickle, feeling somewhat that she too was being affixed to the wall along with Cabot's clocks, began bowing her way out, not only convinced there was no story here, but incredulous she could have spent this quarter of an hour in the presence of a convicted rapist.

"Ready for another session?" she heard her host say to the Reverend Cross, as she walked to the door. But Cabot Wright was already opening the door for her, and said, this time in what seemed to Mrs. Bickle an imitation of the West Virginia accent of Reverend Cross:

"You come back now, Mrs. Bickle, if you need any help."

With this obscure message echoing in her ears, she went back to her own room to think everything over. When she got there, out of sheer nervousness she began to read the manuscript in her room.

7

CABOT WRIGHT BEGINS

T he popularity of Cabot Wright as a criminal may have stemmed from two facts [she read]. He was employed in Wall Street in a well-known broker-age, and he was no respecter of age, raping girls, young ladies, middle-aged matrons, and even elderly women. Anyone who was a woman could be next.

This had kept the suspense high during the two years of his operations. Women waited in the humid fall twilights, in the blistering heat of July, on cold winter foggy evenings when the boat whistles cried all night. Weather never kept him inside. He didn't kill, he didn't bruise, he didn't cuff or buffet. He used, everybody insisted afterwards, some form of hypnotism. He raped easily and well.

Women who thought of screaming did not. Those who began to run stopped short in their tracks. They knew his step, his pressure. There was never any evidence of struggle after he had left. Many called the police, but more to share their experience than to register a complaint.

Marriages were broken up by him, husbands, sons, lovers went out of the lives of the women in question. Nothing was ever the same after Cabot Wright left. During his two years of activity, women could be said to be waiting.

A window would be shattered.

"It's time, Mrs. Van Buren," Cabot Wright would say, stepping into a neat parlor, and unbuttoning his fly. "I haven't but a moment."

"I know," Mrs. Van Buren would answer stoically.

"Then remove your clothing, sweetheart. You can leave on the light."

EVERY GOOD MORNING Cabot Wright walked across Brooklyn Bridge to his Wall Street office and, if weather allowed, walked back again to his four-room apartment on Columbia Heights, which he shared with his wife, Cynthia Abigail Adams, a dress-designer.

Cabot had majored in art at Yale, but on graduation, returning to his home at Tuxedo Park, his father had called him in and asked him how he expected to rise in the world as an art instructor (the only career his studies had prepared him for). Seeing the look of indecision on his son's face, Wright senior had picked up the phone and in a short five minutes secured a position for the boy with Mr. Warburton in the Wall Street brokerage firm of Slider, Bergler, Gorem, Hill and Warburton.

At the time of his graduation, Cabot was going with Cynthia

Adams, whom he had met at some art lectures at the Frick Gallery. Since he was through school, they both felt they should marry and did so a few weeks after Cabot got settled in his Wall Street post, then moved into a four-hundred-dollar-a-month apartment in the Heights, which Mr. Cabot Wright senior helped them pay for until the "young people get on their feet."

Mrs. Cabot Wright senior—Daisy—did not know if generosity like this would be appreciated, especially by her daughter-in-law, but she said no more about the young couple coming to live at home in Tuxedo Park, as she had originally planned for them.

Cabot's mother did, however, have a discussion almost immediately with her husband about what she saw as a new problem, their son's walking the Brooklyn Bridge each morning to his Wall Street job. Mrs. Wright did not approve of this at all. For one thing, as she pointed out to her husband, his son could easily be murdered, second, think of the shoe leather, and finally, it gave the impression he was not successful.

"I say it's simply not right for Cabot to walk the bridge." Mrs. Wright remained unyielding to her husband's arguments that some of the top-drawer executives in Wall Street walked to work. "I'll have to speak to Cabot the next time they come over," she warned.

"If you ever took any advice of mine," her husband told her with unusual emphasis for him, "don't do it."

"What do you mean, don't do it?" she flared.

"We've got to let him make up his own mind how he wants to get to work!"

Daisy was reduced to silence by her husband's emphasis.

He continued: "It's not important if he walks the bridge or doesn't . . . Besides, he's married. He's begun a new life. Forget your old role and relax so we can enjoy our trip to Florida."

"Relax so we can enjoy our trip to Florida," Mrs. Cabot Wright repeated. "My dear Kirby." She put her hand on his lapel. "Dear old Kirby, how little you understand a mother's heart or her responsibilities."

"And we should also remember once in a while that Cabot is only an adopted son!"

"Kirby!" Daisy warned him. "Stop right there."

"By Christ, I think he's forgotten it himself!"

Daisy wept now, daubing her eyes, and said in a low voice, "I'm afraid he hasn't." But she didn't respond to Kirby's astonished cry of "What?" and his appealing look for explanation.

"Well, Daisy," he said after he had let her cry for a bit, "we've got to remember he's made his decision. We both would feel badly if he had *not* got married. Let's be glad he did, glad he has his post—"

"His *Wall Street* post, Kirby," she shook her head.

"Very well, you wished him to become an artist, but he saw the handwriting on the wall!"

"Oh that eternal handwriting on that—"

"—eternal wall," Kirby finished her statement, and laughed. "And remember, Daisy," he went on, "Cabot is technically not an adopted son, but a supposititious one . . ."

"Kirby, you didn't tell Cabot that!" Daisy cried.

"Yes, I told him the day he was graduated," Mr. Wright said.

She looked still more crestfallen, but astonished too, and the tears now flowed in her eyes.

"Let's go to Florida now, Daisy," he kissed his wife.

"You used that word supposititious," she studied the meaning of what he had told her. "You told the poor boy."

"You'll cheer up in Florida, Daisy," he coaxed her.

AS CABOT WRIGHT walked the Brooklyn Bridge each morning, he felt the weight of his adopted parents and the weight of his new wife dissipate. It provided, he was to learn afresh each morning, the one free hour of his day. He felt "prepared," though he did not have anything waiting for him to feel prepared for. The bridge meant so much. He seldom looked about him when he was on it. Though the roar of traffic was unpleasant, and in the distance Governor's Island and Staten Island no longer invited attention, and the Statue of Liberty was often hidden in mist, yet he was up here and not down there, and that was enough to make him feel, like one of the ships below, in port.

If only he could feel less tired. He had never felt tired when he was painting or hiking or on vacations by himself. But now suddenly he felt completely, *finally* tired.

He discussed his tiredness with Mrs. Cabot Wright Junior, who was sympathetically inattentive.

"It's all in the mind, sweety," she tapped her rather high forehead. "Concentrate on being non-tired, concentrate on being tinglingly alive: give, give, dear, to life. What can suffering teach? Nothing. It's coming alive that tells."

Cynthia's excited speech, borrowed from one of the more intellectual women's fashion magazines for which she occasionally did an article, was queerly interrupted, either owing to her excitement over ideas, or her standing in an awkward position with her legs apart, for she made, as Cabot Wright's mother Daisy described such occurrences, "a noise."

Cynthia reddened furiously and said, "I'm sorry," like a little girl.

Until recently unaware both of his wife's philosophic "ideas" from women's magazines, as well as her digestive characteristics, Cabot muttered:

"We all do it, Mrs. Cabot Wright Junior."

"But we *don't*," she contradicted him.

"Did it ever occur to you what you just did is proof you're tinglingly alive? . . . I mean," Cabot attempted to explain, when he saw the look of fury and outrage come over her face. She seized one of her favorite monthly New York magazines and ran off to barricade herself in the bedroom, which was to become a regular practice with her.

As Cabot grew more and more tired, finally, with his wife's reluctant permission, he decided to consult a doctor who was said to have great success with the tired feeling. Dr. Bigelow-Martin, new to the Heights, did not believe in psychotherapy, analysis, the old tried and true remedies for nervous disorders. He was even said not to believe in psychology. Of course he did not treat the "insane," a word Cabot still insisted on employing despite Cynthia's insistence it was meaningless today.

No one, Cynthia said, thought Cabot was any more than run-down. He worked too hard, she lectured him, and perhaps was not yet "motivated" by his after-all-very-recent-translation to Wall Street. Interest would come, she was sure, as salary and responsibility and maturity increased. "We grow, dear," Cynthia spoke to him from under a kind of spectacles, just come into vogue, based on a model one saw in ancient daguerreotypes.

Cabot found Dr. Bigelow-Martin himself a very nervous man, and in a great hurry, although he insisted on taking down his new patient's case history, rather than entrusting it to a nurse.

"A really classic case!" the doctor exclaimed after a series of mumbled comments on Cabot's symptoms. "Suffering from chronic fatigue," he wrote down on his pad. "Good. You know you're tired. Good."

He continued to write everything down Cabot said, even though what he said was both sparse and repetitive.

Cabot Wright was extremely surprised, though not exactly upset, to discover from Dr. Bigelow-Martin that he had been tired, actually, from the age of a small boy.

"You have reacted to your life-experience by assuming fatigue," the doctor explained to him. "But miracle of miracles, you know you're tired. Most people, most Americans," here the doctor coughed, "don't know they are dropping with fatigue. You know you are. That's a hopeful sign." Dr. Bigelow-Martin now rose to his full height. "We'll begin treatments next visit."

Cabot showed disappointment the treatments could not begin immediately, but the doctor was emphatic. Next time was time enough, and he smiled considerately at his young patient's use of the phrase "tinglingly alive," which he rejected as non-scientific.

MRS. CABOT WRIGHT Junior was at work at her drawing-table when Cabot came home from the doctor.

"Did he cure you, sweety?" she asked, laying down a charcoal crayon.

Cabot was considerably depressed. Perhaps he saw the long slow hard climb back to health. He merely grunted and sat down, his straw hat fell to the floor, and he slipped back into the frame of his chair.

"Well, tell me the bad news too," she came up to him.

"I'm suffering from chronic fatigue," he informed her.

Puzzled by the diagnosis, she nonetheless brightened and said, "But that's not going to kill you!"

"But I've had it *all my life!*" He felt the horror more now than he had in the doctor's office.

"Darling, you've not been tired all your life. It's not possible," Cynthia corrected sweetly, but a hint of uneasiness caused her to raise her own voice.

"According to the Doc I have," he said with emphasis. "Just think, Cynthia, to be this way since you were a boy!"

"Come now," she responded, "the doctor, I'm sure, was speaking only figuratively."

She took up her New York magazine again, hunting a column of text here and there among the bright ads.

"You'll be all right, dearest," she said. "And while you were out, I bought you something as a surprise. Some nice Holland beer. Wouldn't you like that?"

He looked at her with an expression that seemed to fall between hunger and amnesia.

"Yeah," he answered when she had put her question again. "Though beer makes me sleepy, you know."

She went out into the kitchen.

"Is being sleepy the same physiological thing as tired?" he called out to her. She evidently thought the question over a moment before answering: "Yes, dear, I'd say they're exactly the same."

"This is the loveliest beer in the world, Cabot," she said, coming in with a tray and two bottles. "Why can't American beer be as good?"

"I'll have to ask my colleagues in Wall Street," he quipped.

"Cabot," she cried, seeing the strange look come again on his face, "what is the doctor going to do to you?"

He jumped at her question. "Cure me," he giggled. He went on giggling for a time. Then he kissed his wife on the face.

"*You* cure me," Cabot whispered.

She gave him a slight peck in return.

"Do you love me?" she said suddenly.

He stared at her a moment before replying.

"I adore it," he said.

"Cabot!" she cried, alarmed now by something different in him.

He had already unbuttoned her blouse, and had pushed her back under his torrent of kisses.

SWEAT POURED DOWN from Cabot's armpits as he walked into Dr. Bigelow-Martin's office for his first treatment. He had never felt so apprehensive since he reported to the induction center for the army.

"We are beginning a new life," Dr. Bigelow-Martin intoned,

putting his hand on Cabot's knee. "You are about to study yourself, see what you yourself do to yourself. You have been tense and tired, tired and tense, puffing and straining, expending far too much energy and getting oh so little back in return. Your case is not exceptional, Mr. Cabot Wright. Indeed it's not. Put it out of your mind that you are different. Your case is, in fact, my young man, the rule. Americans are tired. America is tired. What is the root? We do not know. Is it world-wide? Perhaps, perhaps. Lie down, please," and the doctor suppressed a yawn.

Cabot Wright was already nude except for his shorts.

The doctor, bending over the day-bed where Cabot lay, suddenly with a remarkable show of strength picked him up bodily and put him over a kind of padded hook which had come out of the wall, and hung his patient on it, much as one would a side of beef.

"Do not move," Bigelow-Martin admonished. "No matter how much you may wish to change your position, resist it, simply give in to your fatigue, let go, let go, Cabot, let go."

Struggling on the immense mattress-padded hook which had come out of the wall, Cabot felt very much like a fish— caught but not pulled in. The blood rushed violently to his head. His shorts, which he had laundered many times, snapped, and fell down about his legs. Visions of gauchos riding on the pampas came to him, together with memories of bull-fights he had seen on TV. His forehead was swimming with sweat, he felt his intestines give, spittle flowed freely from his mouth, and his navel suddenly contracting violently seemed to explode and vanish, as will the top crust of a pie in the oven when the proper slits have not been made in it. Cabot felt he was saying *adios* from a boat rapidly advancing from the shore on which stood his adopted father and mother in their Florida clothes, and his recent bride, Mrs. Cabot Wright Junior in her Vogue pattern dress.

When Cabot Wright regained consciousness, Dr. Bigelow-Martin was bathing his forehead with some drugstore witch hazel.

"How did we do?" the doctor was saying.

When Cabot did not reply, Bigelow-Martin waited a bit, then said: "I'll tell you, sir. We did fine."

"Did I pass out, doctor?" Cabot wondered.

"You went to sleep," was the reply. "You relaxed. Probably for the first time in your life."

The vision of the gauchos came back to Cabot.

"Can I tell people about this?" Cabot inquired.

The doctor appeared to be studying his question.

"At least I can tell my wife?" he appealed to Bigelow-Martin in an almost wistful voice.

"Just as you wish," the doctor was grudgingly acquiescent, and he turned away from his patient, humming a tune.

There were certain obvious warnings in what the doctor did not say, and Cabot understood that secrecy and indirection were characteristic of the profession. Yet, as Cabot asked himself, who would want to tell on himself and reveal what he had undergone in Bigelow-Martin's office? Who would believe it?

"My God, you look different," Cynthia said when he came into the apartment. "You look like *you'd* been to Florida."

But Cabot was already unbuttoning his wife's blouse.

———

"I HOPE HE's not charging you too much," Mrs. Cabot Wright Junior said in bed, next morning, speaking of the doctor of course. Cabot had brought her morning orange juice and coffee because he felt it was his fault neither of them had had a wink of sleep till dawn. Irritated he did not reply, Cynthia tossed away her black mask which she wore to protect herself against early morning light.

"Old Bigelow-Martin." Cabot now hummed the same tune the doctor had. "As a matter of fact," he finally came to her question, "I haven't asked the old bird how much he is going to charge."

Cynthia fished some seeds out of her juice.

They had both spent money recklessly, and even with the Cabot Wright Seniors' help, were badly in debt.

"You don't think his fee will be prohibitive, do you, sweetheart?" he stood by her bedside, briefcase in hand.

"Aren't all their fees that?" she snapped. "I remember that time I fell while riding—"

"Well, I'll just tell him he can't soak me too much. I'm newly married, after all, just starting in business . . ."

Furious he had interrupted her, she spat: "*Anybody* could put you on a padded hook without your clothes on and let you pass out!"

As he stared at her, incredulous at the anger in her outburst, she went on: "How do you know he's an accredited M.D.?"

"You, Cynthia, sent me to him."

"Draped naked over a hook," she went back to this. "What kind of therapy is that?"

"You admitted yourself I looked like I'd been to Florida," he

began now to open the door while making his kissing sound
of goodbye.

"It could all be dangerous," she muttered, ignoring his
goodbye.

"So is being tired," he told her. "Bye, lamby."

"Cabot!" she called, but he had already closed the hall door
behind him. "All right," she began to sob a bit, "hang on your
goddam hook." Then she cried in earnest, because she knew
nothing was going to be right between them.

ZOE BICKLE LOOKED up from the manuscript and gazed across
the room. She was astounded by what she had read. Was this
the real truth about Cabot Wright's beginnings? Had Bernie
Gladhart written these pages, even with Carrie's help and
guidance? Nervously, she stood up and went to the window.
In the light of the street-lamp, she saw a policeman going by
across the street, twirling his nightstick. She counted the
five gold buttons he wore on each side of his jacket. Looking
behind him, she saw the words, *High Pressure Fire Service, Main
Pumping Station*, painted on the wall of the deserted building, with some words scrawled in chalk in big letters below:
COOL FOOL YOU WILL NEVER EXECUTE THE MAD SPADES. She
thought back to Chicago and Curt, and reviewed her unhappy
marriage and life, thought of old age and death. She had called
Curt a few times in Chicago, but he sounded more languid
than ever, obviously deep in *Isaiah,* begrudging the time away
from his work, much as if she had come into his room on
returning home from the office. In recollection of another of
Cabot's eccentric habits, she found herself counting her own
pulse. Some of Cabot Wright's odd statements came back to

her now, such as his *"Mrs. Bickle would like to be interested, Reverend Cross,"* which she now felt contained either a great truth or a great prophecy. She sat down in her chair again, and took up the manuscript where she had left off.]

WHILE CYNTHIA DID her shopping in the supermarket or finished her weekly drawings for her fashion editor, Cabot would saunter into the office of Dr. Bigelow-Martin for his afternoon treatment on the hook.

"How did we do today?" was the invariable question put to him by Bigelow-Martin, as the signal that the treatment had come to an end. Once sufficiently conscious, Cabot would reply from the hook in a voice described by the doctor's eavesdropping secretary as "strained honey":

"Fine, doctor."

The doctor was already taking his pulse.

"You're one of my more intelligent patients," Bigelow-Martin said. Then looking at his patient closer, he added: "At least one of my more cooperative. You follow instructions to the letter, and you don't talk me to death. You'll get well, Cabot . . ."

Whether Bigelow-Martin had foreseen the ramifications of his cure or not, some strange and potent *élan* was released in Cabot shortly after the second treatment. At the time of the trial and investigation of Cabot Wright on criminal charges, Bigelow-Martin himself had disappeared, and with him any possible clue to his methods. But under the doctor's ministrations, Cabot Wright came, so to speak, into full manhood. He bloomed, as so few men do, and the very sight of him made women stare, or hurry on, or stop.

Some say that he now gave off a kind of sweetish rich

animal-vegetable odor, such as one associates with the trop-
ics and natives before they were spoiled by missionaries, con-
stricting clothing, V.D., bottled drinks, and candies.

At first Cabot Wright was not aware of his own metamorphosis. Cynthia, plunged into the difficulties of a dress-
designer, did not pay too close attention to him, insofar as
to note the daily changes in his makeup, and spent most of
her time, actually, rejecting his renewed sexual attentions to
her. "We're living in the most civilized city in the world," she
remarked, "and we're not going to do this every hour on the
half-hour, and that's final. What do you think you're trying to
prove? You look so pink and flushed, too, lately. Perhaps you're
eating too much red meat in those masculine Wall Street
restaurants . . ."

Cabot had required ten to eleven hours sleep before his
treatments with Bigelow-Martin. He now slept only four or
five hours a night. He slept stark naked. Often, in the middle
of the night, his wife would wake up and see him with his eyes
open contemplating his form. The fact was, as she finally came
to understand, he was so relaxed that, even with eyes open, he
was not conscious. She would call to him, nonetheless, urging
him to close his eyes so that he would do his best work next
day, and usually he would obey her.

THE CHECK FROM Cabot Wright's father was not always forth-
coming, especially now that Cabot Junior had his Wall Street
post, and Cabot and Cynthia's expenses were increasing by
geometric proportion. Cynthia found that she must work even
more than when she was single if they were to keep their four-

hundred-a-month apartment overlooking the water and the Statue of Liberty.

"Where does the money go?" came so frequently from her mouth that Cabot pinned the words, cut from an advertisement, on the wall above their dinette.

Stingy at heart, Cabot, refusing to plunk down what they were asking for movies and plays, began browsing in a branch of the Brooklyn public library, a pastime which carved up his evening until Cynthia's return from her fashion shows. He developed a sudden interest in books about plants and animal-life, especially such exotic forms as the fish in Asiatic waters.

Rummaging around the shelves for books about his new-found subject, he soon realized that because this was a branch library, there was very little available except for those books forgotten or discarded in the receding tide of popular taste. He picked up one large red book on popular science, long out of date, and read:

SWIMMERS AND DRIFTERS

The animals of the open sea are conveniently divided into the active swimmers (nekton) and the more passive drifters (Plankton). The swimmers include whales . . . The drifters, jellyfishes.

His eye ran on at random, as his hand lifted page after page:

Sometimes when a plant is grown in a foreign country, artificial pollination must be resorted to: the marrows and peaches in our gardens and hot-houses are

commonly pollinated by hand. The red clover never set
seed in New Zealand till the bumble-bee, to which it is
adapted, was introduced.

He read about the Cuckoo-Pint which attracts flies by a car-
rion stench and by the lurid purple of the club of its flowering
axis, and went on to the case of the Red-Clover, in Darwin,
and the ripe flower-head of the Goat's Beard, whose petals
close before midday causing the flower itself to be sometimes
called Jack-go-to-bed-at-Noon.

Cabot yawned widely, and touched his heavy lids with
his hand.

At that moment a young woman in a soft blue sweater sat
down at the same reading table with him, exactly as if she had
come out of one of Cynthia's fashion magazines.

Yawning now almost helplessly, he found at the same time
he could not quit staring at the sweater girl.

His hour of reading about tropical plants and seeds, together
with the warm air of the library, had caused him to break
out in a sweat such as he had never experienced since he had
had to do hard manual labor in the Army. Rivulets of water
poured down his temples, and from his arm pits. He took out a
large silk handkerchief, a graduation gift from his mother, and
wiped his forehead. The cloth came away soaking.

His eyes, smarting with the unaccustomed bath of perspiration, tried to focus on the text:

The flowers are hidden in a large green hood or
spathe, in the mouth of which can be seen the club-like

end of the floral axis. This club attracts flies by its lurid
color and its foetid smell.

Feeling the girl's eyes on him, Cabot Wright loosened his
collar slightly, then tied his Italian all-silk necktie, with severe
stringency.

"Warm," he heard his own word addressed to the girl in
the sweater.

She smiled at him with the calm of one who knew him.

"No ventilation," he whispered, took out a pack of English
cigarettes and laid them down between them. His eyes
continued:

In wind-pollinated plants the adaptations run on different lines. The pollen is dust-like and is produced in
enormous quantities, for the chances of a grain borne
in the air reaching the stigma of a flower of its own
species are remote. The grains are small and light; in
the pine they are provided with two little bladders, the
better to float in the air. Conspicuous corollas are use-
less; they would even be a hindrance, catching the fly-
ing pollen and preventing it reaching the stigma. The
corolla has almost entirely disappeared, the wind flower
is small and inconspicuous. The stamens hang far out
of the flower on slender filaments, dangling in the air,
shaken by every gust. The stigmas, too, protrude—
the crimson filaments of the hazel, the feather of the
plantain, the brushes which hang from the grass ear—
winnowing the air for drifting pollen.

He closed the book with a bang which molested several readers. He grasped the package of cigarettes.

Again he heard his own voice: "Any chance your joining me
in a cigarette?"

Her lips formed the word No mutely, but after a wait, she
got up to follow him.

They walked out into the hallway. The building was undergoing extensive alterations, according to a sign in the hall. A
huge hole in the wall exposed another empty darkened room
adjoining where they now stood.

His fingers trembled so badly as he tried to light her cigarette that she had to hold his hand briefly, the hairs of which
were weighted with drops of perspiration. They smiled at one
another.

"Overhead lights add to the heat," he said.

She nodded in her eviscerated debrained cool sweater-ad
grace: "I'm a bit used to them. Actress," she pointed to herself. "Catching up on the theater files. Am here nearly every
day lately."

"You're researching," he giggled, taking Cynthia's phrase.

A rivulet of sweat slipped from his cheek to his soft gabar-
dine lapel, and the Italian silk tie gave and the top button of
his shirt was exposed.

In his absorption at feeling the droplets of perspiration
descending from his face, he missed something she said to
him. He was about to make some reference to Cynthia's profession, when the girl looked in the direction of the darkened
room next to them, and pointed out gleefully that it had an
electric fan going.

They entered the room to observe the phenomenon.

He saw her lips move in surprise, and then he adjusted his own mouth quickly and solidly to hers. She pushed him with mechanical violence. He hit her lips again, and holding her against the wall, he had, with a routine instantaneity, unzipped his fly. A kind of barking cry of relief came from his throat, while he muttered into her hair: "Get deadly."

A dangling thread of saliva, or perhaps sweat, extending between both their mouths, helped impose silence.

Afterwards, drying himself on mouth and neck with sheet after sheet of paper towel, he decided that she had not cried out for fear of attracting visitors.

"Get deadly," he quoted his own unpremeditated phrase initial to his new career.

8

"YOU COULD COAX IT OUT OF ME"

fter reading these pages on the early career of Cabot Wright, Mrs. Bickle did what a few weeks earlier she would have considered daring. Nor would she have done it now, if she realized what time it was—two in the morning. She went to Cabot Wright's room, carrying the novel in manuscript.

She knocked twice and the door was opened for her by Cabot Wright. He was not surprised she had come, and seemed to know for what purpose she was here, for he put his hand out tentatively for the manuscript. She handed it to him without a word.

Before she could say more, he had closed the door upon her. Though she stood there for what seemed some time, there was nothing for her to do but return to her own room. It was then she looked at her gold watch and saw the hour.

———

HAVING REGAINED HER room, Mrs. Bickle sat down in her easy chair, and perhaps as much worn out by the events of the past weeks as by the lateness of the hour, she went to sleep. She was awakened from an uneasy doze by the sound of reveille coming from Governors Island. Then she was startled, if not terrified, to see someone sitting across from her. It was Cabot Wright, of course, dressed in what must once have been an expensive dressing-gown, stained by breakfast and with one sleeve badly in need of sewing. She recalled that he had had this article of clothing on when she had knocked at his door some hours earlier.

He nodded and, giggling as usual, said: "I'm returning your call."

Her own action with regard to him had deprived her of any grounds for indignation, criticism or indeed appeal. He knew obviously what she was in Brooklyn for, and that she must be a person who would stop at nothing—she saw that her "falling" through the glass sky-light into his room must be construed by him as a form of reckless intrepidity, the hardened ruse of a dyed-in-the-wool newspaper woman and adventuress.

In the feeble dawn, she questioned her own motives in having gone to him and handing him the manuscript of Bernie's novel. Her action seemed now to her an abject appeal for help on her part. She realized she did want to write the novel herself, just as Princeton Keith had suggested. Some stifled cry of authorship buried by her marriage to Curt must be asserting itself in terrible Brooklyn.

Instead of saying anything to the point, she suppressed a

groan, and said in her old Chicago manner: "Since you've lost your memory, Mr. Wright, I don't suppose you can tell me if what you've read is authentic or not. That is, if you did read Bernie Gladhart's book?" and she looked at his hands which held the typescript pages of the novel.

"This manuscript?" He giggled briefly again, and took off his glasses. "I read it . . . no, I've not lost my memory for consecutive events," he began. "I remember the separate details when once they're put together for me. You see for nearly a year I read nothing but stories about myself. In newspapers, magazines, foreign and domestic—me, me, me. All the time I was in prison it was my story that was being told and retold. I read so many versions of what I did, I can safely affirm that I couldn't remember what I did and what I didn't."

He raised his right hand as if gesturing in sleep.

She was about to ask him how true Bernie's fiction was, when he went on, as if to answer for her:

"Did I do all this?" he tapped the sheaf of manuscript. "Yes, I'd say so, but it still reads wrong. The facts, I mean, are put together, the beads are all strung along like they were mine, but there's no necklace. The press and TV stories were also like that, you see—everything people said, then and later, describing everything about me to a T, including those things I didn't really know about myself. For instance, this manuscript points out at the beginning that I was a supposititious child, which I didn't really ever remember hearing as a term until I was out of prison and a magazine told me about it. Nor did I know my exact wrist measurements until a lady journalist, helped by a police captain who'd put the tape around me, said my body weight was ideal in line with the circumference of my wrist and height. My complexion was described with the exact artist's color and shade, my excessive perspiration was counted in drops, together with a chemical description of odor and content, and there was of course my blood count and blood type. Who didn't know these things who read the dailies?" He giggled hard now. "If you'll excuse the detail, which I know you will because you're a writer, the size of my glans penis was testified to in court and got into print, but the extenuating fact is that I never saw the Brooklyn housewife who described it, and certainly never assaulted her, even in the dark. I read somewhere, in school, that Louis XVI had his puce coat torn to shreds during or after being guillotined, and my silk Brooks Brothers suit was slashed and divided by female spectators the first day of my trial. Yet I've heard my own life so many times, I can say I'm a stranger to the story itself. If somebody told you the story of your own life, Mrs. Bickle, in New York newspaper English, wouldn't you disremember yourself too?"

"Do you mean to say you'd know your story if somebody told it to you, but you couldn't tell it to anybody yourself and be sure you were right?" she inquired.

He looked at her brightly. "How can you express it so well?" he wondered.

"If that's the case," she rose, "I'm afraid this is the time for me to go back to Chicago."

"But why?" he was deeply disappointed.

"You certainly know why I'm here," Mrs. Bickle was a bit

indignant at his question. "I'm not on a vacation," she surveyed the room, "and you've just told me I can't get what I came for, which of course is your life."

"Of course it's true you're not the first to try to write it," he seemed to be studying a plan.

"But you're quite good at knocking down all comers, aren't you?" She sat down again and looked in her purse for a cigarette.

"That's not exactly true," he came over to her chair and looked down on the crown of her head. "No, sir. Besides," Cabot Wright went on, "I'd rather like to tell you what happened to me, all in one piece, so to speak. If, that is, you could coax it out of me. Do you have that kind of time, Mrs. Zoe Bickle?"

She looked up then at something in his tone, and perhaps remembered he had been a rapist.

"If you could coax it, milk it out, say," he told her.

"Sit over there," she commanded him, and he obeyed.

He went on with his speech: "The others who came I didn't knock down, like you claim; they didn't have that kind of time. They were interested at first, but they couldn't stay interested for weeks or months. Said they'd never stayed with anything that long. Days or hours were their kind of time, you see. They wanted me really in minutes, come to think of it. An hour is long to their kind."

He stopped talking and she stared at him.

"Let me get this straight," Mrs. Bickle said, puffing away on her smoke. "If I sit, and read to you or have you read, or we read together, say, what Bernie has written, and he's written

a lot, believe you me, you think you might remember e
more to get the whole thing out?"

"Exactly," Cabot Wright said.

"But what will you get out of it?" she wondered. "After all,
when we do get the truth, if it's there, we'll just turn it into
fiction."

"What will I get out of it?" he looked at her mouth. "Well,
Mrs. Bickle, let's say I might get my own story straight. Now
with the other writers, they weren't like you. You're slow and
disinterested, as I told you in front of Reverend Cross. I believe
you can wait long enough to coax me. I believe so."

"I can wait forever," she told him. "I've waited all my life,
and besides now I'm rich." She laughed.

"Exactly," he said. "That's what I told Princeton Keith."

"You told *him?*" she cried, a bit uneasy if not scared.

"Oh, don't let that worry you. But I told him, and I told
Bernie Gladhart, if I could see my whole story written out
straight, I think I'd be cured."

"What of?" she laughed.

"Cured of being what everybody made me, I guess I'd say,
so I can go on and be somebody else." He giggled, but in a less
pronounced fashion. "Because I was never really the man I
read about in the papers. That is, I suppose, I was never really
Cabot Wright. I was a supposititious child and I fell into the
part out of there being nothing better to do. But if I got down
all that I did, when I was *him*," he giggled, "maybe I could go
on to be somebody, if not better, different. There. I've told
you, I've told Princeton Keith, I've told Bernie Gladhart, Reverend Cross, and I've told myself. We can get started then."

She stared at him for the longest time, and then he got up and handed her back the manuscript she had given him.

IN THE ENSUING weeks Mrs. Bickle read Cabot's own story aloud to him, while correcting, rewriting, and listening to him as in a play-back on tape. Then she read some more, erased, stopped and thought, as did Cabot himself, immured now in her sitting-room. Together they handed the sentences and paragraphs back and forth between them, while poor Bernie Gladhart, in the same building, in solitary misery, practiced drinking himself into the grave.

It was not long before Bernie Gladhart figured out what was going on. As Cabot and Zoe worked on the novel, the original idea-man of the rapist's career stayed in his room drinking, or walked to and fro on the Brooklyn streets. Occasionally he would gaze up at Mrs. Bickle's window, confused and wondering, and at the same time somewhat relieved and even unconcerned over what had happened. As long as Carrie's small checks continued to come—and he knew they would come as long as she wanted to keep him away from Chicago—he felt he could hold on.

Mrs. Bickle, somewhat to her own amusement, saw herself turning into a novelist at a ripe age, while Cabot Wright's life as fiction sprawled and grew under her hand, lumbering on in endless corrections and addenda as it reeled and retraced itself, was interrupted, continued, ran on over lapses of memory, lies, vague echoes, police-tapes, gossip-columns and eye-witness stories. It was a hopeless, finely-ground sediment of the improbable, vague, baffling, ruinous and irrelevant minu-

tiae of a life. If she could not lay down her pen, however difficult her task, it must have her realization that all lives were
like this, and indeed this was proof of life.

"Why did you rape?" she was always on the point of asking, as she wrote and annotated, listened and shook her head,
but she usually withheld her own question because she knew
Cabot wouldn't know.

9

THE YOUNG EXECUTIVE

W hen Cabot returned, after initiating his new career, from the branch library, not finding Cynthia at home, he sat down in his tropical-hut armchair without bothering to light the eye-saver lamp beside him. He snapped on his tiny portable Japanese radio. Ballroom music, so muted and blurred one could not distinguish the separate musical instruments in the orchestra, was in progress, song hits from two generations before that gave him a feeling of mild surfeited comfort, as he mopped himself with a face cloth under his open shirt.

At the height of his comfort he caught Cynthia's unrhythmic spike-heeled tromp, similar to the sound of a circus pony. Then he heard her open the door, key-ring jangling.

"Do you *listen* to that cheap cascade of sound?" she stormed.

"It's background, sweety," he picked small particles of tobacco from his upper teeth. "Hey, I'm getting to like soft music," he counterfeited elation. "Especially old soft. Your grandmother heard this stuff. Anyhow I've had my education in real music," and he imitated modern cacophony.

"Pray don't turn it off for my comfort!" Cynthia commanded, when she saw his finger beginning to touch the tuner. "Nonetheless," she went on, "it's a bit funny to come home and hear you listening to the same piped-in music they play at the supermarket. It's my little surprise for the day," she said, coming closer and looking at him more carefully than was her wont. "What's wrong with you, by the way?"

"Can't you tell?" he studied her almost contemptuously. "No conditioner in the library."

She was almost taken in by his quip, but she quickly asked, "What do you go to the library for?"

"Loose ends, I guess."

"Since the branches have no books," she mused petulantly, "no book, that is, a civilized person could pick up, what did you read?"

"Something about wildlife," he gazed at her, stony.

"I hope this new doctor is doing you some good," Cynthia walked over to the stack of breakfast dishes. She touched a coffee cup.

Cabot lost track of her in the stream of ballroom music now. Then after an indeterminate period he heard her voice coming from the bedroom, whether scolding or commenting he was not sure, if indeed there was a difference.

He looked in on her. She was already in her twin-bed, dressed in her waltz gown, sleep-mask on, her hand turning off the light.

He began removing his clothing unmethodically, slowly, staring at her.

"What have you been reading, by the way?" Cabot inquired, with the thick tones to his voice she had come to know and dread.

"I don't want you to make love to me tonight," she boomed at him, and tore off her sleeping-mask to stare at him.

As he continued to approach her, she cried, "Good God, your eyelids are covered—they're dripping with perspiration."

Putting her sleeping-mask back on her face and slipping off her waltz gown, Cabot told her: "There's nothing wrong that you can't cure."

CABOT'S BOSS, MR. WARBURTON, who dated from the Great Days of Wall Street, was continuously depressed at the way things were going downhill. Like so many men whose main interest in life is making a fortune and then doubling it, he had more than a routine interest in the Civil War. Now he had become less enthusiastic about the subject in the wake of its excessive popularity, and devoted himself instead to his book of "sermons" whose subject was the decline of business civilization in the United States. The word "sermons" was chosen by him with some reluctance, since he was lukewarm to religion, though he had been an elder in the Presbyterian church some years back. But, on the other hand, as he said so often to Cabot, he would not have given two cents for a city without a generous sprinkling of churches and synagogues.

Mr. Warburton had recently tried to break himself of the habit of using the phrase "good business" which, like the Civil

War, was now in the mouth of every pauper and tin-horn in the land. The last time he had used the phrase was a few weeks ago when he told Cabot: "It may be good business to hire cripples and copulate with Negroes, but by God, Cabot laddie, you and I know better."

Cabot nodded and swallowed.

"I've always been satisfied with basing my life on making a fortune and centering myself around the System," Mr. Warburton went on, "but today I'm surrounded by men *and* women whom *nothing* can satisfy one way or another. Present company excepted."

Although Cabot was unusually tired from his previous evening's encounter in the branch library, listening to Mr. Warburton was one of his principal duties and he simulated attention as Mr. W. ("Warby") touched on the subject of women in business.

"They are the very hell over here," he heard the old man say, meaning women in Wall Street. "Talked with this Crozier dame the other day who controls or claims to control most of the beer they drink out West. Do you know what the fool is really interested in? Artificial hand-painted eggs—all she cares about. Hasn't been a wife to her husband for twenty years, they tell me. Hand-painted eggs. Can you beat it? Has thousands of them in her insured collection, and claims the best ones come from the Iron Curtain countries. Has no use for her own native land anyway. Abroad most of the time. But, as I say, controls all the beer out there in the West."

Mr. Warburton continued this morning's sermon with his favorite bitter remark of the day that He (God and sometimes

Uncle Sam) was dead and knew it, but they (the fools who were taking over) were buried already and did not know it. Cabot and Mr. Warburton laughed together at this sally.

Once during his morning listening period, Cabot had nodded and swallowed hard as usual, but then added in a voice he felt was too low for Warby to hear. "O.K., everybody knows this, Dad," Mr. Warburton, who was the soul of formality and rigorous etiquette, had paused in shocked silence and then, repeating Cabot's remark in unbelief, had finally broken into uproarious guffaws, in which Cabot insipidly joined. "O.K., everybody knows this, Dad," Mr. W. had repeated, tears of laughter in his eyes. It was from that time on that Cabot had been "in" at Slider, Bergler, Gorem, Hill and Warburton.

This morning, as if to show suddenly that all this amiability and manly horseplay belonged now to the past, Mr. Warburton cleared his throat, shifted his knees, then spread his legs majestically as if, Cabot thought contemptuously, there was still anything between them the years had not shrivelled. Then a peremptory nod from Mr. W. brought Cabot half to his feet. He supposed that the morning listening period was at an end.

Today, however, as happened every so often, Mr. Warburton had planned an added ceremony to follow the Sermon: coffee with, one supposed, more jokes.

"Sue of Short Hills will do the honors," Mr. W. referred to his aged secretary Miss Watkins, and he rang the bell for her.

Miss Watkins entered with shorthand pad and pencil, but Mr. W. indicated by a special movement of the skin of his forehead that the coffee urn was to be tended to and that it would be refreshments, not dictation.

"Yes, that's the ticket," Mr. Warburton mumbled from time to time, addressing nobody, while Miss Watkins poured coffee and cream at last for the two executives.

"I thought we needed a little caffeine, Sue of Short Hills," Mr. Warburton quipped, "because our young General Partner here, Mr. Wright, looks like he'd lost a good deal of sleep yesterday night."

Cabot flushed and touched his eyelids briefly.

"Didn't you now?" Mr. Warburton was sure he spoke roguishly and he winked at Miss Watkins.

Cabot made a motion with his head which resembled putting his neck in a noose more than it did a bow or nod.

Miss Watkins retired, and the two men sipped the weak brew she had prepared for them.

"Coffee all right?" Mr. Warburton inquired after they had sat some time listening to the motor of the air conditioning unit.

"Fresh tasting," Cabot nodded.

"Strong brew wreaks havoc with the liver, I'm told," Mr. W. solemnized. "Let me tell you something then," he continued in Presbyterian elder tones, and suddenly snorting. "It's better to lose sleep at your age, laddie, than get too much. Americans sleep and lolligag around too much for their own good. Sow the wild oats if anything," Mr. Warburton advised.

"Don't forget, sir, I'm a married man," Cabot yawned briefly.

"You kids today all get married too young!" Mr. Warburton was indignant. "Before you know what life or people are about. It's nauseating." He mumbled over his coffee. "When I was your age, I hardly ever got more than four or five hours sleep at a stretch. Out every night. Poker, this, that, the other," he was suddenly vague. "And I've always laid it to keeping awake long hours that I've made for myself the berth I'm occupying today!"

Mr. Warburton relaxed then, laughing, and Cabot mused over the fact that the old bastard considered himself without a grain of doubt one of the eminences of the great metropolis of New York.

"Of course I sowed my wild oats damned near a half-century ago," the old man reflected. His mouth turned down until his lips were a thin white line. "Isn't that scary, Cabot? A half-century ago! By George, the passage of time is one thing that can frighten a fellow into running right out of here, without his hat, down to the river, if he let it. But, by God, laddie, I don't let it, and I won't. Keep the mind and hand occupied, that's the ticket.

"Now speaking of that," Mr. Warburton placed the fingers of his hands in the shape of a tepee, "Cabot, my lad. Of course you know how highly I esteem your father. Your foster-father, that is," he plunged into thought then, and Cabot knew he was in for something more serious even than the Sermon. Perhaps, who knows, he was going to be fired after all, despite Mr. W.'s long indebtedness to Cabot Wright Senior.

"Cabot, I've got my eye on you for the future," Mr. Warburton managed to say, but he avoided Cabot's eye. "The somewhat distant future right now, but coming as sure as sunrise."

Mr. Warburton closed his eyes as he might have done when he was an elder.

"I've had our good Sue of Short Hills prepare you a little

something," Mr. Warburton now faced Cabot and rang the buzzer.

Cabot felt the color drain from his face.

"Miss Watkins," Warburton said when his secretary entered. "That envelope I spoke to you about, please."

The sound of the expensive air-conditioning unit nearby contrasted in Cabot's mind with the unoiled defective electric fan he had listened to last evening in that room in the branch library.

"We've prepared you a little something, my fine General Partner," Mr. Warburton spoke in a manner peculiar even for him, "and we hope you will want to accept it." As if surprised at his own use of the word "we," Mr. Warburton fell back on his habit of placing his fingers before his mouth in tepee-shape. He whistled mournfully through his fingers.

"Now, Cabot," Mr. Warburton studied the envelope Miss Watkins had brought. "I want you to take this in the spirit in which it is offered. And by the bye, both your parents have been informed of what I am doing." He handed Cabot the envelope.

Tearing it open, he saw of course that it was a check. "Christ, Mr. Warburton, two thousand five-hundred dollars!" The young General Partner next got out in a kind of ghastly whisper "Severance pay?"

"Nothing of the kind, not by the remotest suggestion," Mr. Warburton bellowed but Cabot's phrase, it was easy to see, had touched a nerve.

"You're a valuable fellow around here," Mr. W. intoned,

"and, by God, I reward valuable fellows." Wheeling about then in his chair, Mr. Warburton continued: "But the situation is, Cabot, and the fact is: you're tired!"

Cabot rose from his chair, about to cry, "Who told you?" but Warburton was going ahead:

"Probably, Cabot, you're one of those, as I hinted a moment ago, a modern American who sleeps too much. I don't know your habits, of course, nor do I intend to pry into them like the goddam Government. But facts are facts. In my generation nobody was tired. God damn it. The word was unknown, not allowed in decent company. But that was then. This is now. Cabot, I want you to go away and rest, or do something you feel like doing, don't rest, God damn it. Explode maybe. And your parents wish this too. By the way, do you walk the Brooklyn Bridge to work?"

But on the word *explode* Cabot swallowed the weak coffee the wrong way down, and some of the liquid painfully went through his nose, simulating hemorrhage for a moment, which caused additional irritation and loss of time on the part of Mr. W.

In dismay, Cabot let the check slip from his finger to the carpet, and Mr. Warburton picked it up at once with the professional proprietary grasp of the banker, and handed it back to his young executive.

"You've gone stale in your work! I've already told your father!" Mr. Warburton thumped Cabot on the knee. "In my day nobody got stale, because, by Christ, we didn't dare to. But I know times and periods change. I learn that lesson every hour. We live in a less vital world today, Cabot. But I've got my eyes on you and I feel you are one of the ones who *may* go on. It won't be my world, of course, not by a damned long shot, I'm resigned to that, but I think, I believe, you are one of the ones who may go on up and onwards. Were you a football player in college by the way?" Mr. Warburton inquired suddenly, an expression of desire and hope in his expression.

"The second team," Cabot said, irritated that the swallowing of the coffee through his nose had imparted an unwonted lachrymose flavor to his tone, which he did not at all feel or desire.

"I see," Mr. Warburton replied, and assumed his habitual tepee pose with his fingers. "Well, that hasn't got a good goddam to do with what we're talking about. Let me close with this thought. I believe in you as I believe in no other man in this organization but, Cabot, by Jesus Christ, I'm waiting for results!"

Mr. Warburton had gone white.

"Mr. Warburton," Cabot said, standing up, "I believe I am your man, sir."

Cabot wondered later how he had made this statement. He decided that he must have heard it on his Japanese portable radio, when it was advertising, while he was partially asleep.

But the statement worked. It electrified old Mr. Warburton, brought the color back to his lips, and made him stand up and pump Cabot's hand.

"That's the ticket now, laddie," Mr. W. exploded, wreathed in smiles. "That's my Cabot . . . Go away and have a hell of a time, laddie . . . One hell of a one . . . Do you hear, you good-looking son-of-a-bitch . . . And what is this talk you are worried about being a supposititious child? Don't you know your father Cabot Wright Senior has implicit confidence in you? Implicit. As do I. Now go away and explode! Explode, my boy."

Mr. Warburton punched Cabot in the ribs and then in the solar plexus, which was the way, Cabot realized, these things are done.

"And for the sake of God and these goddamned United States, don't come back with that sleepy look. Give up sleep for the good of the nation, Cabot!" And Mr. Warburton roared with laughter as Cabot left.

Downstairs, in the Alexander Hamilton bar, Cabot ordered a double brandy and fingered the check from Mr. Warburton. He was almost sorry that the old bastard had not fired him at once because he knew the two thousand five-hundred dollars, yes, those little embossed figures, were the first step down, if not out. He could see Cynthia already halting in her application of her Princess Gray cold cream when he told her they were "required" to take a vacation. Cynthia hated vacations, never liked to leave New York and never went away unless the trip could be combined with some "connection" with her career, business with pleasure.

Having been potlatched by Mr. Warburton, Cabot Wright remained on in the Alexander Hamilton bar until he was too drunk to walk the Brooklyn Bridge back to his apartment, and took the subway at the Bowling Green stop. Later that day at home, looking out over the confluent waters of the Hudson and East Rivers, he gazed at the Wall Street towers, and had the distinct impression he had flown in over the water and the Bridge.

Mixing three kinds of vermouth, all bitter, with an immense shot of rum, he began thinking of Mr. Warburton's icy wrath of the preceding weeks:

"See here, Cabot," the old man had said at that time, *"I've put up with your goddam nonsense about long enough. We are here to get things done. Right? as the New York Hebrews say. All right then, we won't worry about our feelings and our personalities, our motivations or our own little aspirations. Work, Cabot, that's the ticket, work, and get on the winning team. The team, Cabot, goddam it, the winning team. What does the geography of Down Town stand for, my boy? I told you the day your Dad and Mother sent you fresh in here. The winning team will decide, goddam it, and you're a member of it."*

"The winning team is you, you old white-haired crud," Cabot mixed himself a second pitcher of rum-vermouth, and then sat down at Cynthia's typewriter, and began writing a letter to Mr. Warburton. Not knowing the touch system, the typewriter under his fingers sounded like an old-fashioned sewing machine making a false hem. Cabot was scarcely aware what he was saying in his letter of resignation, and after signing it in swooping letters, he put it on a table nearby.

As dusk fell over the edge of the Wall Street towers, Cabot's day-long depression warmed itself into a kindling triumphant sense of victory. He imagined having wrung from Mr. Warburton both a speech of apology, and a testimonial in praise of Cabot's "performance," together with a statement in which the old man said he would resign for the good of the firm, that is, the team. At the last moment, however, Cabot had insisted old Warby stay on, but with fewer responsibilities, no decision-making powers, no authority to hire or dismiss personnel, a considerable reduction in salary, and a diminutive office facing the powder rooms and the freight elevator shaft.

"What are you looking at out the window this time of day?" Cynthia quavered, coming unexpectedly into the room. She touched her hair-bow gingerly.

"The job and man I left behind, lover," he replied, and he raised his face and his glass to her.

"Have you been home all day drinking?" she leaned over him, but on whiffing the air did not kiss him. "Bloodshot as a St. Bernard," she examined him. "Well, give me a taste," she took his drink, and sipped a bit.

"What kind of a concoction do you call that?" she wondered, still tasting.

"Mr. Warburton gave us two thousand five-hundred dollars to go away on," Cabot said loudly, holding one hand over his eye as he gazed in the direction of Down Town.

"Let's not have any of your sick jokes today," Cynthia cautioned. She began folding the fresh linens she had picked up from the laundry on her way home. "And please don't joke about money tonight. I've had a day."

"Here's the check, dear girl," he extended it to her.

She peered at it.

"You've been fired," she said. "Dear God, that's all I needed."

"Oh, this is only the first step to my getting the sack," he informed her. "They're firing me when I go back." He bristled, and looked brave, as perhaps he might have looked had he been on the first football team.

Just then as she closed one of the drawers the letter Cabot had written to Mr. Warburton fell directly at her feet. Stooping to pick it up, her eyes were riveted to the irregularly margined triple-spaced words, giving the effect of having been branded on the paper by an iron.

Dear Gray Forks,

I have decided that rather than accept your crummy two thousand five hundred dollars which all men on or off the team know how you came by, you can take same and apply as poultice to your piles. How about giving some to your alum-pussed wife so she can go out & hang one on for a change? I take it, Gray Forks, you won the goddam money at either poker or recent market swindle. It will be one hell of a relief not seeing you or the frog-throated eunuchs of either sex. Am having a hand-carved marble stool with cherry colored throw of General Ike and Dick the Nix to replace the wooden seat where you park your old sagging white cheeks so many hours of the winning day. Am also forwarding to your home 80 foot mural of General Mac conquering Asia with his hat on.

Cabot W.

"Did you send this?" Cynthia kept staring at the paper.

"Why don't you take your clothes off, silly," Cabot replied. "It's nearly dark out."

Turning, she slapped him smartly over the mouth.

Rising very much like a star half-back, Cabot picked her up and carried her writhing vigorously into their bedroom in order, as he told her, to make her distinguish between a paid vacation and severance check.

10

TWO CATASTROPHES

C abot Wright, in addition to that long hard nine-inch sword he wore from then on all the time at the left side of his shorts ("Wounded by my own blade again! Condition brand new, never misses a volt!") until he was restored to equilibrium by police brutality and his prison stretch, now underwent two tragic events that, together with his state of permanent erection, made his coming return to Wall Street a mere anticlimax.

The first catastrophe was Cynthia, of course. Her growing fear of and contempt for his physical presence finally made coitus or, as she preferred to call it, sexual commerce, impossible for her. She had always feared, as she wrote in that final letter to her mother, the thought of a life growing in her body. To her pregnancy was now synonymous with death. She therefore barricaded herself.

If Cabot had remembered the story of Pyramus and Thisbe, he might have applied its lessons to the last days of his married life. Locking herself in her own room, Cynthia forced Cabot to communicate with her entirely through the keyhole. Putting his mouth to this aperture, her husband would call out, begging her to be reasonable. Weeping, Cynthia would reply she would never come out again.

"Sweety, do you realize what this means in law?" Cabot inquired, keeping his pupil to the keyhole. He had to repeat his question several times before she understood. He then recalled for her a conversation his father had had with a young working-man in a similar difficulty: if the wife continued "not to yield," divorce would be permitted and, in some states, the marriage would be annulled.

"I've yielded, God in heaven knows," she responded, "more than the laws of nations could require." Her voice was coming from behind a fashion magazine, and was muffled though intelligible.

Then he heard her weeping into some kleenex.

"You've changed, you're the one who is not himself! Ever since the night you came home from that branch library!" Her voice was going through a metamorphosis, and she sounded more and more like a child in the first grade.

"The branch library!" He recalled this event now, as if for the first time, and closed his eyes. "All right, Cynth, pour it on!"

"You don't need to act like a doped-up animal," he heard her little girl voice, and he could visualize the hair-bow she now incessantly wore. "Yet that's how you've been ever since the day you saw Bigelow-Martin. I think you've just decided to act out a part, not caring how I feel or what happens to our marriage. I don't see how we can raise a family, in any case, on what we earn. And I'm sick and tired of your parents' attitude."

"My foster parents, if you please."

"I'm not thinking of divorce, mind you," Cynthia said, a bit worried, to judge by her strange breathing. "When you come to your senses, we can settle down to living together again. But I just don't know why you have to pretend all of a sudden you're an animal, sweating and panting and rushing. You're not yourself, and if I had any respect for, or trust in, your Mom and Dad, I'd tell them how you are now," she cried. "But I've never been close to your mother. Your father never stops long enough to listen, one can't say a thing to him, and they wouldn't believe what I told them in any case because I can't believe it myself." She dissolved again in tears.

"Do you want me to quit seeing the Doc?" Cabot inquired, moving his eye back and forth over the keyhole. He had never been very adept at looking through keyholes. As a college boy, at Yale, he had often followed his classmates to a particular keyhole and while they had seen so much, they claimed, all he ever saw was a fuzzy portion of wallpaper. As he peered into Cynthia's room, all he could get his vision focused on was some part of a windowshade, or a dress hung over a chair.

"What has seeing a doctor got to do with you turning into a sweating panting beast?" she countered. "Go to the doctor or don't go. It's immaterial. No M.D. is going to change you, if you ask me."

"All right, Cynth, old girl, if that's your last word," he got up from his squatting position in front of the door. "I've tried to be reasonable. I guess you'd just rather draw fashions than be a woman . . ."

"Yes, you can say *all right!*" he heard her smothered voice growing more faint and more like her own mother's until he almost thought the old girl herself might be in there with Cynthia. But of course Cynthia's mother was safe away in Oakland, California.

On the whole, Cynthia's outward behavior remained unremarkable until, toward the end of her self-imposed confinement, she began mouthing garbled imitations of the headline announcements that came over the radio. She would cry out, from time to time, things like:

"EAGLE SCOUT CONFESSES TO OFF-COLOR DEED.

"WALL STREET BROKER SLAYS WIFE, MISTRESS, AND THIRD WIFE'S LOVER.

"CRIMES OF PASSION INCREASE, CRIMES WITHOUT NAME ALSO UP.

"F.B.I. OFFICAL DEMANDS MORE SUNDAY SCHOOLS STAY OPEN.

"RACE RELATIONS DELEGATE BLAMES MOST NEGRO CRIMES ON BLACKFACE ARTISTS.

"MOTHER OF TEN MAKES INDECENT ADVANCES TO Y.M.C.A. LEADER."

Cabot, after his key hole interview with Cynthia, went on the prowl for several days. He slept in Central Park and emerged alive, rode the subways, inhabited the Automat, strolled down 42nd Street, and went to see Hell's Kitchen. As Princeton Keith later pointed out to magazine editors, an entire book could be written concerning these hours in Cabot Wright's life. Descriptions of the places he passed alone could fill countless pages of major American prose, with flash-backs to his Army career, long meaty paragraphs concerning the women whose breasts he had studied off-limits, the glances of guilt, hesitation and fear which he exchanged with passers-by, and finally his leaning against a lamppost or railing to get his breath. There would be long poetic descriptions of his reveries, with phrases or entire sentences in French, for the satiny weekly New York magazines to sandwich between their vermouth and plumbing ads.

Returning to his and Cynthia's apartment one early afternoon (the clock on the mantel said 12:03), he was surprised to see their friend, Leah Goldberg, seated in the big arm chair looking him square in the face. Immediately she rose, and putting out her hand, her face warm and troubled, she was ready to tell him at length about Catastrophe No. 1.

Only this morning Cynthia had gone to the supermarket to shop, shortly after it had opened its doors, so she could have her pick of the freshest fruits and vegetables, before the crush. She had walked up and down the aisles with her cart all morning, taking nothing down from the shelves and ignoring customers and clerks.

Then toward the middle of the morning, she had begun to act "disturbed." She began throwing cans on the floor, but so haphazardly and gradually that the clerks thought for a while

the cans were falling by accident. After too many repetitions
of this sort of thing the manager, Harry F. Cowan, had rung
a bell by which he summoned extra help. While he was con-
ferring with the assistants, Cynthia methodically began flinging cans and frozen goods to the floor. The ice-cream hostess,
Miss Glenna De Loomis, attempted to salvage as many of their
Dairy Maid frozen products as possible, but Cynthia then
began to throw the articles at the fluorescent lighting fixtures.
Just before the police and rescue squad came, she had moved
back to fresh fruit and vegetables and had managed to throw
in the air nearly all the pomegranates, persimmons, apples,
peaches, and Jerusalem artichokes she could get her hands on.
Then in a rush toward the front of the store, she had over-
turned three entire shelves of detergents and cleansing fluids.

When she was seized, her beautiful frock was spattered with
the leaves of vegetables, the juice of mashed fruits, and spilled
ice cream and detergents, but the police were most gentle
with her and led her rather easily out to a waiting ambulance,
where she was strapped down to a litter and given an injection
by a young internist. She immediately went to sleep.

Leah Goldberg explained that she had been there only by
sheer accident. Irving having got the day off and driven her
over to the supermarket to buy staples for the coming weekend, when they were expecting house guests. Leah had, of
course, tried to comfort Cynthia, but the latter seemed hardly
to recognize her.

"Cabot, you poor fellow!" Leah Goldberg cried, wishing
to impart sympathy, but with accusation, reproach, indignation and blame on her sun-tanned face. She explained that she

wished to pick up some of Cynthia's clothes to take to the hospital.

"Help yourself, old girl," Cabot walked in the direction of the liquor cabinet.

Peering around impishly at Leah, who was continuing to stare at him, he said, "That was the one thing that kid loved—duds!"

"Haven't you had enough to drink already?" Leah cautioned him, as he poured himself a shot from a bottle he had taken from the cabinet.

"I'm never drunk," Cabot said, which was near the truth.

Mistaking his wish to drink for deep grief, Leah had come up close to him in order to give comfort, and Cabot had absentmindedly taken her hand. He did not release it.

"Cynthia kept herself locked in there," Cabot nodded toward his wife's bedroom. "Couldn't even get a look in at her through the keyhole."

"You must be calm," Leah told him, not daring to try to release her own hand from his grasp, seeing with unease that far from being upset he was perfectly calm.

"You understand, Cabot dear, what I've been telling you," Leah Goldberg went on, her hand held stiff and trembling in its trap. "Cynthia had the complete thing, you understand, a real breakdown. She was shopping for *you*, at the time, poor dear—for food, that is," she added nervously. Leah now got her hand free and dried her eyes with some of Cynthia's own tissues.

In the guise of comforting her, Cabot patted her arm, and then energetically pressed his mouth to her hair. A somewhat strong odor, mixed with a kind of brilliantine whose perfume was unfamiliar to him, stimulated his nostrils. He pushed Leah securely against the back wall so that she now faced the Wall Street panorama across the river.

"Cabot!" she cried, feeling something in their combined posture that puzzled her.

But his face and expression, as it had in the case of the young woman in the branch library, began to work its effect on Leah Goldberg. Her mind became hazy, she muttered something about poor Cynthia again, then suddenly gave an incongruous titter, while at the same time, she seemed unconscious that he had opened her blouse and taken off her bra.

Leah was completely silent when he pressed himself gently but relentlessly into her, as standing they both pressed their combined weight against the wall. She had the helpless expression of a woman who has fallen under a slowly moving car, and watches studiously as the wheels go over her body. She felt Cabot's panting and his intense joy of relief, and coming fulfillment, as he worked himself into her, with a kind of charitable and selfless exertion about him like one remedying some mental discomfort of her own. Her mouth fell against his thick soft hair, and her spittle, suddenly released as if from a well, flowed freely and ran down the front of his face to his own mouth.

Then collapsing under her confusion and her terror, Cabot, with the cry of relief still stuck in his throat, extricated himself slowly from her body, carried her methodically to an easy chair, and then gave her tumbler after tumbler of tap water.

As they sat together, his head over the general situation of her mons Veneris, with Leah weeping somewhat convulsively at first and then regularly and quietly, Cabot gently massaged her nipples.

CYNTHIA'S CONFINEMENT IN a mental institution paved the way for Cabot's successful return to Wall Street more than any other event could have. His playing the role of a youthful Orpheus around the office prevented anybody's "reviewing" his future for a while.

"Warby," as Cabot Wright recalled in one of his long police-tape interviews, "like nearly any American you could hit by spitting from a high building, was a congenital sentimentalist. The thought of Cynthia going mad made him all gooey and got him out of my hair for a while."

The day before Cabot's second tragedy, he and Mr. Warburton were seated in one of the old man's favorite restaurants, on Fulton Street, an oaken-panelled place as big as four barns, with private rooms upstairs and downstairs. They were in one of the private rooms now, and Warburton was pouring Wild Turkey down his throat almost as fast as he could gulp it. "Cynthia will come out of it, she's that kind of a girl," he assured his General Partner. "Will fight her way back. Determined chin, if I ever saw one.

"Laddie," Mr. Warburton now got down to business, "we're going to put you in charge of Monthly Reports."

Cabot's face fell, to use one of Mr. Warburton's own favorite ways of describing the reaction of his colleagues, and of course, it was a facial expression never to assume in the old broker's presence. But when he remembered what Cabot had been through, he forgave his having allowed his face to fall.

"Wonderful training for a chap like you," Mr. Warburton was in full and loud enthusiasm. At a look of uncertainty from Cabot, he elaborated: "Monthly Reports are a damned serious phase of our work. Be great to have you on them."

A few months back, Cabot had told Warburton he would resign rather than be in charge of Monthly Reports. "It's a stenographer's work," he had shouted then at the end of that interview. "Am I a frigging typist?" And though Mr. Warburton had cautioned him then about exploding in his presence, Cabot had been firm: "I'll be goddamned if I do your Monthly Reports."

And even now, with all his great fatherly interest in Cynthia's going off her rocker, both Mr. Warburton and Cabot appeared to be hearing again their row of a few months past, as if on play-back tape, and at that moment they might have posed for an advertisement for dictation machines.

"Agreed then, my boy!" the old broker vociferated over his Ramon Allones cigar.

Cabot said nothing, and did not even go pale. Later he wondered what would have happened if he had repeated his earlier tantrum, and refused to write Monthly Reports. This time, drinking his French cognac, sinking into the rich leather of his chair, with the soothing ubiquitous oak-panelling behind him, he could only say yes of course to Monthly Reports.

Mr. Warburton had immediately slapped him on the back, spilling a long ash, and crying, "That's the ticket, boy!"

Cabot had smiled faintly and Mr. Warburton, wanting to say something assuring, had then stumbled for words, the sure sign of an even more unfavorable attitude toward Cabot than before his General Partner had taken the enforced vacation.

"I know what you're thinking," Cabot had helped the old man. "You're thinking, 'The son of a bitch still looks tired.'"

Mr. Warburton had turned purple with laughter, then stroking the back of his head, said gravely, "Well, who wouldn't, laddie, in your shoes? Good God, with your better-half in a mental home!"

A FEW DAYS later, summoned unexpectedly to Mr. Warburton's presence, Cabot fully expected to be fired once and for all. Instead Mr. Warburton had some black crepe on his arm. Cabot was already rehearsing his "speech of relief" at hearing the news of his dismissal, though he thought the touch of mourning was a bit much even for Warby.

Warburton began: "It is my melancholy duty to inform you that the first great tragedy of manhood has happened to you, my boy."

Cabot heard the sentence and thought it applied to his dismissal. Sitting in a swivel chair, looking out the window over glass buildings and old brown church steeples, sweat again began to seep through his cotton undershirt, and though his body suffered, he knew he couldn't care less. In fact at that moment he believed he would have been indifferent if he had been told the thermonuclear bomb was being counted down to go off. There had been so many threats, warnings, auguries, coming catastrophes, ends and beginnings of ends, cataclysms and Armageddons. What could you do but not care?

At that moment Mr. W. put his hand on Cabot's shoulder, and the latter of course jumped slightly. "Now, now," Mr. Warburton was patting him. "It's your parents," he almost whispered. "Your Mom and Dad, Cabby . . ." He removed his hands

from Cabot's shoulders to wipe his glasses, for tears were coming from his creased eyelids. "You couldn't have picked a finer
pair of people, let me tell you, to grow up with."

"What's their problem?" Cabot finally said from behind a
linen handkerchief with which he was drying his neck.

Mr. Warburton did not appear to take in Cabot's inquiry,
for he was continuing with his announcement:

"While pleasure-cruising in the troubled waters of the
Caribbean, my boy, an incendiary bomb fell on their yacht,
setting it afire immediately and sinking it. Your parents,
Cabot, perished instantly. There is no doubt on that score.
Hope is idle. However, they did not suffer. I can reassure you
on that . . ." He brought out a crumpled telegram from his vest
pocket, and prompted himself. "Now, as your father's solicitor
and also the executor of both your parents' estates . . ."

"My foster parents, Mr. Warburton," Cabot said in a loud
voice.

When Mr. Warburton merely popped his eyes at him, Cabot
went on: "You knew I was supposititious. Think we discussed
it once."

"I'm aware of your origins, sir," Mr. Warburton cried with
passion, for he felt that any interruption at a moment like this,
and with regard to an announcement such as he was making,
was not only inexcusable but in appalling bad taste.

"Who my real parents were," Cabot was going blithely on,
"well, as they say in the funny papers, you search me." He
laughed quickly and then tightened his mouth.

"In the funny papers," Mr. Warburton repeated, and then
studied Cabot with serious scrutiny for, as he knew, great grief

sometimes masks itself in incoherent remarks just before the bereaved one collapses. He therefore placed his arm again on Cabot's shoulder.

Shifting under Mr. Warburton's pressure which was meant to comfort, Cabot placed his hand now under his undershirt, working to stop a twin rivulet of sweat which had begun to race unevenly over his pectorals, one stream of which was racing down toward his abdomen.

Mr. Warburton on observing this behavior immediately rang his buzzer, and Sue of Short Hills responded.

"Brandy," Mr. Warburton said to her.

"I'm not surprised the news has unhinged you, my lad," Mr. Warburton now spoke in quiet and uneasy tones to his General Partner. "After all, it's your second blow in a very short period of time. And your most acute. We can always marry again in this country, but where are we going to find parents once we lose them? Grieve openly, my boy, don't hold it in. Grieve." He patted Cabot's shoulder briefly again.

Going back to his desk, however, Mr. Warburton repeated aloud to himself: "In the funny papers! By God, what do you make of that for a remark."

Addressing Cabot, then, in a loud business-like voice, he went on: "My boy, you realize now that you are a wealthy man in your own right. Easy street and that kind of thing." He cleared his throat.

Sue of Short Hills reentered with the decanter of brandy, which Mr. Warburton took pontifically, waving her out of the room.

He poured Cabot a drink, got ice from a nearby container,

and handed him the brandy on the rocks. He made no offer to help himself, as he had had a snort a short time before.

Cabot drank thirstily, while getting out the words: "Just the same, Mr. Warburton, I'd like to have a chance with those Monthly Reports . . ."

The old man looked at him appraisingly, cautiously.

"I mean, what would I do without work?" Cabot proceeded. "I can't just walk the Brooklyn Bridge and back, with no excuse for doing so, can I?"

Mr. Warburton showed his involuntary respect for the newly crested millionaire by changing his mind and pouring himself a brandy.

"My wife in the nut-hatch, my parents killed in the revolutionary Caribbean," Cabot faced him threateningly. "By God, you owe me those Monthly Reports!" He was close enough now to see the older man's dentures. "How about it, Warby?"

Mr. Warburton winced when he heard so young a man call him by nickname, but he overlooked this also in light of what had happened. He smirked, however, perhaps under the sting of the lack of reverence, squared his shoulders and advanced to the window in General MacArthur strides.

"Holocaust as it is," the old tycoon orated, "almost Biblical in its conclusiveness——" He could not go on, and wheeling around from the window to face Cabot, he blurted out, "But you're rich as Croesus!"

He studied Cabot's face, but evidently saw nothing on it which informed him of anything.

"Tell you what I'd like to suggest," Mr. Warburton approached the bereaved man again, putting his arm around him. "I'd like you to take the day off, and I'd like you to have luncheon tomorrow with my wife Gilda. You've heard things about Gilda, of course you have. Discount them. She's frail in health. You know, she doesn't see many people. Kind of a hermit of late. But take the day off. A woman's sympathy and kindness are what you need as of now. I won't accompany you tomorrow. But I think Gilda's the ticket. Just step out of my office a moment, will you, while I phone her and have the arrangements made certain. Will you please, laddie?" Cabot was amazed at this suggestion of Mr. Warburton. Only the very top brass were allowed to meet his wife. Cabot knew he was really "in."

Before he was able to do much in the way of drying his chest and arms of the bath of perspiration he had inflicted upon himself, Mr. Warburton himself popped into the lavatory and informed Cabot that Gilda would be more than delighted to have luncheon next day. Then as Cabot adjusted his clothing, Mr. Warburton put his arm around him again and patted him with mechanical rapidity on the ass. "Keep the old spinal column straight," he told the bereaved. There were no longer tears in the old man's eyes, and the hard vague look of the hyena was back.

"And if you feel so disposed, God damn it," he finished, "call me Warby from now on."

"Thank you, Mr. Warburton, I will," Cabot replied.

11

LUNCHING WITH GILDA

T he succession of incredible, though (to Cabot) unin-
teresting events, that made him all at once orphan,
widower, newly re-employed, rich, respectable
and criminal, did not overwhelm him in the least. They made
him want to go on doing as he pleased.

He sat in his four-hundred-dollar-a-month apartment and
peeped out the windows with a pair of Army surplus binocu-
lars at the historical panorama anchored in the waters of the
rivers Hudson and East. He could still smell the perfume from
Cynthia's clothes. Just before she had lost her reason, she had
gone clever and begun using men's colognes, which had been
the style in her day. He giggled as he savored that last phrase,
in her day.

He decided to phone the institution where Cynthia was
safely immured, and inquire about her. "Condition satisfactory," a voice, obviously recorded, informed him. He then
asked the voice what condition satisfactory meant, and the

voice repeated the single word, satisfactory. No visitors was
still the watchword. It reminded him that in his own office
when his secretary was said to be not at her desk, one knew
she was in the pee-parlor making up or something. His wife
Cynthia was crazy as a bat in hell but her condition was going
to be satisfactory, he would be told, until she died of old age.

Cabot listened to the phone ring every so often. Sometimes
he answered it in a disguised voice, again he did not. After
all, in his new character of orphan-widower, rich-office clerk,
arrived-criminal, he didn't exactly see the point of answering.
What could anybody tell him now, after all?

GILDA WARBURTON HAD been drinking, Cabot realized, immediately she had opened the door of Mr. Warburton's house on
Fifth Avenue, overlooking Central Park.

Looking at his hostess, under the chandelier of the hallway,
he remembered having seen her at a charity ball with Cynthia earlier that year, a woman of indeterminate age, much
younger than her spouse, with a popular wig of the hour, a
breast alight with jewels, flashing in cadence with bracelets of
gold and platinum, and a stale dank gin breath.

"The wife of the great broker!" Cabot wanted to exclaim
as she ushered him to a chair. "Where are your servants?" he
was about to inquire, surprised by the lonesome silence of the
mansion.

She had already anticipated his question, and was giving
her popular lecture on how, in the current of the present, she
had got rid of her European servants (though they were loves)
and had engaged colored personnel. The latter had brought

her deep satisfaction and peace, had given her, as an American, and through their character as Americans, a closer touch with the realities of the present. Furthermore, this new relationship between employer and servant had revived for her her wonderful Alabama childhood, when she had known oh so many marvelous marvelous Negroes. She shaded her eyes with her palm.

"I feel deeply close to this wonderful new awakening nation within us," Gilda continued. "Our sterling colored friends," she looked away at the flicker in Cabot's eye, "noble people with a grand tomorrow . . . Brady and Anna (she named her personnel) are slow, but they're gold."

Gilda finished her speech as she gave the signal for Cabot to march with her into a huge anteroom. Still leading the way, she ushered him into a cavernous parlor, where he slouched into a creamy gold divan.

"But here while I talk about new nations and tomorrow, dear young Cabot," Gilda raised her voice, "your own loss, poor boy! What can tomorrow mean in the face of such a terrible sorrow?"

She placed her index and middle finger over her frown marks, perhaps in prayer.

"You knew there were two, I gather," Cabot remarked, moistening his upper lip.

Gilda turned her head briefly in his direction. "Two?" she said. "Ah, yes, two parents," she seemed to echo, for her left ear, if not turned just right, often missed a crucial word or so.

"Two losses," he corrected. "Cynthia went off her rocker last week, as I informed Warby," Cabot remarked in a voice adjusted for deafness, while he looked about to see if there might be drinks cached away nearby. "She went just a short time before the explosion took off Mom and Dad."

"Cynthia?" Gilda pondered, thinking perhaps Cabot had reference here to a servant of his own, for servants were a permanent source of attention for Gilda Warburton.

"Our cocktails are on the way," she thought best to change the subject, for she understood the nervous motions of her youthful guest's hands as arising without a doubt from the discomfort of thirst that she too suffered. "Any second now," she reassured him, and glanced inquiringly at her white nail polish.

Then reconciled to the slowness of her new servants, she went on with a short speech: "I feel it's an imposition for me even to ask you here," she spoke now in soaring tones, "but Warby thought you should see somebody. Staying in the office is out of the question, as of course is being alone."

"Oh I intend to go back to the office, unless I get word to the contrary."

"Oh I didn't mean that," Gilda cried, much too emphatically. "Warby would *never* allow you to leave him! Not in a year of Sundays!" Though her voice was shrill, her lack of conviction was paramount. She therefore escaped on to: "But who is Cynthia, dear fellow, if you'll pardon an old woman's paucity of information."

Cynthia was my wife," Cabot intoned. "Went out of her head last week in a new shiny supermarket. Good place for it, as Leah Goldberg more or less said outright. Worried too much, you know, Cynthia. Dress-designer. Tense and keyed up over everything. I blame it on our not having a car. But we couldn't afford everything and live in a nice neighborhood like we did. Choice between an apartment and a car, and that did it."

"Leah Goldberg is a friend, I take it," Gilda considered this name, improbable though it was in her circle of acquaintance.

Then firmly, and with great assurance, she said, "I had no idea at all you were married, dear boy. Warby never mentioned it. Do you suppose he didn't know it also?" She laughed. "Certainly he never even hinted at this second tragedy of yours, or your first one, whichever the order. He always speaks of you as one of his boys. And all the time you've had a wife, and now, as you say, she's—well gone mad, to put it truly."

A paroxysm of giggling overtook Cabot at that moment, and Gilda herself could not restrain a sudden burst of laughter on her part.

"Life is so terrible!" she announced, still laughing.

A tall Negro servant entered with a tray bearing two over-size cocktails.

"Brady, here," Gilda commanded as she saw him begin to go first in the direction of Cabot. "This is Mr. Cabot Wright, Brady," she coached. "A General Partner in my husband's firm."

The cocktails distributed, Brady was about to leave, when hearing a cautious whisper of his name, and a loud "Thank you," he turned back, and then receiving Gilda's permissive dismissal, exited.

"I'm still training Brady, as you must have observed," Gilda pointed out when the servant had left the room. "As I said, I want to have a part in their future. My European days are over. I remember my own Alabama roots more and more, and

I feel I've earned my Afro-American servants. It's only fair for all of us." She quickly sipped her drink.

"To Africa!" Cabot raised his glass.

Gilda thought for a moment before raising her own, and then amended Cabot's toast to "Let's drink prayerfully, if I may say so, Cabot, to your own uncertain future. Africa will wait."

They drank on that, and it was this drink, actually the fifth pre-luncheon "taster" for Gilda, that seemed to reach her, for she swiftly became very flushed and from then on lost a good deal of the thread of conversation.

Brady entered, however, almost immediately with another tray of cocktails.

"It was good of Warby to think you would like luncheon with me, in any case," Gilda said while muttering some reproof *sotto voce* to Brady, while taking her new glass and snatching up a watercress sandwich. "Warby has (that will do, Brady) an occasional good idea from time to time. I speak of the human world, mind you. I know nothing 't all about his business genius, which I am told is on the breathtaking side. He makes piles of money and that impresses the outside public.

"Shall we tell Anna luncheon in five minutes?" Gilda called somewhere in the direction of the retiring Brady, her vision now not quite allowing her to spot him.

"Let me admit it. I adore Negroes." Gilda asseverated, when the door had closed behind Brady. "Adored them, mark you, before they were in all the newspapers."

"To Africa, Gilda," Cabot tilted his glass at her.

She thought a moment, and then said, "If you insist, youthful Cabot, if you insist. To Africa! It's a big toast, though."

"You're big, Gilda," Cabot said sweetly, so that she accepted his remark, after a glance, without comment.

Studying him a bit more closely now, Gilda remarked, "Grief hasn't spoiled your looks, my dear, I'm glad to report to you."

As they tasted their drinks, Cabot made smacking sounds which she was not aware were echoing hers.

Gilda said, "I don't know whether I'm big or not, come to think of it. Did you think Warby's big?"

"Off hand, I'd say why ain't he, Gilda," Cabot replied.

"What about off-the-cuff?" Gilda wondered.

"On or off, I'd say he was big," Cabot replied.

"Hmm," she considered his remark. "What can I say to comfort you, though, charming boy? We've given Africa and Wall Street the benefit of our doubts. What about you? Where do you come in?"

"Maybe luncheon wasn't the right idea," she went on. "Maybe you should have gone to a Turkish bath. I hear they're great for grief."

"But remember I'm not grieving," he assured her.

"Ah, you're going to have the delayed kind," she considered this. "That will be awful. Perhaps luncheon again at that time, what say?" She caressed him with her eyes and her tone. "I hope you'll like what we're having to eat. So few of my friends think highly of my menus. They've spoiled their taste buds beyond the power of satisfaction. At least you're a man. Hunger does a lot. Anna always has something palatable because she's on to hunger. I love Anna. She's black as midnight, but I'm not sorry I changed from the European plan. After all, I'm Alabama myself . . ."

"Tuxedo Park was unaware of any problem, I guess," said Cabot.

"You must think of it in this way," Gilda puckered her lips, and Cabot noticed her mouth was still beautiful. "See where we are, I mean, my lad. We are sailing in troubled waters, all of us, high and low, white, black, brown, speckled, or mottled. God bless all colors, say I, since we're together and can't do anything about weeding things out now if we tried. We're afloat in rotten climate and lunatic weather besides."

Cabot put down his glass slowly.

"I'm afraid," Gilda said. "Aren't you?"

He was still wondering at her fear when Brady announced luncheon.

Cabot and Gilda went into the dinning-room arm in arm, but Gilda insisted that Brady seat her so that he wouldn't lose his lesson.

"I've got to train him, and I've got to exercise my responsibility," Gilda said, when Brady had gone out of the room again. "I've got to give them their chance. He's got to have a real beginning somewhere, and this is where I'm giving it to him. Of course there's wax in his ears and he sniffles, and there's a kind of smell at times—why pretend. But I've got to give them their chance."

Staring at her soup, she asked, "Cabot, are you afraid?"

Cabot said he was sometimes, but didn't think about it.

"Don't you like turtle soup?" she inquired as she noticed he was not touching his bowl.

He took a mouthful then and said "Ahem."

"You do feel a little consolation here, I hope. Of course

you've lost everybody you had in the world, haven't you?"
she suddenly narrowed her eyes as she sensed the enormity
of it. "That you can sit up at all is wonderful," she praised
him. "Cabot, you're wonderful," she applauded him. "And grief
doesn't mottle your complexion either. It turns mine to coffee
and grime. You have auburn hair, too. So few auburn-haired
people in my life now, except for wigs."

She pushed back her plate. "I know Warby must be hell to
work for . . ."

"Oh it's all me frankly," Cabot volunteered.

"I doubt that. He's not human at all, you know. This quality has kept us together, I suppose, nonetheless. But he's just a
troll, a mammoth mummy with a motor, but no soul."

"Don't you see him sometimes as a shoebill?" Cabot
inquired, thinking aloud as her mention of animals carried
him back to his reading at the branch library.

"Shoebill?" she considered the word if she could not visualize the thing. "I'm afraid you've got me there," she wiped her
chin slowly with her napkin, and studied her guest narrowly.
"However," she proceeded, "the only relationship one can have
with Warby is working for him. Not with him, please note.
Yes, that's the way the boat rocks." She threw her head back in
the attitude of one about to vocalize.

"And now here's the sesame fried chicken," Gilda greeted
Brady as he entered. She touched a drumstick with her index
finger. "Sometimes I run Down Town for luncheon with
Warby," Gilda went on. "Feel such a blamed prisoner in this
house, and my servants are so good to me during the day.

Sometimes I could almost scream. Ever get tired of being treated so *nice?*" Gilda put the matter to Cabot.

He stopped chewing a moment in an effort to think it over. "My life is largely paper work," Cabot confided.

"How would one describe my life, do you suppose?" his hostess looked at her forkful of dark meat. "Dressing up and getting there takes the day," she said. "I don't write letters any more, though in my day I was a minor Mme. De Sévigné. Phone calls finished me. Dial just anywhere at present, call up California or London or Nice and say, 'I hadn't a minute to pick up the inkwell. How are you?' Half-listen to this and that, and goodbye again. So miraculous and yet so unsatisfying, so spooky-unreal to hear people's live voices when you know you'll never see them alive again if you both live to be 200. It's already like talking to the River Styx. Writing letters to people was better, but who has the time or will power any more? Do you know, Doctor told me when I cry I double my metabolic rate? But, Doctor, I said, when I write a letter it must quadruple it. I was always so emotional. Warby, I know, hasn't heard anything I've said since 1930."

Cabot finished his chicken and pimento potatoes.

"Speaking of writing," Gilda went on, "I used to be on speaking terms with this retired novelist Princeton Keith, now turned big-time publisher. He was the rage for a year or so as a writer, and do you know what from? Framing me in a novel of the epoch—oh, before you were born or thought of! I always have the feeling, too, he's waiting to frame me all over again . . ."

Gilda looked thoughtful, and then very sad. "The whole world was his prey, Cabot. Since you mentioned animals— what was it, the Bluebill? —well, do you know what Keith has on his wall, along with the heads of wild beasts. Well, on his wall is the head of an animal that is the friend of man. There on the wall with wild boars, tigers, and snow leopards."

She began to cry.

"Is it a horse?" Cabot began to guess.

Gilda shook her head.

"A collie?"

"No, no," she seemed to scold him, drying her tears. "It's a camel, dear friend."

She cried a little more, and rang the bell for Brady.

"Keith didn't shoot camels too, did he?" Cabot hadn't both- ered to tell Gilda he knew the game-hunter in question.

"He couldn't shoot," Gilda looked at him with tender con- descension. "Princeton put me in a book once," she remi- nisced, looking at the design on her china. "*Clarissa, Mistress of Sam* was the title, best-seller, book-of-the-week selection, you know—they go in for dirt, you see, if the prose is a bit refined. I was a prostitute in it, with just a *soupçon* of the lesbian. Can you imagine it now? I was, you see, Clarissa. Warby was going to sue Princeton, when he realized . . . But you're not concen- trating!" Gilda cried, staring at Cabot.

Her guest sputtered something.

"But why should you concentrate, you dear thing, with all your grief? How do you do it, Cabot? You're of heroic mould. I know I'm boring you, but it's better to bore you than have you sitting alone overlooking the Statue of Liberty and all that water flowing out to sea. I've tried to be amusing. And I gave the luncheon, so forgive me, for Christ's sake . . ."

Sobbing, Gilda rushed out into a side room and closed the door behind her.

Cabot Wright sprang up with alacrity after her, and pounded on the closed door. "Gilda, come out at once. I must see you!"

Brady entered at the moment with the dessert plates and doilies, and exited after a hooded glance of wonder and surprise.

Cabot managed to open the door of Gilda's retreat and went in. She was sitting in a large fat chair, in what was a small den-like chamber, blowing her nose. Her wig was a bit crooked.

"Gilda, dear lady," Cabot said, "forgive me if I seemed inattentive or offended you in any way."

"Offended? You couldn't do that, dear child. It's too late for anybody even to try to offend me. No, it has nothing to do with you. I'm an old recluse, that's all. I know I've bored you, and besides I can't remember in a prolonged conversation what topic's been covered and what hasn't. Luncheons are a workout! People are a workout! And I'm not very well," she cried hard now remembering her metabolism.

Her diamond necklace flashed in the subdued light just as she finished talking.

"You look so absent-minded when you perspire as you are doing now," Gilda remarked. "Shall we go back to the table for our dessert, like soldiers?" A worried look passed over her eyes and brow.

"I think dessert is out of the question," Cabot told her.

"How gaily you put it," Gilda smiled again. "I suppose you think I'm plump enough besides."

"I hadn't thought so, Gilda," Cabot sat down beside her. He put his hand on her white arm.

"Shan't we return to the dining room just the same?" she wondered, wistful.

"Just to give Brady his lesson? I think not."

"Dear Cabot," she tried to remind him of his loss.

"It's deadly," he said the word. The sting of his kiss warned her too late.

"I have servants!" she cried. "Am expecting callers!"

He had already begun to remove her clothing.

"Negroes understand just about everything, especially concerning grief," he assured her, going to work in earnest. She smiled, still hoping perhaps that grief explained what was happening.

"I'm old enough to be your grandmother!" she appealed to him when she saw how deep they were.

"Let Doctor decide," Cabot told her.

"Mrs. Warburton, ma'am," Brady's cautious baritone came to them through the panelling. "Dessert's on."

When Mrs. Warburton did not respond, the servant called through the jamb of the door: "Peach Melba on the table, Mrs. Warburton, please."

There was a long pause and then Brady's drowsy voice again came to them: "No dessert course then today, ma'am?"

There were some smacking sounds from the room off the

dining hall, the sound of a chair toppling, and then the phonograph began playing.

Brady exhaled heavily, took the last of the dishes away, then
paused just before he began to go through the swinging doors
that led into the kitchen.

A heavy crash in the room into which Mrs. Warburton and
her guest had retired made him hesitate just a moment before
he let the doors close on him and the two untouched Peach
Melbas.

12

THE BEGINNING ROOM

D id I mean to bang 'em and blow 'em and make 'em feel they were mine?" Cabot Wright had rephrased the question put to him by a row of medical experts and detectives. This was long afterwards in jail, after his capture and incarceration, when both his accent and diction at times resembled that of the great beating heart of inner Brooklyn.

"Well, did you, Cabot?" an elderly psychiatrist inquired with routine medical kindness.

"O.K. I'll sit in for some vacationing best-selling crap-artist for you," Cabot is said to have replied. "I'll tell you, gentlemen and cops. The older the hen, the richer the gravy. But you always want to know why. Search me. I was sick—I can go this far—sick of the young marrieds, the professional brief-case smarties, the sun-bathers from the Hamptons comparing their browns, the baseball addicts, race and fight pros, sports-car nuts, TV glaucoma people, jeans-wearing faggots of forty, ginger-beer voices of the off-track betting baboons."

Cabot thought some more under the Hiroshima bright lights: "Murder may be an indoor crime, but rape needn't have any backdrop and shouldn't. It's an everywhere sport. I raped everyone through boredom, so maybe then I chose the thing I felt would bore me the most, dumb dames. You are not as bored, gentlemen, listening to me as I am to myself, which disappoints me. I surrendered to boredom knowing there couldn't be more to it than itself. Wasn't boredom the only experience I could latch on to, considering what Wall Street had for me? Next to dying, boredom is the most. I knew only boredom was possible then, because there is no time for pleasure today, you can just allow yourself that second-and-a-half to hear the message, which is always an ad. I more than half-heard it, and I think that might have been Cynthia's trouble too. She had been hearing and reading and then drawing for a living nothing but ads all her life. Feasting on them, poor little twat, by day and having them again by night in New York classic fiction, *The Shepherd in the Pie, Gooey and Girly,* and the Great Boy Writer's Gentile successor, *Your Rarebit Is Running.*

"We were digesting our own personalities which somebody else had given us in the first place, and it all backed out up on us before we could cry puke. The business of winning finally gave us one too many hellos. By Jesus, we were overstimulated and turning over too many new leaves at once, we went haywire."

———

ALTHOUGH STILL A member of the firm of Slider, Bergler, Gorem, Hill and Warburton, Cabot Wright, by reason of his becoming an heir, could no longer be listed merely as a General Partner. While a more suitable name was being found for his changed status, he sampled his new-found leisure. No longer going to the office so assiduously, he discovered around him, in the novelty of off-hours, a world whose existence he had neither known nor suspected, the army of persons who know no routine labor.

He had thought that businessmen and stenographers, career women and elevator operators were the entire population, and that those left behind were housewives and children or small groups too nondescript to consider. By being semi-retired at 26, he found a whole population which did not walk the Brooklyn Bridge or go by subway to midtown Manhattan, or commute to Long Island. Neither were they all over 65. There were the young and the very young among them. Some were, he supposed, heirs like himself, while others were the unemployed and unemployable—a monster statistic whose real numbers both press and government concealed under stock phrases.

Everywhere he saw those engaged in race-track betting, gambling and other related pursuits, professional dog- and cat-walkers, disappointed unpublished writers, longshoremen unhired or laid off for other reasons, plain clothesmen resting until their suspects turned up, photographers, reporters hoping to run into stories, worried businessmen out to think things through, senile Spaniards who still discussed Franco, young men in Bermuda shorts, the crippled, ministers of churches getting ideas, social workers out "in the field," shoe

clerks off for a smoke, nursemaids, homemakers, cooks, and
children not at camp.

The boats screamed prior to departure from the Columbia pier, air-raid sirens occasionally rehearsed their cries, gulls
flew sleepily overhead, and the Wall Street towers stared back
at Cabot from the other side of the river.

Deciding to look like everyone else, Cabot put on summer
slacks, a soft sport shirt, and sun glasses. Before he left his
room, the desire for a whiff of present-day reality made him
turn on his tiny Japanese radio. He heard the words of a song:

> *"Everywhere in our free land,*
> *our only land . . ."*

sung by youthful male altos, followed by the rouse of the
march song for Beer, the democratic get-to-gether drink.

A dialogue followed between a woman with a low contralto
and a man identified as her husband concerning plans they had
laid for a vacation in the Adirondacks, with Victor, their 8-year
old son with an I. Q. of 180, this dialogue being succeeded
instantaneously by Feminine Hygiene Ad, followed, while
the last note of the preceding sounded, by Health-Larynx-
Cigarettes. A chorus of Swiss yodellers then spoke of men's
body odors as contrasted with those of ladies. An expensive-
dentured M. D. lectured for 30-seconds on baby's heatrash, and
the listener was then returned to the low contralto who read a
funny joke in the presence of her husband (already identified)
from a list of jokes known as "Buzzie S.'s At-Home Talks" (the
genius child).

Then an eighty-piece band played, with background of mixed chorus of 14 middle-aged men who sang a religious number, after which came the religious quotation of the day, plus appeal to attend church, synagogue or tent of your radio sponsor's choice, followed by a chorus of the sons of the middle-aged men singing *a capella* for Mooney Cement and King Bar Beer. A father whose voice had earlier spoken to the M. D. concerning his baby's heatrash, then urged all to buy shares in freedom and appealed again to attend church of radio sponsor's choice, but if as yet you had not chosen church, go at once to the free psychiatric clinic nearest you, where you would be given a telephone appointment.

Adjusting his trousers, Cabot went out, not taking the time to turn off the radio, and hearing again in the hall the contralto's shared laughter (with identified husband), and the parting strains of the chorus of youthful middle-aged men singing

"Keep it free, keep it free . . ."

On the wall near his apartment building, he saw an old-fashioned obscene word misspelled, and although obviously a trap laid by the borough police, since the chalk lay in open view on the walk below, Cabot picked it up, fumbled for the extempore inspiration, and then wrote the word: JITTO.

There are no streetcars in Brooklyn, though there are the remains of the tracks that were once laid for them, and of course nearly everything of the old city was being abolished. "The bull-dozers are coming to you and to me," Cabot thought. "They will flatten the old Federal homes, so dear to so few, the yards, the shrubs, the tea-rose bushes, tear down the fancy bird-houses, the immaculate greenswards, though leaving a few golf-courses founded by Italian candy kitchens, and a statue of a Scottish caddy who found the ten thousand dollars and returned it to the owner only to receive a dollar reward, on which he founded his chocolate biscuit factory and became a Flatbush millionaire."

IT WASN'T LONG before Gilda, in a drink coma, squealed on Cabot Wright. Later, sober, she denied her own story, leaving Mr. Warburton high and dry, but still obsessed.

"Did he touch the little woman?" he kept mumbling aloud Down Town. Finally, after soul-searching and rereading many of his own Sermons, he confronted Cabot. He blurted out his accusation suddenly and unexpectedly, but the look of calm innocence on young Wright's face immediately convinced him of the impossibility of the charge. He realized the young man had never insulted his wife, that she was not well, and so to forgive him, forgive her, forgive everything.

Warby knew that a boy who had just lost his parents, and seen his wife break down in mental illness, certainly wouldn't have insult and rape on the brain. Impossible. And again that fine wholesome look to Cabot. Open any newspaper to the photographs of captured rapists, and see their faces. Blood will tell. No, Gilda was just not well, after all the fortunes they had spent on specialists, rest cures, and Wisconsin vacations. Just goes to show you no amount of cash can buy health. Most precious thing in the world. Nothing equal to it. Old John D. knew that with his stomach ulcers. Without health, damned little to be grateful for. All the money in the world can't equal it.

Despite Cabot Wright's convincing disavowal, Mr. Warburton then and thenceforth seemed to lose his appetite for information. He ceased perusing the *Wall Street Journal* (he had given up the *Times* twenty years before), hardly touched his food, and in many ways looked more ill than Cynthia Adams prior to her celebrated breakdown at the supermarket.

EACH MORNING, IN order to comfort the not-to-be-comforted, Cabot walked the Brooklyn Bridge as in his obscure days, and stepping into the old broker's office reassured him each day that the charges were absolutely false. On those very days on which he was denying Gilda's charges against him, young Cabot was raping women and girls at the rate of about $1\frac{1}{2}$ per diem, by that meaning, in weekly statistics he raped about 2 an evening or afternoon, and fewer for some reason over the weekends, perhaps because women are more apt to be accompanied by sons, husbands, or other loved male companions in the cessation of work periods. Such was his incessant ability at rape or, as he testified to an attentive police-interrogation squad, his uncanny power to "have his way with them."

EATEN BY A hidden malaise, Mr. Warburton grew weaker and weaker by the day, and finally was advised by a young business colleague to consult a new physician, who had recently put up his shingle in Wall Street, and who was having sensational results with both older executives, and younger partners who were below par. Name of Dr. Bugleford.

Then another event transpired in Mr. Warburton's domestic life which made Cabot's real or fancied overtures to Gilda of secondary importance. To explain fully its impact on Mr. Warburton, one should know that although he had been born and raised in the East, all of his ancestors, like those of Gilda, were from the South, and he was proud of his heritage. That is, he was proud of being from the East and the South, and his loyalties were sometimes strained, though his principles were always clear.

Going to Gilda's room "to have it out with her" a final time as to whether Cabot had molested her or not, he had heard a scene of such intimacy between Gilda and her butler, Brady, that the Cabot Wright episode was, he now believed, a ruse on Gilda's part. At first he could not believe, quite naturally, what he was hearing outside Gilda's door, but living as he was, at the end of a civilization, nothing was surprising, he supposed. It was nightmarish enough, when he went back the following evening to Gilda's room and heard the entire scene between her and her Negro servant repeated.

"So it was Big Smoke then and not Cabot Wright!" he could only mutter. It was then he told his secretary to telephone Dr. Bugleford. "Troy has fallen," he said of himself. All his life he had scorned doctors and therapy, believing that medicine must be employed only in such mechanical matters as a broken limb, or to staunch the flow of blood.

The reader, in this case the listener (Cabot Wright eavesdropping on his own story as novelized by Bernie Gladhart and revised by Zoe Bickle) has already met Dr. Bugleford, when he was Dr. Bigelow-Martin. Having had to leave the leaf-

shaded blue-stoned pavements of Brooklyn Heights in order
to escape a possible charge of malpractice, Bigelow-Martin
changed his name effortlessly to another and set up practice
on Lower Broadway where superstition, in a district so close
to national pulse and strain, has always been rampant, especially in moments of crisis and naturally induces a flourishing
patronage of herb-doctoring, health cures, astrology, fortune-
telling, bone, muscle, and nerve realignment, not to mention
new-thought parlors.

The doctor received the distinguished Wall Street personality in an unusually beautiful consulting room, on the floor
of which rested a carpet, snowy as a llama's belly. Because of
Mr. Warburton's age and an old football injury, Dr. Bugleford
waived regulations and agreed that he would not require him
to take off all his clothes for the present, though this was his
usual method, to see the entire human radish stripped of sub-
terfuge and disguise. In the case of Mr. W. the doctor would
work up gradually to nudity.

While Mr. Warburton consulted his gold pocket watch, Dr.
Bugleford gave his beginning lecture on civilization's woe, the
demented neuroskeletal tension we are all living in, or rather,
expiring under.

"Let's get down to facts and figures," Mr. Warburton advised
him. "For my part I'll leave what kind of a world we're living
in to the preachers and the women." Rising from the relaxation couch, Mr. Warburton explained that he was due back
at his office in one half hour, that he had given up his usual
luncheon at Whyte's, and hoped the Doctor would be through
with his examination in fifteen short minutes.

"The initial examination is over," Dr. Bugleford smiled pityingly (and his expression of condescension was not lost on Mr. Warburton.) "Your disease is America's. Hurry-tension. Knotted arteries and veins. Clogged network of nerves and muscles. Tight brain tissue. It's in every atom of our atmosphere. And when one thinks, Mr. Broker, we're 6 billion muscle fibers encased in 639 muscles all of which have got steel tight with tenseness, isn't it natural, then, we feel bad bad bad? Well, that's my worry, not yours: I'll hunt for the tight spots in your 6 billion muscle fibers . . ."

Usually quick at a rejoinder, Mr. Warburton was struck dumb.

"Ready, Mr. *Warming*ton?"

"Warburton, Warburton, if you please," he corrected the Doctor.

"You are as ready, now, Mr. Warburton, thank you for correcting, as you'll ever be. As in religion, we must, in my science, obey or perish. Do you want to change your life, Mr. Warbleton, or not?"

"Warburton!"

"You needn't raise your voice. I hear perfectly well, and stand corrected, Mr. Warburton."

Mr. W. flushed angrily.

"You are very *very* tense, my dear broker," the doctor moved into diagnosis. "Your disease is America's. America is your disease. Your jaw," he seized this portion of Mr. Warburton's facial structure, "your lower jaw could easily be a steel trap."

Suddenly he slapped Mr. Warburton's chin smartly.

"Release that jaw!" he commanded, slapping the mandible again.

The doctor then rose, a smile bringing into play the myriad wrinkles of his countenance, and said: "We shall begin our treatment then?"

"Now see here, doctor," Mr. Warburton began, but an imperious gesture from the doctor snapped this train of thought in the elderly investor, and he finished with the querulous appeal: "Got to call my office to tell them I won't be coming back right away then."

Mr. Warburton touched his jaw gingerly as if he had suffered an extraction.

"Nonsense, Mr. Warmington," Dr. Bugleford reassured him, "they'll see you when they see you, and they'll see a changed man, let me tell you when they do."

The doctor then placed his index and middle fingers in the corners of the broker's eyes and pressed calmly.

"You'll be going back to Wall Street, granted, a little late, but you'll certainly be going back: be grateful for that. But if you go on the way you are, with that steel-trap jaw, those pounding arteries and tight nerves and muscles, you're headed, without the shadow of a doubt, for an infraterrestrial site."

He ushered his patient into a huge room.

"Ordinary doctors would call this the operating room," he told Mr. Warburton. "I call it the *beginning* room."

Lying down on a huge green couch, Mr. Warburton became aware of the doctor's warm wintergreen breath bending over his right (the good) ear, saying:

"Now my dear sir, I think you must realize that it is the way you act, the way you do, your way of raising your hand or your leg or your salad oil or the fork with the piece of sirloin attached to it, the pitch of your voice, the rapidity with which you lick an envelope, swallow your Jack Daniels, or make love to your wife or whoever—"

"Meaning what?" Mr. Warburton raised his head and roared.

"Lie back, sir," Dr. Bugleford was forbearing.

"You are as you behave, Mr. Warleyton, and how do you behave? I know how you behave, but do *you?* Can you catch yourself in the act of behaving as you? That is what we must find out today."

"Smacks of theosophy, by Christ," Mr. Warburton exclaimed.

"Smacks of what you do," the doctor shook his head. "What you do you are."

"Clear as mud."

"Examine now all over again your chin. You have closed it as an iron trap might close over a grizzly's hind leg. Examine your jaw for one hour, noting the extreme severity of its posture, and then having realized the hardness of your jaw, let it break, dissolve, flow, vanish, turn to flowing limpid water, flowing flowing flowing. Lie back, my good broker, lie back. You are flowing away, out to sea, out to the deep . . ."

Mr. Warburton had been on the verge of roaring again with rage, both at the doctor's theosophy as well as his incessant miscalling of his name, when suddenly he found himself doing just as he was bid. Lying on the couch without a pillow, Mr. Warburton had visions of Gilda betraying him first with Cabot Wright, and then turning to the caresses of the Big Smoke, Brady the butler. He saw the truth during that hour concerning Gilda, but he did not somehow care, there was such a pleasant perfume everywhere, and his mouth seemed to lie open on a bed of drifting water lotus.

WAKING UP AFTER an hour in the doctor's "operating room," terrified by the lateness, by the missed appointments back at his office, Mr. Warburton was still not able to be as angry as usual. He tried to vent his rage on Dr. Bugleford. In vain. Relaxation had already begun, and his personality was changing. He already saw the handwriting on the wall: once he was deprived of tenseness and anger, his business empire would crumble—he would be calm and happy and *penniless*.

Nonetheless, shaking hands with Dr. Bugleford, beaming, he made arrangements for a return visit and, rare for him, paid the atrocious fee quietly and without quibbling, on the spot.

NO MATTER HOW much he grilled Cabot Wright in his office, or Gilda in her drawing room, Mr. Warburton could make no sense out of the affair. Cabot Wright denied the whole thing from beginning to end; Gilda wept when confronted with the question; Brady looked innocent and uninvolved. What Mr. Warburton did not understand was that his wife was more puzzled by what had happened to her than he was, that is she was not sure *what* had happened.

His darker suspicions were to be confirmed in large part that very evening when, after dinner, he purposely pretended to doze in his easy chair, while Gilda was resting her eyes with a slumber-mask, prior to viewing television. Nearly a city block away from his wife in their cathedral-size living room,

Mr. Warburton heard Brady enter with his leopard stealth and grace. Through one half-opened lid he saw Gilda take the butler's hand.

"Shall I serve you coffee here, Mrs. Warburton, or upstairs?" Brady bowed to know her pleasure.

With her free hand, Gilda removed her eye-pads (she had taken hold of his hand "blind" from habit) and nodding, said, "Here, quite naturally." As he set the demitasse down, with a tiny plate on which rested two mocha wafers, Mrs. Warburton covered his hand with inaudible kisses. Brady remained calm, though he noted the slow accumulation of lip rouge on his epidermis much in the same way, Mr. Warburton observed, that a zoo guard will permit a lioness to lick the fingers with which he is accustomed to feed her.

"Beautiful veins on that hand, I wonder what they're called," Mr. Warburton heard his wife speak in a tone he had never remembered coming from her before. "I admire any sign or indication of strength," she informed the butler. "And if I remember my anatomy—I was an art student, Brady dear, long before your mother thought of love," and she held his hand now at a distance as one will appraise a ruby, "I believe the vein I am studying comes out of the dorsal venous network. Indeed I am sure of it." She kissed the hand again, though less thoroughly now.

"Can I retire now, ma'am?" he inquired in a voice she had once described as pure velvet.

"*May* I go?" she corrected him. "Of course, wonderful, wonderful Brady, you may."

She had not released his hand.

"But my dear Brady, you've forgotten my medicine!" she
cried. "How thoughtless of you to neglect me."

"No, ma'am, I have not forgotten," he contradicted her. "If
you'll let me, I have it over here for you . . ."

He motioned to a tray near them.

"Shall I hold the spoon for you, ma'am, as per usual?" he
inquired.

He had managed at last to free his hand from hers.

"If you would be so very kind, my dear friend," Gilda nodded
in the general direction of her digitalis.

Brady poured the red heart medicine into a solid silver
tablespoon, and held it out near her thin blue lips. Just as he
removed the spoon from her mouth, she bit down, holding
his wrist in her teeth, which were, as a matter of fact, still
her own. He made no effort to withdraw from her pressure,
but bending down, surrendered his face to the routine score
of kisses. Her impassioned embrace of his face made him lose
his balance slightly and he more or less fell at her feet, allowing her to deposit kiss after kiss on his crown, "the precious
wool," as she rhapsodized over it, finer, she assured him, than
any vicuña.

"Be faithful," she admonished him gently, "as I am faithful
to you and yours. And remember, beautiful Arab, wonderful
wonderful Brady, we both know Mr. Cabot Wright never paid
us a call, or if he did, left without his dinner. There is no Cabot
Wright. There's only, where secrets are concerned, you and
me. Shine on, Brady, shine."

When Brady had risen from his kneeling posture and left
the room, Gilda rose as limber as a 16-year-old, and gambolled

the full length of the room to where Mr. Warburton lay in a
sleep that looked as deep as eternity. He snored.

Kissing her spouse on the lips, she brought to an end his
trying role as opossum. He looked at her. Only an old soldier
could have been so calm, so silent. Yet she must have sensed
something in his eyes. Perhaps they were too wide-awake for
a man who had appeared to be in such deep slumber. "I want
to talk to you, Gilda," he said.

"Can't it wait until the weekend, dear?" Gilda sat on a tiny
footstool at his feet, looking small, blonde and filial. "This is
my big TV night of the week, you know. It's Tuesday—gaze-
night, dear."

"I'm afraid this is a matter of gravest importance, my pet."

"You're not going to give me bad news about your health,
Warby!" she exclaimed in real displeasure. "I'm too weak to
hear about it, my dearest. I can't bear another cross!"

He was touched, in spite of himself, and almost thought of
postponing their talk.

"No, my angel," he replied to her question, "as to my health,
outside of a touch of coronary, Dr. Bugleford is more than taking care of me."

"Thank God, Warby, thank God," Gilda said, but her attention had gone to the television screen.

"Can't you turn the goddam box off for one ten-minute
period?"

"I told you, dearest, it's Tuesday, my gaze-night. You have
your den for talks."

"Gilda, this concerns our very future."

"Don't tell me there's been another crash or panic. I told

you in 1930, it was the last time I could live through watching you worry on that scale. I mean it, Warby. I'll never go through 1930 again with you. *I'll* jump this time."

"It's not 1930, God damn it to hell, but I don't know if it isn't something worse . . ."

"About our suspicion concerning Cabot Wright," Gilda began sweetly. "I've hit on a plan to prove whether he insulted me or not. It's fool-proof . . ."

"I see," he stared at her with icy dissatisfaction.

"I'm going to have you arrange for Cabot Wright to call on Zenda Stuyvesant."

"Why that old bag?" he exploded.

"She'll know," Gilda told him.

"Know what, for Christ's sake?" he demanded.

"Whether he'd be capable of offending me or not." She lowered her eyes, and looked so sad and sweet that he was again won to her.

"So old Zenda can read minds," he commented.

"She'll know, if you'll only send him to her . . . Say yes, Warby. Say you'll send him."

He kissed her on the nose, meaning, she supposed, he would.

"Gilda, are you aware, my dearest, now let me try to put this as gently as I can, God damn it . . ." She waited and he said quickly: "The fact is, Gilda, you smell lately like a Negress."

"That word is no longer in vogue, my innocent. Sweety, you're so out of touch. If you spent more time with your little wife, you'd be more in the swim."

"I'll make my point, love, if we sit here through tomorrow."

"Make your point, dearest, for I'm attending to the screen now and not you."

"You smell like a Negro lately, and I wonder why."

This time she paused, briefly, but came up with an answer. "I've been using a lotion made from tropical plants, if you please, and I'm really not paying any attention to your question because I know it's an excuse for some other kind of unpleasantness."

"Gilda, aren't you overdoing your attentions to Brady . . . and to Anna, of course."

"You know I am! I have nobody else to shower my affection on!"

"Don't bawl now," he implored, for she was weeping hard.

"Gilda," he proceeded, "have you been intimate with Brady even in a minor way? For Christ's sakes, tell me . . . I'm not going to take action if you have. I'm too old to divorce you no matter what you have done, or are planning to do. I'm too old and too busy to make any change in my domestic arrangements. I regard this as my hotel, in point of fact, and a damned good one it is, too."

"Thank you, Warby, for the additional black eye."

"To go back to my original question, I'd like to know why you smell the way you do lately?"

She gave him one of her more terrible looks, and then said, "I look upon Brady as an adopted son, though a servant."

"And your relationship stops there?" he wondered.

"It does. We go to Harlem, but then I'm studying Harlem. You have no idea how empty my hours are, Warby. You've brought more vacuum into my life even than money, and you've made me feel vacuum in places I had no idea existed. Why begrudge me a bit of color?"

Mr. Warburton rose and began to leave the room.

"Warby, come back here," she called to him. "You aren't going to do anything desperate now?"

"I'm going to the liquor cabinet. Bring you anything?"

She shook her head.

When he returned with his bottle of rye, she took his hand, and said: "I haven't done a thing wrong, Warby, and you know it. I never smell anything different about Brady and Anna, and my sense of smell is superlative. Still, who am I with all day? Negroes. I have to pay to have people with me, you said that long ago, and the Europeans couldn't stand me. How long the Negroes will is anybody's guess, now they're revolting, of course. But if I smell, Warby, that's part of your bad bargain in marrying me. And you don't begrudge me, dearest, a little *mental* romance with African beauty?"

His head was in her lap, for they had changed positions, and he was sitting on the footstool, and she was in the large chair, the better to see the screen with.

"And promise me you'll send Cabot Wright to see Zenda Stuyvesant. She'll know if he did anything wrong or improper while he was having that sympathy-luncheon."

She patted Warby's head, who grinned contentedly.

"Zenda's alive with occult perceptions, dearest," she was watching the screen hard now, and her wrinkles of care relaxed, and her blond curls fell back softly on her head. She continued to pat Warby.

"You'll be sure to send Cabot to Zenda then, my dear, first thing in the morning."

He grunted his assent.

ALTHOUGH MR. WARBURTON was expected at the dedication of the Professional Football Hall of Fame, taking place somewhere in the hinterland of Ohio, and should have departed hours ago, he postponed his flight to call Zenda Stuyvesant and arrange Cabot Wright's coming visit to her home (Cabot had been more than pleased to go), and in view of feeling "awful letdown" over everything, he decided that a few hours with his physician would put him in better physical shape to meet all the decent, wholesome people at the Roller Bearing Axle Empire party in Ohio, where the Professional Football Hall of Fame inauguration was to be held.

Forgetting the doctor's iron-clad rule that nobody visit his office without an appointment, Mr. Warburton opened the doctor's door without so much as pressing the buzzer. The receptionist informed him that the Marriage-or-Death Clinic, a special psychotherapy group, was in session, and he could not see the doctor.

Fearing a long wait might be in store for him, but loath to leave without his needed "tune-up," Mr. Warburton irritably picked up a brochure that explained to the layman the philosophy of the doctor's marriage-or-death philosophy, and what it promised mankind. The brochure pointed out that Man requires Marriage, One Marriage. Any other form of existence for him is impossible, leading to dissent and noxious activity. Then followed Dr. Bugleford's prayer—though as the physician took pains to make clear his Marriage-Totality program did not pretend in any way to replace Jehovah or God. (The doctor had written in one of his best-sellers that there is no First Cause, just as there is no individual man or human personality: marriage is the sole reality and marriage's giant counterpart, Society or the State.) Mr. Warburton then read the Prayer:

> Sole institution of wedded bliss, heterosexual union, the fount and meaning of all human endeavor, the only human destiny, where alone riches lie, Cradle of commerce! Progress! Sole reality! Step in and heal this misdirected son or daughter, or misdirected individual of anomalous sex: join him and or her in the sole human reality, Marriage and Society, and make him, make her, MISTER AND MRS. Amen.

The brochure followed with a resume of the doctor's stirring career, against impossible odds, setbacks, and calumny:

"A GREAT JEW FOR GENTILES"

Dr. Bugleford, in addition to being the founder of Marriage-the-Sole-Reality Clinic, has spent much of his youth and mature life in combating deviation, especially of the male sex and, if necessary, tracking down the deviate. A serious deviate himself at the age of 13, he effected a self-cure by joining the Y.M.C.A. (prior to his membership he was known as a snowball addict, and

threw hard-packed balls at elderly check-room women
and sodomites), and after only 6 months of group activity, decided to run his own program with affiliated
agency for the "tracking down" and cure of deviates,
with his world-wide detective agency, eventually to be
located overlooking Central Park *and* the Promenade in
Brooklyn Heights.

Dr. Bugleford's cure is simple and permanent: the
deviate marries; he has, if possible, 6 or more children, or
adopts this number; he joins the Y, country club, church,
temple, synagogue or tent of detective-sponsor's choice;
when cured, he begins to run his own detective agency
for 1) detecting other deviates (in the bud if possible),
and 2) either having them detained or leading and direct-
ing them to marry, have 6 or more children, or adopt
same, join the Y, country club, church, etc. (*as above*).

Unregenerate deviates such as lyric poets, star-watch-
ers, coffee-drinkers, or Bhang-eaters are arrested and
sent to the Hoover grottoes, or "disappear." *Cure or liqui-
dation* is Dr. Bugleford's motto.

Gentiles describe the doctor as a bearded ghetto-like
mole; Jews describe him as a broken-down German ath-
lete of strong body-alcohol tendencies; Negroes think of
him as a hooded rope-expert from Hattiesburg, Missis-
sippi; Puerto Ricans claim he is a Moslem acid-thrower
with a long axe-murder career behind him. The doctor naturally pooh-poohs all these descriptions as the
work of his deviate-enemies. He himself thinks of himself as akin to the God force but societized in marriage.
He objects to the concept of a personal God and / or

Jehovah, since he maintains God has often behaved as a deviate in history, and Jesus, although once a great Jew for Gentiles, does not fill modern needs, even Gentile modern.

PLAY SAFE = OBEY

The goal and purpose of the doctor's program is simple:

1. Alert and apprehend every individual before he (and/or she) is different.
2. A strong-arm Man for every 3 weaker-armed men (i.e. deviates).
3. World-wide radio system of "hearing" (which would be applied to the rectum ((by tiny wires)) of all newly-born infants) so that the least indication of their becoming deviate (lyric poet, coffee-drinker, Bhang-eater) would be detected from birth on. Cure or liquidations measures then are taken.

Hearing loud choral shouts from a nearby room, Mr. Warburton laid aside the brochure, hastened over to the door, carefully opened it a crack, and saw a group of men and women, with a sprinkling of children, kneeling before folding chairs, intoning before the huge cranium of Dr. Bugleford:

"I will marry, marry, marry & will play safe play safe and obey. We'll be Mister and Mrs. O.K. O.K. Thanks to that institution that makes me go & society hum. Over-all institution! Heterosex fount of progress and fun! Marriage! Marriage! Marriage!

Marriage can be fun! Marriage can be fun! I will marry marry marry! Heterosex! Fun! Money, money heterosex fun! I will marry! Marry! Marry! I will stay married married married! And obey! Obey! Obey! Fun! Heterosex! Life insurance! Life! Heterosex! Marriage! Insurance!"

"For good Jesus Christ's sake," Mr. Warburton said, and closed the door. He picked up his hat, and after a moment to slow his speeding heart and get some wind back into his lungs, he hurried on out, just in time to hail a cabby with the words, "Get me out of this goddam city."

13

FROM GENERAL PARTNER
TO GOD

G ilda knew she must find out two things in order to remain, as she said, a functioning plant (she had given up her attempt of a few years ago to be a functioning animal): she must know once and for all if Cabot Wright had raped her, and if, as a consequence, she had crossed the color line with Brady. She didn't care, she comforted herself, if either event was true. America was coming to an end, she had read in some distinguished intellectual periodical, and what happened to her, she supposed, could not be too crucial. Yet she had curiosity, if nothing else. She must know. If neither young male, the white or the black, had touched her, then she reckoned she could go back to being sick and miserable in her own plant-like way, imbibing certain liquids, and crying most of the time over the way life and time had treated her.

But she must find out: "Was I or weren't I?"

Fortunately, she knew that Warby, before going off to the Football jamboree in Ohio, had telephoned to Zenda Stuyves-

ant about Cabot Wright's impending visit. Gilda now telephoned Zenda herself. Though unusually cold and formal,
Zenda promised Gilda she would see the young man, and give
her "professional" opinion as to whether he was capable of an
act of violence.

Zenda, who had been a former silent screen star, still had
mother-of-pearl skin and lovely big eyes. Not content with
yesterday's glory, she had penned the best-selling *Building
Baby's Wardrobe*, "ghosted" by Princeton Keith (4 million copies in hard-cover; 39 million in paper). Under the tutelage of
old Warby, Zenda had become a top-notch real estate woman
in New York and for this reason, if for no other, Gilda could
always expect some little "half-favor" from Zenda in a pinch.

Zenda, it was perfectly clear, did not wish to do this one
little favor for Gilda, seeing a young man who had, improb-
ably, offended Warby's old girl. What did "offend" mean? Furthermore, Zenda had troubles of her own these days. Family
troubles. Wealth, fame, best-sellerdom at the ghost hands of
Princeton Keith, none of these had brought Miss Stuyvesant
happiness, as she confessed in that brilliant midnight radio
show over the tinkle of wine glasses and clatter of Chicken
Tetrazzini casseroles.

Zenda's cross was a daughter by the former matinee idol,
Horace Ross. Everyone knew the girl as Goldie Thomas, for
Thomas had been Zenda's fourth husband, a noted Boston
attorney, and Zenda had chosen the name Thomas because
she felt it would do her daughter the most good. Besides,
oddly enough, Goldie resembled Mr. Thomas more than she
did Horace Ross.

ldie had become a top-notch model, the highest paid in her field, and the money was rolling in. She was making damn near more than her little Mother had back in the Grand Old 'Twenties. Yet what Zenda wanted for her daughter was marriage and a family. The right young man had come along, a fine upstanding fellow from Madison Avenue, who had wanted to marry Goldie right away. Wilson Cramer was his name. Yet Goldie, rather than fill her leisure hours with young men like Wilson, preferred to be alone, to listen to her FM radio run by reds and degenerates, and go out to dinner with her agent, an elderly man of 44.

At first, Goldie had welcomed the attentions of young Wilson. He had, after all not been connected with the entertainment world and this made him a kind of rarity. He was considerate and thoughtful and often accompanied her when she was to be photographed: in front of the Plaza Hotel, in front of the Cloisters, in front of the UN, in front of St. Patrick's. Wilson's reassuring smile and the look of adoration in his eyes helped her at those trying moments before the camera to make completely successful advertisement photos. Her agent had been ecstatic.

But when the money started coming in, so much of it, and her assurance was at its height, Goldie began to see flaws in him. Wilson's love making—never permitted by her to be brought to fruition—began to tire her. Even without yielding to his restrained, if passionate, importunities she found, though still a virgin, that she looked less and less like what she desired to be in front of the camera. Her skin, after his embraces, seemed less fresh, and there was an expression about her eyes that she did not like. Finally, she summarily told Wilson not to come back. He had done, then, "mad" things, like climbing up on her fire-escape and threatening to jump. These new worries she was certain had aged her beyond her 18 years (in the advertisements she posed as 16). Goldie sent Wilson a frantic night-telegram: "YOUR ACTIONS ARE DESTROYING MY LOOKS. HAVE SOME CONSIDERATION MY CAREER. STOP. I HAVE TWO NEW WRINKLES SINCE LAST WEEK. STOP. FRIENDSHIP MUST END. REGRETFULLY BUT POSITIVELY. GOLDIE."

Calm after sending Wilson this ultimatum, Goldie considered that one day as sure as winter was followed by spring, her ideal American man would arrive. Kneeling before her satiny coverlet, Goldie did not pray for the ideal American husband—just yet. Her prayer was always very short, for she was very tired from being photographed, and she needed the long hours of dreamless sleep to keep her beauty and look 16, but each evening kneeling on the same identical place on the carpet, she could always manage to get out: "Please God, Hollywood. Please, dear God, Hollywood. I must go." She knew it would come. Wilson had been sure it would come, too. She would be—in an era without stars—a star.

In bed, with her cucumber night cream carefully applied, Goldie was about to whisper faintly again, "Please, God," when her mother, Zenda called her on their intercom phone:

"If you hear me talking with somebody below, dear, it's a young man Gilda Warburton is sending over. Cabot Wright. She wants me to size him up. See if he has criminal tendencies. Ha!"

WHILE ZENDA STUYVESANT sized up Cabot Wright, she regaled him with stories of her silent picture career way back before

Cabot was thought of, her triumph as the author of the best-seller *Building Baby's Wardrobe* under ghost supervision of Princeton Keith, and her final fabulous success as a real estate magnate, with acknowledgment to Warby's tutelage and kind efforts.

Then she told Cabot Wright she would admit immediately to owning at least 50 brownstones in and around Fifth Avenue so that the two of them didn't need to carve into the shank of the evening arguing about that! To her discomfort, Cabot did not laugh at this remark, which everybody else "new" always found so funny.

Desperately she attempted to entertain him while she plumbed his depths. At first she saw nothing in his appearance to suggest crime or offense. If anything, he was very Wall Street, boring despite the butter-milk sweat on his upper lip, a sure sign, she knew, of youth and vigorous physical health. It was his red hair, nearly fire-house in shade, and his mouth, too full for that of a broker, which raised phrenological danger signals.

Zenda then told an anecdote about her blind voyeur-lover. Seems while still a silent star, Miss Stuyvesant was greatly admired by the blind multi-millionaire cattle-rancher, O'Hara Morgan. Spent all her vacations in the late 'Twenties with him. He never touched a hair of her head. Only made one demand on her, and she was glad to comply as it did not deprive her of dignity. She did it as kindness, pure kindness, to O'Hara and all the world would agree with her if it knew the facts.

"What O'Hara loved for me to do," Zenda said, "was bathe nude in his immense swimming pool at an hour specified by

him. Then he would sit at a comfortable distance from where
I was to go in, and have me describe to him in detail—for, be
advised, though blind as a cave of bats he was not deaf, had
ears like an owl—how I took off each stitch of clothing, bit by
bit, this one, that one, the other, until he would say, 'Are you
completely bare, Zenda, love?' when he would go crazier than
a row of boys at a burlesque show, in the days, that is, when
boys cared about girls and there were shows." She sighed. "I
used to come over to O'Hara sometimes still dripping wet and
give him one innocent little kiss on his ear lobe. Dear, dear
O'Hara. There's nobody like that today. Because nobody likes
anything today, that's why. It's a nation of frozen jellyfish . . ."

As Zenda later explained to Gilda Warburton, while the
two girls wept and commiserated together, it was after she
told the anecdote about O'Hara (what a damn fool she had
been to tell that story) that she saw the peculiar look about
the young broker's passionate mouth on which the drops of
butter-milk sweat were pouring, the suspicious bulge of his
left-side trousers, and the words she heard with unbelieving
ears: "About ready for your roll in the hay? I can keep my eyes
shut too, old doll . . ."

"I have a young daughter upstairs," Zenda had implored
him, and then she had heard the statement that could come,
of course, only from a psychopathic: "You'll do, old pal. As I
say, autumn honey is sometimes sweeter to the taste than that
from the spring hive."

"You wouldn't!" Zenda now begged him.

She was already lying back on the factory-fresh Louis XV
divan, as Cabot, to use his own phrase, pumped the origin of

life into the old girl, while interrogating her about her daughter upstairs. Panting heavily, in spite of herself, her head hanging over the end of the divan, Zenda begged him not to go upstairs and "disturb" little Goldie.

As Cabot buttoned up and mopped his neck of sweat, on bended knee Zenda said: "If you touch that child you'll ruin her career, which has just begun. She's got to stay looking 16 for her model job, mind you, and one thing of this kind— You're from a profession! Think of hers, if you won't of her or me!"

Then Cabot suggested that her daughter Goldie could, after he had finished with her, perhaps pose for middle-aged women's ads, and make even more money. "Take it from me," he said, "middle-aged women are in and besides run the nation."

Cabot went upstairs.

Painlessly gagged and tied, Zenda waited below while Goldie, upstairs, was brought to terms with reality or, in the young broker's abominable phrase, having her hymen separated from her vulva by an expert. As the mother lay in her thongs, though her cheeks blushed as her mind told her they should, she realized she was not entirely unhappy about what was happening to Goldie. Her daughter had always been such a snot—Zenda was thinking this even as she heard the peculiar light and heavy sounds above indicating speeded activity by a sex criminal—and maybe she would find out what life was about, poor dear. But her daughter's career, Zenda feared, was over.

———

IT WAS GOLDIE who untied her mother after Cabot Wright had left by the fire-escape.

"My precious lamb," Zenda began to comfort her daughter. "It hasn't aged you a bit, love. You still look sweet sixteen."

Goldie had already looked in the mirror and knew her mother was lying, as usual.

"I'm not hurt, precious, if you aren't," Zenda feared the look of calm rage on Goldie's face. "Shall I summon Doc?" she asked her daughter while she rubbed her arms frantically, trying at least to restore circulation there.

"A lawyer," Goldie commanded.

"Why a lawyer, dear heart?"

"This happened in your house," she told her mother.

"Darling!"

"I was attacked in your building. By a friend of your friends."

"Goldie, child! Please."

"I was raped. My career's over. You know that, and by God, you'll do something about it!" She walked over to her mother and slapped her smartly over the mouth. "I'll sue you! You incapable old pouch. I'll have it out of your bank account. This happened in your house, and you'll foot the bill for your negligence."

Zenda now struck her daughter full in the face.

"I'll put more than wrinkles in that snotty face of yours, you spoiled little tramp. As that young broker said while he was doing me, maybe you'll earn more with a middle-aged mug than as the empty-faced little snip you were when you still had your cherry!"

As Zenda struck her again smartly, Goldie spat in her mother's face. Zenda put up her fists then, and let her daughter have it. Goldie fell at her feet, conscious but no longer struggling or talking. All she could get out was: "I wouldn't put it past an old has-been like you to have planned this!"

MR. WARBURTON'S SUICIDE took place exactly twelve hours after a delegation consisting of Zenda Stuyvesant, Goldie Thomas, and Gilda, the widow-to-be, paid a call to his Wall Street office, convincing him, they claimed, beyond a shadow of doubt, that Cabot Wright was a sexual monster who had performed the deeds ascribed to him on the persons of his wife, Zenda, and Zenda's child, Goldie, and how many other innocent victims, beyond conjecture or documentation.

Miss Watkins ("Sue of Short Hills") was reluctant to report to the board making the investigation of Mr. W.'s death that after the women had left, she heard the old financier laughing heartily, alone, for an unusually long period of time. (This was explained by a friend of the family as undoubtedly rising from hysteria and temporary depression-reaction.) Warby had subsequently called in a notary and altered his will, and this was ascribed by some, in view of Miss Watkins's report of his "laughter," as evidence of insanity.

Although planning to retain a battery of lawyers to obtain Cabot's conviction and sentencing, Mesdames Stuyvesant, Warburton, and Thomas suddenly made no further moves when they learned the contents of Mr. Warburton's will. Warby, it became known to the world, had appointed Cabot his business successor and the sole executor of his estate, and referred to him as "my adopted son in point of fact."

"To all intents and purposes," to use a phrase dear to that great literary critic of the pink 1930's—Cornell Dicks, now a successful investor in his own right—Cabot Wright was now head of Warby's firm and, if you will, empire.

"From General Partner to God, how's that!" Gilda had cried, when mulling over the provisions of the will. Between sniffles, she mumbled, "Hypnotism! Diabolic sleight-of-hand!"

It was now clear to the girls, that if they brought charges against Cabot—as Zenda Stuyvesant, with her real estate, business, and Hollywood background, pointed out to Gilda— the newspaper publicity alone, in view of what it had already been in the past, would blacken them forever. All burden of proof would rest on them, the girls, and would any of them get off scot-free? Zenda answered her own query in the negative.

14

CABOT READS TO MRS. BICKLE

P rinceton Keith remained avid for the manuscript of the full story of Cabot Wright. He was dying to enter the lion's den of Al Guggelhaupt and show him the most fantastic novel his firm had ever published, the most current, the dreadfullest, the most "in."

Mrs. Bickle had to tell him the sad facts. So far as the novel they had all been writing was concerned, Cabot had covered only the main biographical rapes—Cynthia, the Sweater Girl, Leah Goldberg, Gilda Warburton, the Stuyvesant ménage, mother and daughter. Beyond these were 360 more rapes, according to testimony in court, and newspaper files. Who were these women? Where did the crimes occur?

Cabot Wright literally did not remember. He recalled only the parts of his own story that Mrs. Bickle put down and read to him. While she read, he could corroborate a bit, add a detail here and there, a comment, a nod, a giggle, no more. But when she stopped, he had nothing.

The gap which they especially needed to bridge was the period of his life after he rose from General Partner to God—in Gilda Warburton's words. This was his rise from a young broker to an heir and inheritor of Mr. Warburton's empire, in which Cabot not only had lost most of his money by foolish investments and wild spending, but committed the major part of his rapes and won for himself his claim to the name of criminal.

No matter how much the Chicagoans talked to him, he could only smile or giggle again, and tell them nothing more occurred to him.

"Get it out of him!" Princeton Keith commanded both Bernie and Mrs. Bickle.

While Cabot walked up and down in Mrs. Bickle's apartment, thinking, trying to recapture a bit of his memory, she suggested as a change of pace that they do something with Mr. Warburton's *Sermons*, which had had such a marked influence on Cabot in prison and were, as he admitted, one of the sources of Cabot's "cure."

As Mrs. Bickle listened to Cabot read the *Sermons*, they were, she thought, too "plain" and even perhaps too "pointed," in an old-fashioned sense, of course.

The mausoleum of wrath, indignation, hatred, loathing, distaste, weariness, ennui, nausea, surfeit, and animadversion that had been the real Mr. Warburton lay buried and flowering in these diatribes against all and everybody, including himself. He had hated everything except baseball, football, and boxing, and finally he hated them as well, especially boxing, for he saw these noble sports as the pawn of criminal minorities who had come over in cattleboats and risen to offices of power.

"If I had my way and the strength to do so," Mr. Warburton's voice seemed to be filling the room again, "I would open a permanent window on Wall Street and continuously vomit through it for the next 25 years. However, nothing will clear the air. PLAY BALL!"

Cabot felt, Mrs. Bickle realized, that with Warby for the first time in his life he was actually talking with another human being about something. When Yale and the Army and his supposititious parents had been Cabot's façade of reality, everyone talked *around* everything. Warby considered Cabot a failure and Warby had been, Cabot was sure, more than half-right. The old broker had railed a good deal, of course, against the new Wall Street and the new America, and he had hinted at the total failure of human nature, history, government, the cosmos, and god. But as he had perused the *Sermons,* Cabot had had the shattering feeling of entering into some kind of reality.

"America, which began as a society of men with plans, confidence, and good blood in its veins," Warburton wrote, "has ended in a shambles of scrofulous obscenity and barking half-breeds in which nothing worth selling or connecting is hawked, barked and exposed in its inadequate meretricious shine to a nation of uninterested buyers. Young and old have suffered and are suffering a series of consumer hemorrhages from a non-attendant civilization that has only noise, confusion, pumped-up virility and pornography. It is a nation of salesmen, imbeciles, retired faggots, strip-tease sluts with nothing above or below the navel any more (the pathetic attempt of America to simulate sexual vigor is as unconvincing as her fame as a great hive of business organization). America's single role at present is to militate confusion, dirt, hollowness, race transvestism so that she can pass as quickly as possible into the cosmic scrap-hole of non-existence."

Cabot next read the section headed, *"Swear it, Swear it, U. S. A.":*

"The great thing about the American consumer is that it is filled before it is ever empty, glutted without knowing the feeling of either hunger or satiety, the organs of America so easily manipulated and ready for any surgical, plastic, or other adjustment the Master Masturbator may believe ready. Thus faggots are in charge of sexual makeup for women and men, stimulating the gonads of baseball players, prizefighters, captains of industry, farmers, and small-town grocery clerks saving up to become drag-queens on Manhattan's West 72nd Street, to say nothing of decreeing that women shall resemble lead pencils without a hole for refills."

"The true sexual orgasm in America takes place today in the popcorn bag in the movie theater on your right, before a base-ball game on TV while chewing 80 percent fat hamburgers.

"Pleasure died 40 years ago in America, perhaps further back, in a wave of carbon monoxide, gasoline, cigarettes for dames, the belief in everything and everybody, tolerance for the intolerable, the hatred of being alone in silence for more than 20 seconds, the assurance that immortality was Americans eating all-cow franks, with speeded-up peristalsis while talking to a crowd of fifteen trillion other same-bodies eating sandwiches, gassing cokes, peristalsing, and talking, while baseball-sound-movie-TV tomorrow's trots off-track betting howled roared farted choked gagged exploded reentered atmo honked bawled deafened pawed puked croaked shouted repeated repeated REPEATED, especially SAY IT AGAIN LOUDER SAY IT AGAIN, stick that product in every God-damned American's mouth and make him say I BOUGHT IT, GOD, I BOUGHT IT AND IT'S GREAT IT'S HOLLYWOOD IT'S MY ASS GOING UP AND DOWN AGAIN, IT'S USA, GOD, and if you can't get it in his mouth and make him SWEAR IT SWEAR IT USA, stick it in his anal sphincter (look it up in the dictionary, college graduates, on account of you didn't have time to learn it in the College of Your Choice)."

Under the section of the *Sermons* titled "When the Day was Shorter the Moon was Nearer," Cabot read of Mr. Warburton's taking the subway on those rare occasions when his chauffeur was ill, or he was in a crotchety mood and needed anonymity. It was the sight of Miss Subways ads which may have contributed to his suicide. These "girls" in early middle-age, photographed in wigs, wanting to make the grade if the price is right: "I will do anything within the framework of advertising, radio and Money-Street; will mortgage my pudendum and that of my Mother and Sister (the latter a confirmed nun)." Miss Goona Hartshore, for instance, Madonna Subway of the Week, says she has dabbled in pianoforte, handball, easel painting, wigwam handicrafts, advanced underwater breaststroke, and now works in a dental surgeon's office as bill collector, but of course hopes to make her debut on Broadway soon, with a little luck.

Deafened by the songs and choruses of the laughing hyenas

of disk-jockeys blaring out their cancerized larynxes in the corridors leading up out of the underground, Mr. Warburton continued on the case of Miss Subways: "She will consider any reasonable offer. Morals or big salary no obstacle. Sings and dances. Performs normal or irregular coitus. Will do anything, absolutely anything to make her debut. Stop. She has just been informed by the Patriotic Bunting Society that this can be construed as American. Question: "Will coitus be a group sport of the future?"

"You won't believe me," one *Sermon* began, "when I tell you because nobody sees American anymore but me, but I'll tell you anyhow. One day walking down one of the narrowest streets in the Wall Street section, one of my mindless strolls, I stopped before a violet window-display, saw a sign in a private ladies' Swedish massage parlor, a sign not meant to be seen presumably by the general public, certainly not by men of my walk of life. I saw these words:

"A beautiful potential screen star* whose name cannot be revealed until the house lights go on, not yet 20, will perform the entire operation of scientifically cleaning her anus with our new love-petal facial tissue on our private TV-for-ladies screen. Live. She will demonstrate that only with Love Bloom tissue can one's fundament be scientifically cleansed but not stimulated or chafed. Learn true scientific daintiness know-how & be safe for that special date or business appointment, ladies. In our Wilma Thom-

* Goldie Thomas

son Memorial Auditorium. 8 star coupons honored in lieu
of admission fee."

And thousands of paragraphs later, Cabot read the section
of "Faggot-fever, or virility-fantasy: Common to many a Wall
Street executive, many American men are now so unsure of
their erectile tissue, their virility, they are afraid to be seen
in public in the company of another man or even other men,
unless a banquet is in progress. I call it faggot-dementia, a
term of my own, as I long ago (ten minutes) planned to sever
connection with that Bohemian mountebank on whom the
Nazis have bestowed their own mentality, Dr. Bugleford. An
executive now should be accompanied by a woman. Any pair
of tits will do in a restaurant or lunch-counter. Makes a better impression with silk stockings in public. Fear of reality,
America. No country ever put on such a false front over the
human mask. And they say it is falling. Fell ages ago. Take
this headline: The model agencies complain that the male and
female models (faggots all) are still not thin enough, and Dr.
Clancy Ridgeway O'Brien Fuchs has settled that, I have just
learned, like this. He combs away with a newly invented surgical knife any suggestion of excess flesh on the face, and a little
accident of his has spelled fortune for himself and his clients;
the agency went mad over it. Fuchs uncovered a bone under
the buccinator muscle so that the model was actually photographed showing a tiny bit of his and or her calcium there (this
model later posed for all the men's wear, she is duo-sexual ad-
wise). A success everywhere. Most models now undergo this

safe and painless surgical operation on their *os zygomaticum*. Their *os nasale* remains covered, I'm informed."

"Consider these United States," Mr. Warburton wrote. "It's the time when the country has less virility than ever before, when the men are more faggoty than all the frogs who ever lived, and the women dyed-in-the-wool irregular anaesthetic whores, and the whole communication media devoted to sex-unsex. All America talks of nothing but sex, my boy, and there isn't a stiff pecker or a warm box in the house.

"I feel like a man too weak to turn off the radio which goes on through all eternity advertising trading stamps, beer, and tasty fags to Jewish-Negro-hot-box music. Am I responsible for the stinking level of American life to any degree? I must answer, I am. I know what is coming, Wall Street in Moscow or the Congo, New York a Black Metropolis, with the Negroes speaking in an Irish-Jewish-Italian accent, and the few white men left, in the role of male nurses.

"My book of *Sermons* perhaps may be found one day, and the truth told, but I fear not. There will be only the radio advertising purple & blue stamps, and cancer papers. Even garbage will beam radio messages.

"I used to know the rich when the men were men and the women people. I can still see *them*. Can't really focus on the freak parade that's them today. And then everybody's rich who can raise his right hand and screw somebody. Put on your glare-goggles and take a look at them today, see their Florida tan in the winter, their South-American ski-slide burn in the summer, their jewels, their fish-eye gaze, their big air of

'Heard this before, Joe,' their mountain sickness from going up to the Waldorf Towers.

"Under all their diets, vitamins & makeup, their reducing-rooms and mental love courses, their 2,000 mile a day travel schedule, today's rich, skinny as skull and cross bones, look fat and are. They're fat and getting fatter and the Rich's secret is to look like anybody today; their children gaunt undernourished, shabbily clad, their model a Harlem pusher. It's all part of the Rich being bigger and greater, hoggier and nastier than the first Rockefeller, Carnegie or Ford ever dreamed. They want to be in to stay, even if in masquerade, and so they look fatter than ever, dirtier and blacker and more like nobody than nobody who ever lived."

At the end, Cabot read a baseball hero's testimony that Warby had clipped from a newspaper: "I try to get my thinking straightened out before every World Series game and during the playing of the Star Spangled Banner, I close my eyes. My prayer is gratitude, gratitude I am a citizen of this wonderful U.S.A. and that God has given me the ability to do the thing I like most: Play ball. I don't believe in asking for help to win."

"Play ball!" Cabot continued, and suddenly rising, he saluted an imaginary flag. "Peace to your ashes, you mixed up old mummy," he intoned.

15

THE YOUNG PHILANTHROPIST

fter the death of Mr. Warburton, Mrs. Bickle heard from the rapist's own lips, Cabot Wright became not only a well-known philanthropist donating rent-free flats to derelicts, but continued his own special philanthropy, raping his victims with disinterest and tender unconcern. The police kept a list of "possible" suspects. Cabot himself might as well have worn a different disguise for each criminal attack, so various were the forms and faces attributed to him by those whom he attacked—a Black Muslim, a Puerto Rican degenerate, a longshoreman amuck on canned heat, an Atlantic Avenue dope addict, an escapee from numerous penitentiaries, and a noted Jewish nightclub comic.

Cabot's prey always knew his touch, his presence, his tarry laugh, ending in whees and giggles.

He was called the Anonymous Coon, the Kosher Jack, the Eternal Tar Baby, working with his weapon into the far hours of the night. Somebody's disillusioned lover, husband, daddy, a pimp to the unknown of his own body, who patiently unsheathed his dagger in the night.

Cries echoed cries as dark settled over Brooklyn.

A woman falls behind a hedge and shouts "Mucker!"

They are waiting by the river,
They are waiting late tonight,
For his tool is hard as cobalt,
His dagger gleams like light.

"Unsheathe your dagger!"

Cries go up as hallelujahs tell everybody it's happening again. Boats whistle, there is the rumble of the subway down in the guts of Brooklyn, a scavenger lets fall the lid of the garbage can, muggers drop their brass knuckles. "RAPIST IS OUT! ANONYMOUS COON STRIKES AGAIN."

"Many of my victims thanked me, however," Cabot went on to remember, still talking to Mrs. Bickle. "Take Bertha McIntosh as an example. Bertha had been connected with the Department of Health for many years, and she was certain that too many people were living under my roof. On the death of Warby, I began filling up my brownstone, which I had purchased, with people, friends, or finally, strangers who needed free rent.

"One early fall morning Bertha McIntosh rang my buzzer. By some odd chance, I had not yet gone to my Wall Street office. My arrest was in the air. I was paring my toenails after having had a really rough time trimming the nails of my right hand—the battle to appear decent in public! Had my Abercrombie and Fitch socks on, but had not adjusted the garters which rested on the cow-hide high shoes I affected, though to tell the truth I walked the Brooklyn Bridge better without them.

"'Wrong door,' I told Bertha. She showed her inspector's badge.

"'Cup of black?' I offered her the pot and nodded to a cup and saucer.

"'Why, maybe I might,' Bertha McIntosh said. Boldly she poured herself a cup, took it in her hands, 'I merely wanted a confirmation or denial from you, Mr. Wright, if you were allowing more than three persons to occupy any of your rooms. You are the landlord, I am told.'

"'Who were you told by?' I grinned. 'I mean you make it sound so goddam passive.' Bertha McIntosh began to feel uneasy when I grinned and giggled.

"'I don't rent rooms, Miss McIntosh, sir. This is all church property, so to speak. The Islamic Federation come and go all hours. I don't receive a penny intake from them or nobody. Hardly hear a word of English all day long and believe you me my English was going downhill the day I moved to Brooklyn. But seriously, unemployment in America has its biggest head-quarters right here. I came into an inheritance not long ago. Warby's suicide you've read about. Gilda not expected to live either. Well, take a look at an heir, Bertha, not a landlord.'

"'To get back to regulations,' Miss McIntosh said, consulting a sheet of instructions which a superior had handed her that morning. 'You say you're on church property here,' she wrote down the statement.

"'I'd say so,' I nodded.

"'All right then,' Miss McIntosh tried to smile, showing her bridge. She drank her hot black coffee. I grinned at her.

"'I could show you some of the church rooms,' I told her.

"'You call yourself, I believe I am right in saying this, a philanthropist,' Miss McIntosh went on. She waited awkwardly for my reply.

"'Someone has written down here," she consulted her notes, 'that you have so listed yourself.'

"'Where?' I wondered.

"'On the telephone,' Miss McIntosh said. 'To my superior.'

"'Yes, I can call myself a philanthropist,' I told Bertha. 'I give away a lot,' and then, Mrs. Bickle, I couldn't stop giggling.

"'Are you listed as a philanthropic society?' Bertha McIntosh continued the interrogation.

"'Don't suppose I could list myself as such, as all I do is give out free rooms to whoever needs one, I don't phone the Government I am doing it.'

"Bertha McIntosh was even more unfavorably impressed by my giggle than she had been by my grin. And I am sure, Mrs. Bickle, it was my giggle led to my arrest later on (the Puerto Rican girl with the pimples knew what that giggle meant, let me tell you).

"Miss McIntosh's showing me her disfavor by a curled lip was her first mistake, you might say.

"'I'm afraid I'll have to report this entire matter to City Hall,' Miss McIntosh beamed and got up to go. 'Thanks for the coffee.'

"'I'm afraid I wouldn't do that if I were, or was, you,' I said.

"'What?' she said, a kind of green ivory shade now.

"'Wouldn't tell anybody I'm not a society,' I explained to her.

"'Mr. Wright,' Miss McIntosh said, 'I'm afraid you're asking me to disobey my superior. I'm doing my job, after all . . .'

"'See that banister on the winding staircase?' I pointed to this early twentieth-century work of art, copied from Federal interiors. She stared.

"'Hop on it, and I'll show you what we're talking about.'

"'Good morning, Mr. Wright!'

"But I had already picked her up and placed her on the banister.

"'Get your little panties off and we'll see who's who,' I encouraged her."

As Mrs. Bickle made an eyeshade of her left hand, she learned that Miss McIntosh, like all the rest of them, didn't do a thing. Cabot went on: "Bertha cried a little after a while, shucks, and the exertion had tired her too. Sitting together, we two, after it was all over, as she drank and drank more coffee with generous helpings of rum, I said: 'Bertha, everybody is screwed in America to protect the innocent. America is sports is fun. Get American, kiddo. Get American.' Then as I looked at her again, I said, 'God, Bertha, do you look guilty!'

"I'm telling you all this, Mrs. Bickle," Cabot Wright continued, "in order to lead up to a certain letter-confession which Bertha penned after she began to go straight again, and which I keep in my breast pocket . . . Her entire life had been as unpleasant as though she had been tied under the posterior regions of a huge mammoth, such as a rhinoceros. 'I felt a monster crouching over me, and I was powerless even to show nausea, such a conformist had I become.' Bertha McIntosh speaking, mind you. She has put on 10 pounds and is the picture of advertising, rosy, beaming, nice toothpaste grin, and an outgoing manner recommended by churches. She never speaks of me, but is grateful, and here's what I've been leading up to, Mrs. Bickle, as I've sat here and heard with you most of the story of my life, except for my career as philanthropist and 300 odd additional rapes I can't quite remember. Bertha McIntosh is grateful I showed her the way.

"Her name is now Mrs. Dirkey. Had I not approached Bertha that late fall evening, she would have continued to believe in her mission as a municipal agent, thought that her enforcing of the law was as important as the revolving of the celestial sphere, and would have died an old maid. After I had loosened her up with (quote) my philanthropy (the pain was just as terrible as an aunt of hers in Elkhart had told her, intolerable, inhuman, such pressure, and yet after it was all over, *memories*) Bertha, as I say, gave up her fine position in City Hall, quit reading intellectual magazines like *The New Yorker* and *Red Book* and went back to Staten Island, which had been chewed up a lot by bulldozers but was still home to her. She married Fred J. Dirkey, a retired housepainter and wheelbarrow repairman, and they planned a family. To tide things over a bit, she opened the frankfurter-stand and became adapted to and dynamically integrated in this way of life. I still send Bertha Hallmark greeting cards whenever I have time to pick a card up. She wrote me this letter of thanks, you see, explaining that had she not met me, had she not had this experience, painful though it was, she would never have found herself, never married, never found the happiness she seems to have achieved with Fred Dirkey. Unfortunately, Bertha has not been able to become a mother, which was always her most cherished ideal but Fred, retired, needs a great deal of attention, and she has found caring for him and his wants an answer to her unfulfilled maternal aspirations. Mrs. Dirkey has a beautiful disposition, and engages in the interesting recent hobbies of collecting butterfly nets and early post-Victorian paperweights. She will always, she says, be grateful to one Cabot Wright."

A FEW DAYS after Cabot Wright's marathon hear-and-answer-back with Mrs. Bickle, in which he had to remind her four or five times that during his heroic career as rapist he had not been deaf, he summoned her out of bed to make a date for the following night. By his desperate tone and hard breathing, she took it to be a matter of some importance. He promised her a sheaf of documents he was getting from a Wall Street safety-deposit box, and said he would turn these over to her, Bernie Gladhart, Princeton Keith and company for making him immortal in a novel. The place of their rendezvous was downtown, at his old stamping-ground, Hanover Square.

They met in a little park near some dead trees, facing an old brown building called India House. Nearby were the Cotton Exchange and several other buildings looking like stage sets. "We can sit here, Mrs. Bickle," Cabot said after her arrival, "and not be overheard." He looked around him. "Damned odd note here tonight. There are rats all around. Two just scurried past my outstretched shoe."

"Since I'm from Chicago, I'll feel right at home." Mrs. Bickle sat down on the bench over which he had spread some tab-loids. "You're right!" she looked around her. "What a stage set this is. I love India House."

"How can I tell you what I want to?" Cabot Wright said.

"You violated some girl here, of course," Mrs. Bickle prompted him.

He struck his thigh. "Matter of fact, yes. Want to hear about it?

"I was well known to the newspaper audience," he went on, "when I did the girl over there . . . As a matter of fact, they were hot on my trail when I got her here at Hanover Square. No rats then, so far as I know. Imagine rats in Wall Street! Sat here many a night in those days wondering what I was up to. But I didn't bring you here to tell you any more about my rapes! And the soft eyes of the ruminants are on us in the dark, Mrs. Bickle! You can put that in your book of memories.

"Yes," he continued, "old Hanover Square near Wall Street. I heard, on this particular evening, an older lady warning a younger one, her daughter, about the dangers of being a single girl in New York, Wall Street no exception, spookier than uptown, and the dark is something you just have to put up with. A sexual instrument may be plunged into you at any moment from any quarter. *Officer, help! My daughter has fallen on the prong of a youthful degenerate who singles out the opposite sex. Give a hand here!* Little knowing that many an officer has sworn an oath to aid and abet the act.

"I had walked over to a restaurant noted for its seafood, and there spotted these two females again, mother and daugh-ter, complaining this time about the dinner menu: 'I don't believe I'll have the gray sole, my dear,' mother said. 'Name's too depressing.' 'Try the red snapper, love,' daughter said. 'Can never go wrong on that.' After a two-course dinner of snapper and biscuit tortoni, mother and daughter parted right outside India House over there.

"I stepped right up like a Jehovah's Witness on Saturday night and engaged the girl: 'May I trouble you for a direction, young woman?' asked I. (Etiquette book warns never to say *Miss,* far from correct. *Lady* is suspect, and reserved for tramps and canned-heat addicts. *Young woman* rates hit-parade usage, and of course it was my choice.) 'Patty, where are you going with that young man?' mother called from a block away, having turned round in an intuitive sense of impending evil. But Patty had already without the shadow of a doubt taken a shine to me. That long fish-dinner with Mother! Ready for anything, Mrs. Bickle.

"We, she and I, vanished into one of the de Chirico alleys. I pulled her gently but with absolute never-let-you-go grasp into a hidden puddle beneath a watch-repair shop, dug hurriedly as you would hunting in warm wet soil for a diamond or opal dropped from a purse, found the 'place,' old familiar *belle chose* with my vivid hand, the veins dancing now under the only excitement that matters outside of war—grope, push away any dressmaking obstacles, there I have it in my hands, and just a question of a moment to unpop, and the mother of course screaming as though she did not at first blush know what was going on or what had to be done. First things first. There at last, girl too surprised to do a thing, and me pumping into her what life feels is never too good for anybody, right up to her lungs, you would think from her moans. 'This is my only pleasure, lady,' I called back to the mother, 'so why be a kill-joy?' Yes, my only pleasure. The only thing that ever made anything seem worth while. Call it a crime, that's a good old girl, for the mother was calling a policeman on the emergency telephone: 'Come quickly, officer! A dagger of meat has pierced my precious jewel. He is entering her basket of joy. She isn't screaming, officer, so I'll bet she's bleeding. Oh, my dear little Patty. Can't you get here in a helicopter, officer? Oh, God, it's too late already! Officer, officer, he's had his way with her! He's buttoning and calling it a night. Stop, degenerate, moron, stop! God, Patty, speak to your little mother. She lies there like a broken kewpie doll. Pray speak to me, darling. Are you going to open your eyes again, do you think? Are you wounded, my angel? You'll never be the same, it's a fact, my dearest, but you're going to get well, and we'll go to Vancouver together and never come back, that's right, dear, we'll go away together, only do get well for mother.'

"In Hanover Square," Cabot concluded, "the policeman got a good look at me, saw my race, religion, build, sedentary character of spine, tilt of hat, F. R. Tripler necktie. I was typed. My arrest was only a matter of days."

Mrs. Bickle looked down on the inscrutable flagstones.

"Homesick for Chicago?" Cabot Wright inquired.

He put the sheaf of notes, manuscripts, jottings and documents which told all of his story into her hands. "Here," he said, "now immortalize me."

"I'm afraid it may not be possible," she said to him. Mrs. Bickle was strangely moody. Then suddenly she saw them! She grabbed Cabot's hand. Screaming as loud as any of the women he had raped, she buried her head in Cabot's breast.

A procession of rats was hurrying past them, in the direction of the water, one of the last ruminants stopping a second and exchanging a look of indifferent malignancy with Mrs. Bickle.

When the procession had vanished, Mrs. Bickle began crying, and he patted her nonchalantly, correctly, as a father will a daughter he has loved but married off and grown indifferent to.

"I thought old Chicago had trained you better," he spoke in nursery-tones to her. He yawned.

"Rats," she gagged. "I can't stand the sight!"

"Do you suppose Manhattan is sinking that the rats should all be leaving in a body like that?" he wondered. Then beating on his forehead he said, "God damn it."

"What is it?" Mrs. Bickle looked more worried than ever.

"Where's my brains?" he inquired. "I can't remember!"

"Remember what?"

"The other thing I wanted to tell you, Mrs. Bickle. You don't think I brought you to Hanover Square just to tell you about the lady who wouldn't eat gray sole and give you the rest of my dossier. No, there was something else."

"Well, try to recall," she said, but there was no interest in her face or her expression.

"Oh, I'm cured of raping people, if that bothers you," he snapped at her. "And I'm entirely cured, except for bad memory and the fact that I can't laugh. Still can only giggle . . ."

She nodded.

"But I did have something to tell you, and it's slipped clean out. Maybe in a month or so it'll come to me."

"I'm afraid that'll be too late to tell me," she said.

"Why is that?"

"We'll be back in Chicago by then, I imagine. My assignment seems to be done."

"And they won't publish the novel?" he inquired.

She shrugged in reply, then looked apprehensively about her as if she feared to see more rats. As she left Hanover Square, she turned back and saw Cabot looking at her intently. She had the oddest feeling she might never see him again.

LIKE THE GREATEST pugilists, baseball stars, football giants, Cabot during his period of philanthropy was continuously sore. His exertions—he lost 20 quarts of perspiration on more active days—spared no section of his anatomy. His bones sometimes ached like those of an old man. His veins and arteries, subjected to the supreme tension of ancient battles in times of Hannibal, Caesar, Napoleon, General Grant, throbbed deliriously.

He ate cut-rate bottles of aspirin by the handful. Yet his strength always returned after exertion—a freshet, a throbbing vigorous spring river of seed, turbulence, overmastering desire tore at his scrotum, sent his *membrum virile* bouncing thrashing flailing against his abdomen astrain to reach his umbilical scar. The flesh in its exertion to rise seemed to tear the rest of his body, he was devoured by himself like Scylla by her own canine appendages. He was covered with sweat from head to foot, flowing with smegma, and lying back in his chair fanned himself unrhythmically with pieces of cardboard from his laundered shirts. Like a metamorphosed creature half-emergent from his life in water, he could smell only the organs of reproduction. His mouth itself seemed to be full of seed. His ears heard only the grinding pumping of coitus in all nature's sounds and voices. He heard flesh tear as he extended his feet to walk. The whole earth contracted, tumesced, stiffened, pumped, exploded, dissolved into thick viscous fountains. In the country, speeding in his rented Peugeot, the sight of the Milky Way made him whimper, saliva fell from his open mouth, he became incoherently excited, moaning and whining, nearly barking.

"I'm gone!" he cried, and he knew it. Whatever had happened to him, he would never be back. Everybody, anyhow, was dead but him, he felt, and he was repopulating the earth, a bladder of erectile fruit, anodyned pain and seed.

Cabot Wright read now of himself as the Anonymous Coon, active in the Heights of Brooklyn, but sometimes for a change of diet wandering as far South as Red Hook and Cobble Hill. Cabot Wright, the press claimed, hid in garbage cans and/or bushes, jumped out, had his way. The tarry night hid his race, or the island from which he stemmed (Jamaica, Cuba, Tobago, Haiti), but the epithet ANONYMOUS COON stuck. Race hate is everywhere, kiddy, and the biggest haters are on the polyglot racial committees stamping it out.

"ANONYMOUS COON STRIKES AGAIN." The Mayor in an extraordinary gesture, cut off two hours of his luncheon, and doubled the policemen on the beat, and anybody who looked odd at all was to be immediately apprehended and carted off. There was also an alert for blackface artists, as Negro groups claimed the Anonymous Coon was a white man with a charcoal make-up kit.

Reading of his night exploits, Cabot at times gave out what simulated a tee-hee, but was of course a giggle, for he looked just the same as ever, slightly-used Wall Street, impeccable collar, lovely he-man complexion, serious turn to his mouth, straight-ahead eye, erect bearing (dig that bulge), Ivy league, wife nuts (he scot-free), parents dead (he alive). He loved reading the headlines:

"DEMON ASSAULTER OVER THE HUNDRED MARK:
MORE EXPECTED TONIGHT. CITY COUNCIL BELIEVES WEEKEND
WILL SEE MOST CONCENTRATED NUMBER OF RAPES.
PERCENTAGE SOARS."

"LOVELY RESIDENTIAL NEIGHBORHOODS TURNING INTO
WILDERNESS AS MANIAC-DEVIATE ROVES AT WILL:
FEAR MANY MORONS WEAR POLICE UNIFORM,
EFFECT LEWD ACTS."

"ARE POLICEMEN BY CHANCE RAPING OUR WOMENFOLK
AND OUR WOMENFOLK NOT RAISING SUFFICIENT ALARM?
QUERIES BY JEANETTE THOMAS MCKINLEY VAN BUREN HART,
NOTED WOMAN COLUMNIST AND AUTHOR OF THE
CHURCH-APPROVED BOOK *Where Are Our Bowling Mothers
Tonight?*" (*Columnist*.)

"We must arrest and arrest until we find the culprit," Miss McKinley Van Buren Hart, who is syndicated in 5,000,000 papers and magazines, urges. "She is willing herself to spend a night in jail to prove her own hands are clean."

"SHOULD POLICEMEN WEAR CHASTITY BELTS ON THEIR BEST
SUITS IN VIEW OF SUSPICION ONE OR MORE OF THEIR
NUMBER MAY BE THE ANONYMOUS COON-DEMON RAPIST?
MISTER MAYOR, ANSWER THAT ONE OVER YOUR
FIFTY DOLLAR PLATE LUNCH." (*Editorial.*)

"ARE TOO MANY POLICEMEN ENGAGED IN CHASING
DEVIATES MAKING GRAND OLD U.S.A. A POLICE STATE?
ASKS A PINK-ORIENTED BRONX HOUSEWIFE WHO HUGS HER
FM SET. ANSWER: LOOK WHO ASKED!" (*Right-wing magazine.*)

"DECORATED MARINE CONFESSES HE JOINED FORCE IN
ORDER TO PERFORM PRETERNATURAL ACTS WITH OTHERS."

"IS YOUR MOTHER A DEVIATE? YOUR PROOF."

"DR. BUGLEFORD JUST APPOINTED BY MAYOR TO REGISTER,
CHECK, INTERVIEW, FINGER-THUMB, CODE, SENTENCE AND IF
NECESSARY EXECUTE ALL DEVIATES BY MORNING."

"DRAGNET FALLS OVER ENTIRE RESIDENTIAL
MEGALOPOLIS ALL NEW YORK ADVISED TO MARRY
OR BE MENTALLY ILL: LOWER MARRIAGE AGE TO 13,
SYNDICATED WOMEN COLUMNISTS URGE. MANDATORY
HETEROSEXUALITY IN THE Y.M.C.A. BILL PROPOSED FOR
FEDERAL LEGISLATION."

Cabot's comeuppance came unexpectedly—at the hands
of a pimply Puerto Rican girl, who had seen a vision of Our
Lady in Flatbush. It is true she charged that Cabot had merely
molested her, not raped her. So strong was religious feeling in

the nation at the time, however, together with prosperity and indignant belief in racial equality, that Cabot, despite his social and business position, was arrested. At the police station he was beaten with the usual rubber hoses and night sticks. Then to the astonishment and debilitating pleasure of the police lieutenant who was grilling him, the culprit confessed to having committed over 300 rapes in Brooklyn and vicinity, U.S.A.

During the trial that followed, scores of women testified they recognized Cabot as their physical assailant. He never denied one of these accusations. He was very tired, more so than when he had first consulted Dr. Bigelow-Martin, very bored, and America did not interest him.

The prison sentence handed down by a court that was more puzzled than vindictive was mild, and would have been possibly milder, many brilliant journalists believe, had Cabot not queered much of his own defense by giggling. *Giggling*, mark you—not laughing. He couldn't laugh.

16

ONE FLEW EAST,
ONE FLEW WEST

 ernie Gladhart was angry and dejected at the way Mrs. Bickle had spent the last few weeks in the company of Cabot Wright, ignoring him. He had gone out in a huff, looking for trouble, as in his old free days, and before his prisons. About to go past the Iron Kettle, a dull coffee house where washed-out denizens of Greenwich Village tried to start a new life, his attention was arrested by a striking colored man wearing an unusually white straw hat with a pink band unknown to this latitude. The expression of his face, his complexion itself, the pearl perfection of his teeth told Bernie at once that this could not be the Brooklyn uncertain status-mad American Negro. The man walked like a prince, and was obviously not impressed by anything except what was inside him.

Bernie, as he was to tell Carrie Moore via long-distance and as he also told Mrs. Bickle, saw an Ideal Man and, in his despairing and yet stubborn mood, decided to love him. Had

he not appeared at that moment, Bernie often wondered later
what would have happened to him in view of his having been
himself sold into white slavery as the factitious author of a
novel he had long since had no connection with. Would he
have resumed his petty derelections and crimes, become a
full-time alcoholic, sold himself to dope-pushers?

Bernie followed the man with the wide-brimmed foreign
hat down leafy streets, past Federal mansions, over blue-stoned
pavements, until they both came to the Promenade with its
benches. His dark-skinned prey seated himself under a street-
lamp and Bernie, more desperate by the moment, seated himself next to him, then almost immediately introduced himself.

His new friend accepted the introduction in the manner
in which it was meant. They exchanged the necessary information about themselves, Bernie learning that his chance
acquaintance was Winters Hart, from a town in the Congo.
He had got a job in a phonograph company and was waiting for
his wife and three children to come join him as soon as he had
some money. Taking Winters Hart's left hand in his, Bernie
held his friend's dark finger on which he wore a wedding-ring,
and pressed the finger and the hand.

Far from being annoyed at this liberty, Winters Hart was,
to tell the truth, relieved and pleased. Isolation in a racial
democracy, as he was to tell Bernie later that night, as they lay
in Bernie's bed together, isolation, no thank you. As for these
American colored people with their immediate ambitions and
small souls, and washed-out posture, their timid arrogance
and hunger for the White, again no thank you. "You can keep

Black America, Bernie," he returned his new friend's pressure, "if it means working all day to turn white."

"I hope this will be as deeply a felt relationship for you as it is for me," Bernie told Winters. It was his Chicago affability, perhaps, as much as his own personality, that won the Congolese over.

"But why talk so much, Bern?" Winters Hart had said. "We're doing good, right as we are, but don't talk to let each of us know just how good we are doing. Americans always explain me how they're doing a right thing. We're just doing something, Bern, was in the cards, and so no explanations please. A little pressure here, a little pressure there lifts the weight of the world from the heart, but no need to celebrate it by way of explanation."

Bernie smiled at these wise words. For the first time, in his friend's arms, he felt some warmth in the cold sea-fog city of Brooklyn.

WHILE BERNIE SLEPT peacefully, spoon fashion, next to the heart of his Congolese friend, Mrs. Bickle was thinking about the manuscript she had just turned in to Princeton Keith and company. Mrs. Bickle felt she could now relax a bit from her strained assumed passive disinterest in the presence of Cabot Wright.

Two weeks passed while the publishing empire of Guggelhaupt was assembling the novel, assisted by checkers, ghosts, stenogs, under-editors, whole staffs working till late at night. During this period, Mrs. Bickle heard not a peep from the man whose life was being prepared for the millions. She felt the need, with a suddenness that disturbed her, to hear more from Cabot. A hundred questions filled her mind about his career. Now that the truth had been told as fiction, and was to be sold as such, now that she and Bernie were "rich" by former standards, she wanted to find out, if possible, the truth as truth.

"He was so obviously *not* a rapist!" she kept repeating to herself. Yet more and more she realized that what he had said to her, and listened to in her presence, must have occurred: he *had* raped and raped and raped, apparently without interest. He had to complete his mission. Had he completed it?

Cabot's final last "look" at her puzzled her now more than when it happened. She decided to talk to him. Going down to his room, she knocked weakly on his door. She waited. No sound of any kind.

Her heart slowed its beat, for she already felt she knew what had happened. She saw that "look" of his again. At the same time she knew she must find out more. This need came over her furiously like the burning necessity for water in fever.

Entering Cabot Wright's room, she saw an envelope standing upright on his desk. She picked it up and then looked apprehensively about her. There was no writing on the envelope itself, though it was sealed for somebody, obviously her.

She looked about the room, examining quickly. There were the same ticking clocks, thirty or more, the atrociously heavy encyclopedias, medical dictionaries, books on anatomy, pathology, the big dictionaries of foreign languages. His clothes were gone. And there was a flat non-human smell in the room, meaning he had been gone some days. She opened the envelope. Inside, the letter was addressed to her, as follows:

Mrs. Bickle—

It is too bad you were beginning to show interest. My story is not yours, after all. Neither am I, though that was coming too, so far as you are concerned. I am nobody's now but mine own, so my disinterest in you remains the same. However, I found you an ideal ear, and tongue. What is more, everything else you may have been, for instance, a woman, was missing, because you have stood by others so long. You were just right for me at the precise time I needed a rarity like you. Maybe you were never a woman, maybe once you were. Still I gather you feel you should act like one a bit. You do have a mind, but your ear and your presence are you. Hats off, I suppose, for that!

You are and always were, Mrs. Bickle, a mature American matron. I am writing this to you because your disinterest in me, which was decaying rapidly, may return. I may drop you a line, as they say in prison, when you get back to Chicago. I may as well tell you that you are going back without any doubt to the gem of the prairies. Princeton Keith is *not* going to publish that fucking novel the ghosts have been writing about my life. They haven't even thought up a name for me. You'll hear about it. Them not doing the novel, that is. Well, so long, Mrs. Bickle, and don't feel grateful just because I do to you.

You listened and you told me. I saw me all in one piece together like in a movie, and as a result I'm free. I'm grateful, but I don't want to pay you back my gratitude. You're not my type.

Cabot Wright

P.S. I am going to take up disguises for a while, I think harmless ones. Think I may be a preacher further South or maybe some kind of a quack healer. Just white-face disguise, though, as I never swam with the current. Hear from me, old girl.

Mrs. Bickle's mind, recovered from the shock of the letter, raced over a number of topics and ideas, the peculiar style in which he had written, the thought that rubber-hoses, night-sticks and ex-boxers' fists during his third-degree police nights and days must have taken a lot out of his former self. Then she admitted her own strange muted growing, call it love or fascination for the man who said he violated—but that would be another novel for another editor.

The truth is, without her being in on the secret, that when the police began their so-called brutality on him, and prison finished what they had started, not only his *membrum virile* went from "At-ten-tion!" to "Pa-rade rest!" to "At ease!" but the bite which had been on so long, the huge false-teeth which Business America fastened at his jugular was *off.*

BERNIE GLADHART ENTERED her room at the very moment that Mrs. Bickle had broken down, crying softly. The letter was in her hand, and Bernie had immediately read it at an angle, while sitting beside her and comforting her.

"You got out of it easy," Bernie petted her. "Think of it in that way."

"He believes Chicago is as remote as Peking," she cried. "A real Easterner, over and above all the other things that are amiss in him." She dried her eyes.

"We've got to see Princeton Keith," Bernie pointed to that part of the letter which attempted to dim their hopes. "Something tells me they've sent him to the cleaners."

17

REJECTION BY THE GOETHE
OF PUBLISHERS

feel like the hollow space inside a statue," Princeton Keith told Mrs. Bickle and Bernie, as they sat
in his Park Avenue apartment on whose dazzling
white walls hung the latest paintings. Princeton's bags were
packed, and Princeton's accent had lost nearly all its New York
edge. If not pure Southern Illinois, it was no longer Eastern.

"We're all going home. Isn't that a goddam note?" Princeton
touched his temples with an ice cube.

"What title did you finally give my novel?" Bernie inquired
suddenly. Princeton Keith gazed at the Chicago novelist benev-
olently, but didn't reply. He swallowed more of a pink drink he
had not asked his guests to share. It might, they realized, be
medicine in any case. Indeed after each sip, he coughed.

"Al Guggelhaupt," Princeton recited, "in many ways *is* New
York. New York today. He's not one man, mind you, but eight
or perhaps eighteen. Changes personalities as the light is
modified from dawn to dusk, mixed of course with our atmo-

spheric gravy here in Gotham. Has ruled, old Al has, American publishing as few men have. Granted, he made me. Now he's broken me. Does he stand for anything, Al Guggelhaupt? Yes, he does."

"Forget it all, Princeton dear," Mrs. Bickle got in while the editor coughed desperately after another nip at the pink drink, and then soothed his throat with an outside application of the ice cube.

"Al Guggelhaupt believes he resembles, and as a matter of fact does resemble, Johann Wolfgang von Goethe. Ever hear of him, Bernie? Of course you haven't, so drink and shut up." Princeton shot angry thunderous looks out in the direction of Madison Avenue. "I would be the last to deny he looks like Goethe, whom I never finished reading anyhow. But Al also resembles Wilhelm II, Emperor of Germany, known to fuckers of the past as the Kaiser. As age has dried Al up, making his extreme height a bit bowed, and his fifty-dollar luncheons have suited him up with a better than average pot, he also resembles Bismarck, the moulting William Jennings Bryan, and in the belly the exiled Napoleon Bonaparte. In other words, look at him at any stage of his development and you see a bloody bully. I drink to the bastard in genu*i*ne admiration, if horror," and Princeton raised his pink drink, though he changed his mind and did not quaff it.

"I've seen him, this great man in publishing," Princeton intoned, "stand before his 10-foot Italian mirror in his Park Avenue cathedral room and mutter the patronymic 'Goethe' as he gazed at himself. Of course, Guggelhaupt, though a culture-hound of the first order (in this resembling his great

counterpart in British publishing, a Jew who embraced Christ
at the age of 40 as his Personal Savior, I refer to the late Clyde
Wagenknicht), has always been passionately wise in dollars and
cents. During the Depression, when the world of thoughtless
intellectuals admired his bringing out books nobody thought
would sell because they were both dirty and well-written, Al
G. even then never lost a real dollar on a book he published . . .
Now he's through with life, I know the signs, and his cashier-
ing of me is the tell-tale give-away. No, he wants to lie down
in an early grave of roses, he considers he's been the Goethe
of publishers, and that's enough. He wants to give up, and so
he's sending me packing—there are my goddam bags I've had
ready against this contingency for twenty-five years—after
him promising me I'd share in his distributed empire."

"Oh, Princeton, sit down," Mrs. Bickle finally said, after he
had risen and staggered over to them.

"I'll sit down, my fine bitch, when I've come to you in this
story," he replied. But he sat down, eyeing Zoe, then said:
"God, you fucked your life as thoroughly as anyone can."

"True enough," Mrs. Bickle replied, "but please don't get
any drunker," she warned him, "if that pink and red drink is
spirits."

Disobeying her, Keith rose again, came over to where Mrs.
Bickle sat, and kissed her on the crown of her head.

"This little lady," he began speaking in the tones he had
always used at the National Best-Seller Book Awards, usually
engineered by him, "this little lady has given her all to literature. Married a writer of talent, and kept her own greater
talent in the kitchen where nobody could smell anything but

her cooking. You're too goddam good for everybody," he told
her and sat down.

"I'm coming now to us," he put on an immense pair of
spectacles and looked blindly about the room. "Al had given
the go-ahead sign, mind you, before he disappeared into
Prague or some other place he and Corinna, his wife, always
got into without visas, unlike the rest of the citizenry. Mind
you, before he disappeared into Hungary or Georgia, he had
given me the nod on Cabot Wright, said he felt the country
was ready for a book on rape, that he believed the times were
ready for it, and if the times were ready, the Establishment
would be ditto. Mind you in the 'Twenties every stylish sex
book had his imprint. Guess he thought he was going to live
over those elegant old pervert days with Cabot," he turned to
Mrs. Bickle briefly.

"Al Guggelhaupt, in other words, turned on an avenue of
green lights for Cabot Wright. *'Have him jab them in every paragraph'* were his exact words. Oh, he and Corinna have the
language of hardened pirates *chez eux,* let me tell you. Goethe,
you know, was queer for kitchen sluts, perhaps that's what old
Al would like to live up to at heart. *'We'll buy it!'* was the last
thing he said to me before he jetted to Europe, speaking of
course of Cabot Wright. *'We'll buy it, Prince!'* . . .

"When he comes back, I see the nasty ambiguous turn to
his lip, the little that emerged from beneath his Bismarck
mustache. I knew then he'd been hobnobbing with old Doyley Pepscout, the king of the daily reviewers, who believes, if
you know the New York literary scene, and I know you don't,
that prayer and money should entirely take the place of the

ithyphallos—which means stiff cock, Bernie, in Greek. Al Guggelhaupt, who would not have spit on a Doyley Pepscout in the 'Twenties when he was the publisher of high-class Parisian smut, goes to him, and says, 'Doyley, favor me by reading this book and level with me. Is this a book you think you can praise in your column? Be frank, man, and level.'

"And now hear this, kiddies. Doyley Pepscout wrote the following report for our Goethe." Princeton Keith pulled out of his tight-fitting jacket a sheet of onion-skin, and read:

"I am pleased and grateful, my dear Al—can you hear old Doyley's nasal Cleveland, Ohio twang?—that you should think enough of me as a critic—dig that, him as a critic, when the last novel he finished reading was *Freckles*—to submit to my consideration your proposed novel *Indelible Smudge*—there's your title, Bernie. It is my melancholy duty to inform you, as I would inform the readers of the great family newspaper for which I have written over a quarter of a century, that the author of this work, at best only mildly entertaining, has continued the growing threat of degeneracy and unhappy endings in fiction. There is not the least question of a doubt in my mind that rape can and perhaps should be treated in literature. But it cannot be treated as Mr. Bernie Gladhart has done in *Indelible Smudge*. Nowhere has he shown the relationship of the youthful rapist to happy older people whom we meet every day in offices and homes, and to a happy America. We are fed only on deviation and mordant thoughts without any higher note. The ending is even less edifying than the bulk of the book. I regret to say that this sordid, often obscure book, without visible motive or meaning, is dispiriting, disquieting, sordid, and utterly without reader-appeal. It is, however, well written and uses an extensive vocabulary, so that I found myself consulting an unabridged dictionary. The vocabulary, however, is an unrefined one, and had better not have been employed."

"Goethe Guggelhaupt of course was studying my face as I read Doyley Pepscout's review," Princeton Keith explained. He then went on to recreate the great scene of rejection by the Goethe of publishers.

"DO YOU REALIZE," Al Guggelhaupt said, "and I see you do not, that if he says the book can't be sold, it cannot. Do you see, sir, the death-warrant in Pepscout's last sentence? *Indelible Smudge* is dirty *and* well-written. Do you get that? That's the combination means no Fifth Avenue bookstore will take it, no book club, no book award group even will touch it. You've again violated protocol and produced a dirty *hard* book.

"But just to show you that I didn't accept Pepscout's word as final, I called in, all the way from his farm in Connecticut, America's greatest high-brow critic in belles-lettres, Talcum Downley who, as you know, discovered the Flat-Foot School of Writers some years ago, and could hardly be considered morally squeamish. In his youth he worked at manual labor on the railroad, so he knows men and his own virility has been proved by marriage and family. Yet what does Talcum Downley tell me?"

Al Guggelhaupt here consulted a sheet in Downley's own handwriting, later sent to Harvard for safekeeping: "I regard this book, my dear Guggelhaupt, as morally loathsome. Splendid writing, of course, but to no purpose. We must bring back

America into publishing, Al! You know this, from talks down on the farm with me. And why, my good friend, if you have gone to the expense *and* trouble of having a novel written, why cannot it be extended to 800 pages, the only possible length for a novel? Al, you should recall the words of the distinguished Irish writer of anecdote-fiction, Boke O'Garrell: 'It's not quality we look for in a novel, but mileage.' I'd go even further than Boke here, and employ a word not popular at the moment with other critics, a bit coarse perhaps, but a favorite of mine: *bloat*. I think we should bring back *bloat* into the novel, and have thought so for years. But in order to bring back *bloat*, we ought to remember the only subject a real American novel must always and perforce touch on is *war*. Our fighting men, and their loves as fighting men. Of course I discovered the Flat-Foot School of Writers, our young wanderers on the road, but it's our fighting men—our he's—that make the proper subject of American fiction. Forget rape, Al, and shelve this novel, or let one of the little forward-guard publishers have it, where it won't be taken seriously. Admiringly yours, Talcum Downley."

Al Guggelhaupt then stood over me, apoplectic, goggle-eyed, while I tried to think of something. I finally came up with, "Well, Al, one of the Greenwich Village publishers might take *Indelible Smudge* but we've obeyed those little matters of paragraphing and spelling, and that queers the book with them too."

Then Guggelhaupt came up to me as close as you two kiddies are now. Shaking me by the collar, he screamed: "I have it on bona fide authority, Prince, that we are at least two years

REJECTION BY THE GOETHE OF PUBLISHERS

out of date here! With you as my editor, we've lost touch with
the current! But before I go into the big question of the back-
seat we've been riding in under your rule, let me tell you, I
didn't stop with just the opinion of Pepscout and Downley.
I even called in Corinna who, as you know, is not a bit well,
Bright's disease, I'm afraid. At any rate, during the 'Twenties
I never published a book without consulting her. Corinna had
heard of the Cabot Wright case, and wanted to see it—a very
unusual request for her. I let her read it, though realizing it was
not her cup of tea, that there was actually nothing in it for her.
Corinna was very calm, very judicious about the whole thing,
I must say. She recognized that the obscene sections followed
logic and verisimilitude—her exact words. Then she said she
was violently opposed to my publishing it. Corinna said that
neither as literature nor a work of scatology would it have a
chance with the big public. The workmanship in presenting
the rapes, while very fine, even akin to the highest talent, is
not in tune with the literary Zeitgeist of the moment—Tim
Raisin, for instance, would never go for it, and that practi-
cally spells death for any book in old-fashioned left intellectual
circles, nor would the wide public care for a rapist who is not
driven to the deed by reason of passion, poverty, race or creed.
The rapist ought to love at least two of the women he subjects
to his lust, while Cabot loves nobody.

"But don't think," Al continued, suddenly collapsing a bit,
"don't think I'd let even my own wife's opinion lead me to a
mistake in business. Corinna or no, I called in more people.
I called in everybody, Prince, and asked from A to Z, what's
going on, what's in style in fiction. I even called Doyley Pep-

scout again. He may be a frost as a man, but he has his ear to the ground as a newspaper pro, and though dirt and sex upset him, he knows what kind of dirt and sex is in vogue. Do you think any of the men and women I called in said rape was in vogue or a style in current fiction? I even telephoned old Cordell Bicks, great pink critic of the 'Thirties. He said, 'My dear Guggelhaupt, I'm surprised you don't know. Rape is certainly not in. It's out, been out for years.'

"Do you hear that, Prince? Hasn't been in vogue in publishing for years. And every mother's son knows what is in vogue except you, my dear Illinois farmer's son. Except you!"

"Brief me, then, Al," I asked him and waited smugly for his answer.

"All right then, Prince, I'll tell you what they told me. It's pathetic you don't know." His voice trembled. "It's the age of the black faggot and fellatio, that's what," he whispered. At heart, you know, both Al and Corinna are mid-Victorians and the smut they peddled in the 'Twenties was just French adultery, with a subsidiary plot or two of lesbianism, which really put it all back in the mauve 'Nineties.

"Now that I'm informed, Al," I told him, "we'll know where to look."

"It's too late to be smart about it now, Prince," Guggelhaupt said. "Be as smart as you will, but get one thing straight: you're through, Keith, and there's no two ways about it. You are cashiered. Fired! Right? Right. I've no place in this organization for has-beens. You're living in the past. You are less in step with the Zeitgeist than my piano-tuner or my hat-check girl. Goodbye, and get out!"

———

PRINCETON SAT THERE with Zoe and Bernie who were fanning his fevered brow and comforting him as best they could. His eyes no longer focussed, and it was only a question of time till he would be sick, but during the interim they all felt close and together. They had tried, and they had failed. They were not just out-of-date people today, they had never really been in date, and never could be. And they were all leaving New York, but two of them, at least, were going home with recent money in their pants and the third, Princeton Keith, had pocketed so much in his big days that it would be his own fault if he had to go on poor relief back in Illinois.

That was the last Mrs. Bickle and Bernie Gladhart ever saw or directly heard from Princeton Keith, and it was hard for them to think of him spending the rest of his life sitting on a front porch in the great Mid-West. However, as Mrs. Bickle pointed out to Bernie, this has happened before to great New York literary figures. Having stomped, romped, barked and cried with gay lunatics and square Marxists in their youth, of a late evening you could now see them somewhere curled up in a hammock or wicker rocking-chair, reading Generals Grant and Sherman, a tear on their balding eyelid.

18

"I THOUGHT I'D DIE BUT I LIVED"

ad Cabot Wright understood even the minimum commands given him by Life, you can ask.

He had been born, of course, and toilet-trained, weaned at an average age. Was sent to the Sunday school of his peer's choice. Saw portrait of Elijah, Jesus the Christ, and God in nightgowns talking with other long-haired gents dressed samely. Entered kindergarten under bad-breathed spinster name of Sadie F. Harkness. Early learned to slide down teeter-totter, noticed girls had different behinds than boys, squatted where boys remained erect. Noticed some people had differ-ent skin-textures and were hiding on the whole behind lilac bushes, was commanded to ignore same. Everybody how-ever even then was riding in big cars. Woodrow F. Harding was dead, of course, and Theodore F. Truman called to the chair. China fell to land-hungry boll weevils. C.W. continued his mass-education learning following subjects: salute to the community, with pupil-community-laity participation program, sliding down escalators, wall-climbing and writing, doughnut-break, group training with both sexes, Democracy for little people period, hygiene, physical exercises, leap-frog, Y.M.C.A. salute night, Field Day with basket-lunch, camp during hot months relieves Mother. College of his choice dictated by friend of the family, Ivy Walls, graduated half *laude*, and entered military service where nothing he did was commented on. His majoring in art at Yale seen to be fiddle-faddle necessary in Eastern gentleman, and after service in khaki shorts entered the Wall Street. America expects every junior-executive general partner to marry & exercise his democratic tool. This Cabot, like all upstanding young blades, did, settling in Brooklyn across the water from his work, bought high-powered telescope to get a lay of the land, wife took ill, mother-father disappeared in pink Caribbean revolution. The rest, reader, you know.

Yet once the Chicago crew and the New York printing Czars dropped him, C. W.'s problem began all over again—learning to feel at last, after having been born anaesthetic from the womb. To recapitulate Cabot's problem: Dr. Bigelow-Martin had taken away all his attention except in his erectile tissue, and the police hoses and night-sticks had removed his attention there. But was this not the problem of the whole USA? Under the different Generals, poker-players, country squires, haberdashers, grandsons of whiskey-barons for President, and while America is fucking the rest of the world or putting a yellow island down the incinerator in the name of freedom, wearing Jehovah's whiskers and the tiara of the Queen of Heaven, the fact remains that the American people at home, *chez eux,* to quote Princeton Keith, outside of the aged and aging who are crying their heads off for free doctors and rectal TV, the rest of the USA citizenry, as a noted magazine calls them, from Maine's retired millionaires to the shores of the gilded Yukon, the American people are all head-wise if not physic-wise anaesthetic. They hear, but they don't get it. They see, but the image is blurry. The rain is falling on their TV screens.

"We have all been here before!" the USA cries as it turns over another page on its TV roller. "Ouch, my bleeding piles."

"We can't tell the difference," the child, the dowager, the millionaire kid from the Chicago department store all say, "we can't tell the difference between General Roosevelt and Captain Truman or Professor Eisenhower from Grover Kennedy Johnson. They all look like boys in charge of a scouting party who don't hear the cry, 'timber!' as the big investors screw away in the jungles, in the sugar islands, the pampas and waters of Lake Titicaca, the dynamite beds under the Prado, Habana, Bolivian tin-mines and Katanga. The boys all look alike to me, the viewers cry, except each succeeding President does promise a little more to the arthritic old and the darker niggers. . . . Hark! Now I hear it! Dong, dong, dong."

"You shall have dong, niggers and outfielders, as long as there is health in my General's body! I will give you dong. I am the President."

"We've all been here before!" the USA is crying in front of the little screen.

But they're so tired.

———

AFTER LEAVING MRS. BICKLE, Cabot Wright, still partially without his memory, was in a semi-dazed condition which plausibly might have grown out of his having been emotionally anaesthetic since emerging from the tut-tut of his mother's surprised birth pains. He went on of course to become a supposititious child. "PA-RAD-E RRRRESST. AT EASE, M E N."

In the absence of Mrs. Bickle, Cabot paused on 42nd and Sixth Avenue when he heard Sister Sadie X: "If I could only make *one* of you feel anything." The evangelist always opened her meeting, feebly but repeatedly waving her Bible and flag.

"If only one man or woman stopped here and showed his eye was not glassy with meaninglessness, I would stoop down here on this dirty curb and say, 'Blessed Jesus, I do thank thee.' But I don't see anything but glassy eyes, and I don't refer to your expensive optical equipment. No, dear lost sheep, I refer to something no optician can correct. You are living in the wickedest city which ever existed, making storied Babylon child's play, for at least the Babylonians felt and relished their sins. You sin not even knowing the stab of your wickedness, not even, oh flock, gaining pleasure from your transgressing as did that ancient city on the Euphrates. You sin not through appetite for it, but through sheer spiritual emptiness and bodily numbness.

"If I could only make you feel anything, citizens of the greatest country in the history of the cosmos, but you've had too much from every point of the compass: they've made of every orifice in your body a cornucopia, and you've been stuffed and stuffed and stuffed till you can't budge. You cry More! More! but you can't feel a thing."

As Cabot walked away further West, losing himself in street after same-looking street, he saw the whole of the Continent, as turned into a highway known as Piker. Trees are rubber tires and condoms. Dirt is cigarette butts propped on spark-plugs. The birds, gophers, rats, field mice, wood pussies and summer rattlers are old-fashioned jacks, air pumps, fan-belt, 1928 inner tubes. Everywhere ads tell you what you are about to do & did. The sentiment of moneycups is catching, and all America loves a moneycup. Not a man, woman or child alive today in this beautiful country who does not love a flower called moneycup, whose eyes grow a little moist at the very mention of the modest bloom, whose hands shake ever so little at the thought that somewhere in this great land a field of pure untouched moneycups is blowing in the soft spring zephyrs. Oh for the afternoons of childhood, youth, and of course full maturity. The aged not excepted either. The aged can look out from their mortgaged shingles and see moneycups. America is moneycups, as a great Yankee poet once said while working in the White House for General Woodrow Roosevelt. He had just received an $18,000,000 dividend check from a mail-order house which sells faulty teddy-bears, and leaky bathroom conduits. "America," he wrote, "you are moneycups," and all Americans waved their hankies at him.

This great mid-continental poet felt that General Woodrow Roosevelt should have waged war earlier as he and his wife (now confirmed Easterners) were quite put out that they had not been able to visit England and France (second land of citizenship for them) to spend their mail-order dividends there on Anglo-French culture. (Enumerate, if you would be so kind: antiques ormolu clocks cheese wine wine wine French perfume not-to-be-duplicated spirits Chambertin champagne British preserves—can't be beat, the English never learned to cook, but they're queens and kings with gooseberry preserve and/or damson spread—British china British Chippendale wax-work dummies selected butlers and don't forget tweeds & stout.) When the laureated great mid-west poet's poem, *America Is Moneycups,* hit the newsstands in the big picture magazine called BEAUTIFUL USA, the crush all over the continent was tremendous. To procure copies taxi drivers were seized and carried to the parapets of bridges and tossed over, mothers with baby-carriages were stopped and slapped for getting in the road of the newsstands, pregnant women were warned not to attempt the streets but go back to their kitchen units and make pudding in event of an emergency, truck-drivers with unusually developed deltoid-bicep-trapezius muscles were warned not to attempt approaching the newsstands to get copies of *America Is Moneycups* and finally the President of this country the President of the Grand Old USA had to speak from his sickbed and say, "Both my wife and I promise you that if you will all go home and quit creating a disturbance, which it is your constitutional right nonetheless so to create, we personally, she and I, will send each Democrat under 70 a copy of *America Is Moneycups* with a portrait of us coming down the chimney on the Fourth of July. Amen and God guide you to the polls. This is your personal Jehovah going off the air."

SUDDENLY CABOT WRIGHT could laugh. It was the first real laugh he had ever been able to bring off. The early part of his life, real and supposititious, had been devoted to giggles, and though he knew he would never be at attention fully anywhere again in his body, now suddenly he could laugh. First Ha then Ho, then Ha Ha HAR, HAAAAAA!

Laughter!

And Reverend Cross had come to see him. He had held his young ward's hand as the laughter trickled, flowed, cascaded, came in torrents.

Cabot had told Mrs. Bickle nearly everything or had hinted at what he had left out. He had told his whole story, and she would never use it. Maybe she believed it and maybe she did not, which was better. Now he could forget his own story and himself.

Every day Reverend Cross from the Church of His Choice had visited him, though only for a few minutes, but today holding the culprit's hand against his paroxysm of laughter, the preacher said:

"Cabot, my boy, you're better."

A young man in appearance, Reverend Cross suffered from several spiritual diseases of his own, as witness circles under his eyes, rapid pulse, dry mouth, looking at boys' crotches, talking to himself. But he had renounced life for Christ and this was getting him through the world without being beaten and reduced to a pulp.

"Confession, Cabot, is good for the soul," he patted Cabot's knee.

"Told you everything, already, Reverend."

"But you're not sorry, Cab. You're not."

"I'm not tired any more, either, Reverend. Not tired at all.

And I told Mrs. Bickle just about everything—after I heard it
in that book."

"Pray with me, Cabot," Reverend Cross said. "It won't hurt
you even if you don't believe in it. Pray some with me."

"I was a supposititious child," Cabot said dreamily. "God,
does that reach your guts when you think about it. But I don't."

"Come pray."

"My scrotum is blue with varicocele, Rev."

"Pray anyhow."

"Hold my pulse then while you mutter, Rev."

He heard in sleep-like underwater thunderings the young
preacher's prayer.

"All suffer the deadwood, my boy, having rejected our divine
inheritance. Remember those flowers which you so adored as
a boy, Cabot? The hunts in the woods for snow-apples, jack-in-
the-pulpit, heartsease . . ."

"When I left prison," Cabot confided, "my warden said,
'Cab, maybe this time you better stick to the company of your
own sex.'"

"We must all do what is right," Reverend Cross said, and his
long black lashes were smashed to his cheek by tears.

"What's right?" Cabot inquired, and when he said that the
Reverend Cross looked like his name.

"My mother said that," Cabot reminded the Reverend. "Did
she know what was right? All she knew was life-insurance
would save her when her mainstay kicked the goosepot. But
was she bugged. Both mothers were bugged. They both died.
The hand of no-return carried them off without their collecting on their forty years of fleshpot bleeding. Where was my

real parents, Rev.? WE SHOULD ALL DO WHAT IS RIGHT. Excuse
me while I use my new laugh. Let me tell you something, Reverend Cross. You bug me."

Pacing up and down, the preacher said, "You have set yourself up against God and man, and especially against yourself.
My boy, you are in a state . . ."

"The ugly truth is," Cabot shook his head, looking out the
window at the incoming steamer from Cartagena, near Fort
Jay, "religion hasn't got anything on the ball. It's all Daddy-
rattling and pious alarm."

"I will continue to pray for you, my son."

NOW CABOT WAS alone again with his non-self. Loneliness
feels so good after the mythic contact with the social. Dreams
become clear, and nightmares are no longer attention-getting.
One sucks eight or nine aspirins and allows his calloused
thumb to rest on a quilt. The trauma of birth, life and death
pass as shadows on the moon. Mother Nature goes right on
keeping house even though nobody is to home.

"Hello, Central Information Bureau?" Cabot spoke into a
phone. "Weather woman? Are you now or have you ever been
in the pay of a Cosmic Bugaboo? I'm not human now and never
was, is my fuckworthy answer. Thank you for allowing us to
enter your home in the legal frock of spies. We are screwing
you, as you know, to protect the innocent. Thank you and
good morning. Remove the bandage tomorrow. The stitches
are absorbed by the blood stream. You will feel no pain. We
repeat. You will feel no pain. Sold, American."

Lying down on his side, Cabot relieved himself in laughter.

His laughter was like a paroxysm, neither willing nor unwill-
ing. His regions from the breast-bone down shook in helpless hapless hopeless waves of self-relief, which happily for him
was one prolonged orgasm. After all, laughter is the greatest
boon Nature has bestowed on miserable unjoyous man. The
release, the only relief from the pain of being human, mortal,
ugly, limited, in agony, watching Death cornhole you beginning with the first emergence from the winking slit above the
mother's fundament, pulled into existence from between piss
and shit, sorrow and meaninglessness, drudgery and illusion,
passion, pain, early loss of youth and vigor, of all that had made
it worth while, with the eternity of the tomb, the final word
over the hunger for God, the repletion of earth and slime, the
shout of the ocean in the ears of death. Meaning is there is
no meaning but the laughter of the moment made it almost
worth while. That's all it's about. We was here, finally laughed.

"The roof of my mouth fell in. I laughed!" said Cabot.

He lay in the Brooklyn mud, guffawed weakly. He had
laughed until he was in erection again for the first time since
the policemen's nightsticks, laughed some more until he was
limp as an old man, laughed until he mewed and purled like a
new-born babe. Then he lay back on his back silent, weeping
a little from the pain of his laughter, a thread of drivel coming
down from his mouth onto his pointed dimpled chin.

"I thought I'd die but I lived."

That deadly monotony of the human continuity,
The fog is a sea on earth!

19

MAMA'S WELL IS DRY

he runaway is back!" Carrie Moore cried, in her TV nookery on Dorchester Avenue, when she saw Bernie Gladhart come in the door.

Entering Carrie's basement again, Bernie Gladhart sniffed carefully and did not take on that "at home" expression around the mouth and eyes. He had the slouch of a transient.

Putting down his bags temporarily, Bernie tried to avoid studying the changes in the face of his former wife. Carrie had aged and when a woman ages, she goes faster than a man ever can, Bernie reflected. Seeing his look of shock, she blamed her face's condition on TV principally. "It's what they call *television glint,*" she explained, a nervous ailment common in the Greater Chicago area. Dressed as usual, only in her foundation, with her wired bra raising her nipples to the angle of a woman young enough to be her granddaughter, she had a special bit of crape to hang, as she explained, on Bernie's lapel.

"Might as well tell you the worst while you're still fresh from your train ride."

"Is a new fellow living with you?" Bernie inquired jerking his head in the direction of upstairs. He knew, of course, that Joel Ullay had departed long since.

"I'm kind of beyond new or old fellows," she said. "I've got real trouble. I've got bad news, real bad news."

He stared at her and saw that what she said was true.

"If you don't want me, Carrie," he began, "I'll leave of course. Your calls didn't indicate whether you really wanted me or not. But I just didn't have any other place to go, sweetheart, not right away today, I didn't. I'm sorry your book idea for me didn't pan out, though I've got some money for it, of course. Princeton Keith, well, he was really queer for the Cabot Wright story. Dreamed it would crown his career and all . . ."

"He's dead, you know," Carrie remarked.

"What?" Bernie gasped. "Who?"

"The name you mentioned, Princeton Keith. Heard it on the early morning show. Shot himself in his rocking chair, with a big old .45. Think of using one of them!"

She yawned convulsively.

"Is that your bad news?" he inquired.

"Bernie, you bug me," she said. "Of course not."

He noticed how out-of-date Carrie's slang sounded. Her slang, which he used to think was current, he now saw as belonging to the earliest lingo of the Flat Foot School of writers, the old bop men who had all retired from the scene, but he knew of course the passion Carrie had always to speak the latest language, in order for her to feel she was here at all. But her speech was hoary; she was an old jazz-record in an age when jazz is more classical than fun.

"*My* bad news," Carrie cried a little, "is bad news on a paramount scale, and it's baddest of all on account of it's largely all just for me and nobody else is going to feel it."

She cried hard now.

Bernie, who had risen now, and with his head resting on his elbow, against the wall, was sobbing quite hard himself, so that Carrie left off her own weeping to bark:

"What are *you* bawling for, can I ask?"

"Guess it's the shock of his death," he replied.

"Whose?" she wondered. "Oh, that editor guy, Keith . . ."

Bernie wiped his eyes on the back of his hand.

"Well, I'm sorry the Keith man died since it strikes you home this way," she scolded.

"He gave me quite a lot nobody ever had before. But I guess in the end he didn't think I was a writer either," Bernie mumbled.

"Well, then it's unanimous at last," she said.

"You thought I was a writer once, Carrie," he came back to this.

"Ahem," she said. "But that's so long ago, baby heart. So long ago. Mama was well in those days."

"Ain't you well, Carrie?"

"Well, let's say like this, honey. If for example you decide to go on living under my roof, you won't be living in the jet age."

"I won't stop here if you don't want me to," he appealed now to her. She stared at him, her eyes slightly out of focus. "I'll leave whenever you give the word," he bowed his head.

"That's cute to hear," Carrie helped herself to the bourbon bottle. "Matter of fact, I hadn't given your leaving or staying a bit of thought. I did think about your appetite, your belly that is, on account of you eat a lot. When I found out your train was arriving I called up the Chinese Chop Suey Parlor on Fifty-fifth street, Wong Duck Fu or whatever the mothy place calls itself now—changes hands once a month at least—and they're sending us over our supper. I hope they've heated it this time. We have some skillets out back though if they goofed. And they're sending a gallon of tea."

"What's your bad news, Carrie?" Bernie returned to this.

"Let me raise the bucket myself, dolly," she admonished him. "Say you don't look so good either, speaking of bad news."

Bernie pointed out to Carrie that he thought he heard the doorbell through the sound of the television set. He walked to the door just in time to catch the delivery boy before he returned to Wong Duck Chop Suey Parlor with their order.

A few minutes later, having dished out from paper cartons the cold rice and chop suey, he poured her tea from paper containers.

"You don't have to eat that grub if it don't suit you, by the bye," she pointed with her paper fork.

"Why don't you tell me your bad news, Carrie?"

"Won't spoil your appetite?" she wondered. She had hardly touched her food. She drank dispiritedly from her paper carton of tea.

Bernie began speaking: "I don't believe anything could happen to me now that would really throw me. I'm throwed, and good. Maybe," he spoke too low to be heard even by her perhaps, "maybe there's always something that can get a guy further down yet, but how?"

"What guy?" she said.

"Where's Joel Ullay?" Bernie inquired.

"I told you all about that yellow bastard . . . Where's your Congolese boy-friend?"

"All I can think about is Princeton Keith," Bernie said, after a long wait. He shook his head.

"Don't change the subject," Carrie said. "I asked you about your Congolese boy-friend. I told you Ullay lit out and why."

"O.K., old doll," Bernie sighed. He took from his wallet a tiny snap of Winters Hart.

"Did you love him?" Carrie looked at the photo.

"Oh almost, that one night," he pushed his plate of food away.

"But not enough to marry him," she went on looking at the snapshot. "Say, that's a weak chin and mouth for a Congolese. Nice hair though and lots of it." She handed him back the photo, and said, "Well, pick and choose, that was always my motto." She threw her plate of nearly untasted chop suey into the open grate nearby.

"Now about my bad news, kiddy," she began. "It's simple like a funeral. Mama's through."

"No guessing games, Carrie. I'm too goddam tired to guess."

"You're too old, baby, you mean. But O.K., you don't have to guess on account I've already told you if you think back. Dig?" she laughed when he did not reply.

He was crying again and that sobered her a little.

"Bernie," she said, "you don't have what it takes."

He cried quite a lot then, and said, in a squeaking voice, "I know it, by Christ, I know it." He broke down then.

Everything that had ever hurt him, everything that had cut and bruised and knifed and festered the flesh, the disappeared and forgotten blows, together with pus and lymph and canker seemed to burst and come out, as from a huge broken sluice. His breakdown froze her.

"What's it from?" she whispered. She put her hand down on his, but he shook her off roughly.

"I got to get out of here!" He started up.

"Don't want to hear my bad news?" she cried. "Hear it anyhow!" she cried, as she slipped and fell by his side. "Hear Mama's bad news! Got to hear it."

He paused, gazing at her, at the same time drying his eyes in the manner of a small child.

"I'm dead, Bernie," she held on to his hand to rise from her sprawling at his feet. "That's my bad news. Change of life, honey. I've gone through the cemetery gates, and the hearse is parked till the burial."

"Change of life," he nodded, still rubbing his eyes.

"Last week it happened for sure. Doctor says it's premature but for permanent. Mama won't ever be herself again. I don't know why it's hit me the way it has. Was on the wagon most of the time you were away, but knowing you were coming back, I began again."

"Oh, I'm sorry, Carrie," he groaned, but in her scrutiny of him she saw he was only sorry about himself and well, how could she blame him.

"You don't have to send me a telegram to show how busted

up over it you are," she remarked at last. "I've closed the Wedding Bower by the way. Closed it after that lily-white snob of a Ullay cleared out, after sticking me for his bills. I've turned it into my store room for paint and turpentine. I mean the Wedding Bower."

"The Wedding Bower!" he cried with something of his old look and old voice. "Why that seems a trillion years ago, Carrie."

"That's the telephone," she informed him. "I got good ears even with this disease I picked up from TV. Go answer it, it might be Jesus." She poured herself some more cold tea while he was at the phone, looked at the bourbon bottle a long time, then didn't reach for it.

"Who is it?" she scolded when she saw him talking longer than hello-goodbye, and with a pleased grin on his face.

Looking at her video screen, suddenly she raised an arm, threw a heavy ash tray at the set, screaming:

"Take off that wig, you two-headed cunt!"

"Carrie," Bernie called to her, "would you mind, please. It's Wurtheim Badger of all people."

"Who?" she vociferated.

"Badger. The guy that owns the used car lots and all. Remember when I sold for him? He's talking business to me."

Bernie turned back to the phone and said, "Imagine you calling me on just a hunch, Badge."

"Well how about that," Carrie said. "Employment in the offing."

Her head fell down now on the table by Bernie's nearly untasted dinner of chop suey.

"I will, Badge, for Christ's sake, yes. Take care of yourself. I'll be fine," his voice drifted over to her.

She looked up as he came back into the room, and said: "You've picked up a lot of new ways of talking since you went to New York. You're not you."

"Carrie old girl," he patted her quickly on the cheek.

"And you're not sorry I've had my change of life. It's not real to you on account of *I* never was real to you."

"Sweetheart, I got to go to work. He's got a job for me, Badge. Don't you follow? It's a miracle. He didn't even know I'd been to New York. Do you know what he just said. Said I was the best car salesman he ever had in all his years here on the South Side. That put the refill in my pencil when he said that," he mumbled joyously.

"Going to work," she stared at him, disgust and surprise both in her voice.

He picked up his grips.

"I got to get this job, honey," he was half-apologetic. "I been in the out and out. Brooklyn was a real duck in the pond. I felt I was in the asshole of the cosmos. It was nothing, sweetheart. They couldn't even make a phony of me. I was an imaginary fart they couldn't blow away."

"You don't need to talk dirty to make me feel at home. On account of I am at home," she said. "So get out if you want out."

"Bye, Carrie."

"You won't be back then?" she eyed him with concern. She drank some more of the tea hurriedly to snatch at some part of soberness.

"As you said yourself, kid, the Wedding Bower is closed,"

he congratulated himself on having had the luck to think of this, as he was trying to get out of the place. "I figured I was through here, anyhow, after I found out about Joel Ullay, but I wanted to stop in and say hello."

"You wanted to do the right thing," she nodded jerkily like a figure in the Fun House. But then she put her hand on his forearm and pressed, saying: "But if you ever did find yourself with your ass out again and no place to park it, cold and hungry—just for the night, you understand, come back. Come back anytime." She kissed him wetly on the mouth.

"Thanks, Carrie."

"Thanks but no—is that what you mean?"

"Thanks," he kissed her.

She followed him over to where he leaned against the street door, his back to her, holding the heavy grips.

She kissed him on the nape of the neck.

"It's just as well, Bernie, I guess. Too much water under the bridge. Been through too much now to even know I'm lonely."

"Please, Carrie," he wept a little again.

"For Jesus sake don't bawl any more," she flared up. "Don't bawl, you hear. Go sell cars, for Christ sake."

"If you want me for anything, Carrie, call me, and I'll come." He still kept his back to her.

"Boy, does that cheer me," she said. "My bad news evaporates when I hear your voice. Goodbye, Bernie. Get it out of here."

When, from outside, he heard the sounds of her rage and bawling, he opened the door again to say: "Carrie, you call me up now, d'you hear?"

"I'm not afraid of bad news like some people," she stared at him, as if confused about the passage of time. Perhaps she thought he was returning hours later.

"All right, Carrie," he said. "I love you anyhow."

"Big help," she said. She dried her own tears now in the predilect manner of Bernie Gladhart, on the back of her hand. "You ain't done bad for a prison graduate," Carrie said drily. "You may as well keep going ahead, Bernie, now you've started."

"Carrie," he held tight to his grips now, "you call me."

She closed the door hard this time.

Back in the room the TV set, perhaps owing to the slam she had given the door, came on thunderous. The "Cuba, You'll Live Again" program was still in progress. A girls' band of 40 played American patriotic numbers, the pertinacity of which was that each and every señorita instrumentalist was an exile from the red Caribbean dictator, and had expressly learned the United States national anthem only recently. A Sousa program then followed.

"The one with the saxophone in the second row is the cutest," Carrie Moore said, and she poured herself some more bourbon for her cold tea.

20

"THE WAY I FEEL NOW"

ou act," Curt Bickle addressed his wife some weeks after her return from New York, "and you talk as though you were going to write the story of this youthful rapist yourself."

"But you know perfectly well I won't," Zoe Bickle reassured him, and Curt smiled with relief.

"You're a bright, brainy and even handsome woman today," Curt wiped his spectacles free of blur and stared at her again with complacency.

It was true. Mrs. Bickle had put on weight so that she looked better than she ever had before, her complexion shone, her eyes were bright, and her laugh had lost its edge.

"Believe you me," Mrs. Bickle said, "there was this temptation to write Cabot's story, after Bernie's failure, and with poor dear Princeton dead by his own hand. Well, what has stopped me from finishing the book," she told her husband, "is our culprit himself. He has begun to write *me*. I didn't tell you before because I hoped they would stop—Cabot Wright's letters, I mean. Maybe they are going to stop, now that he's left New York."

She opened a little box Curt had seen but paid no attention to. She drew out a letter, enclosed in a post-office stationery envelope, and read:

> After the roof of my mouth fell in, I saw how every-thing really was, Mrs. Bickle. That was before I could yet laugh—I'm now as you might guess a really professional laugher—yes, my giggling days are over. To think you—thank you—were the first person to listen to me all the way through.

Mrs. Bickle paused, and Curt looked away, embarrassed. He was ashamed, she knew, like all of us, of the human in his human nature.

"Where will a man like that end up?" Curt Bickle said, at last, in a kind of aside.

"A boy like Cabot?" She considered the question. "Perhaps his letter gives us a clue." She continued to read:

> Having sold all my property, including a row of brownstones—you will remember how rich I became when I inherited Warby's empire—well, nearly all I inherited is gone. I'm cleaned out. Philanthropy by the mile, unwise investments, and so on. I wanted to get clear of it too. Gave away a lot.

Curt yawned because it was eleven o'clock, but Zoe Bickle
went on reading:

My face has broken out in boils and I don't have time
to see the doctor. Besides New York is closed for the
Jewish holidays, there's a mean southerly wind at 10 knots
an hour, and the television set they have in this room is
busted so that I don't have any of the big serious faces
that make me see America, baseball heroes, disk jockeys,
immortal crooners, generals in hats, and living Presi-
dents' wives.

"Oh, how adolescent," Curt said.

As my preacher, Reverend Cross, used to say to me, in
every breath we breathe, life and death jockey for position. There have been 77 billion people who have pre-
ceded us on this planet, but the big news is that with
the increase today population-wise, 1/10 of all the people who have ever lived are alive today. That's the good
thought I want to give you, Mrs. Bickle, before I give
you some of the bad news, the necrology, as the better
newspapers call it. You really do have to know, if you are
going to write the truth about my life as fiction.

NEWS EVENTS & RELEASES:
Goldie Thomas's beauty was nearly completely
destroyed when, riding in her bubble car, she ran into
a fishing lodge in order to avoid a moose which would

not get out of the way in Maine, near a place called Deer
Isle, where she was of course vacationing. Gilda Warburton died by her own hand, of gastric upset, in Manhattan, subsequent to drinking liquid cosmetic, which she
had mistaken for Campari. This is being hushed up as
she had pilfered it from her new colored butler, the boy
who replaced Brady, who by the way joined the Mer-
chant Marine. I don't remember whether I told you or
not, but my first wife and my only, Cynthia Adams, died
of double pneumonia in the loony bin, after never finding out again who she was (some people have luck).

If this letter seems disconnected, it's partly because I
can hear from a neighboring apartment, where they are
not celebrating the holidays, Terry on the vibes playing
"I Love You, Stranger, in Fact I Do."

Well, before I come to the real drama of necrology, I can say what my Preacher says will always bear
repeating, "My own heart was broken before I heard
the Coach say 'Go!'" Yes, Princeton Keith is no more.
I thought that would smash you, as you were childhood chums. A lot he will need to care about auto-
mation. Tell you about a guy like Princeton. He spent
25 years of his life thinking he was permanently land-
marked in New York, even though he was from Illinois somewhere, in fact he thought Al Guggelhaupt
was only the Moon and he was the Sun. What really
killed him wasn't just the quiet of a small town in mid-
America, but the shock to his internal system of not
having those $50.00 a cloth luncheons, with the seven

different beverages. I mean that is a bomb to anybody's
insides. Bladder backs up, great colon nonplussed, liver
no longer tawny, prostate down in the dumps, great
sphincter utterly collapsed . . .

"Oh, for Pete's sake!" Curt cried. Mrs. Bickle went right on.

If you do ever write anything about me, I would half-
like to read it, but am afraid I am more disinterested in
my own life, such as it was, than even you were when you
showed your disinterest at its height. God, did I admire
your non-committed glance, Mrs. Bickle. (I'll never call
you Zoe, 'cause you're the old Ear to me, just drinking
in what you didn't even always get. Thank you for that.)

I suppose even Chicago seems a little Lilliputian with
the jet world all connected up, and the oral contracep-
tive ads going to the tune of "The Old Rugged Cross."
Another friend of mine named Vance Goldanski, who
was writing an article on me for a movie magazine,
dropped dead on the corner of Fifth Avenue and 57th
Street, very young man, had been a French horn player
for 10 years, before he got to be a candidate for the World
Thought Congress. He felt it was time to give up playing
for helping out the world community in trouble, and the
day he signed up he fell over.

But what was always on my mind, Mrs. Bickle, as
you know from all those hours in the cockroach palace on Joralemon Street, Brooklyn, and that night in
Hanover Square, lower Manhattan—and you remember

all those clocks that I had when I hid away in the *See River Manor*—the thought always on my mind was *"Do You think there's a Chance for Me if I ever Find out who I is?"* That's why I've come home to my brownstones in Brooklyn Heights (falling fast), have sold same, and am on my way to extended flight, but this time with myself, and in search of same.

The thought occurs to me that this may be the last time we play our little game of hearing and not listening, Mrs. Bickle. Here I am running out on America, if not myself. That's the funny thing to remember—in case I don't send you more news.

No, what I am getting at is that when I had to have all those clocks going, and you remember how many times I took my own pulse, as though I never expected to hear the Coach say "Go" again, well I've got that one problem solved if no other, on account of I don't have to ask those hard questions that nobody now or any of the other 77 billions ever found the answer to, WHAT MAKES ME TICK? I don't care about that now, Mrs. Bickle, but I do know, *hear* it any way you want, I am ticking as of this letter, anyhow, and I'll write the symbol for the way I feel now, which is HA!

"Well," Mrs. Bickle said, "I guess that will be the last of any letters I ever get from dear Cabot Wright."

"Speaking of paramount issues," Curt Bickle opened his mouth after the briefest of pauses, "you do look around the mouth and eyes as if you might write his story after all."

"Believe you me," Mrs. Bickle intoned, "it's almost a temptation."

Curt waited a little.

"But I won't, pet," she said in a low voice to herself and him. "I won't be a writer in a place and time like the present."

1714